Make It Count

Make It Count

Make It Count

A Bowler University Novel

MEGAN ERICKSON

WILLIAM MORROW IMPULSE
An Imprint of HarperCollinsPublishers

Excerpt from *Make It Right* copyright © 2014 by Megan Erickson.

EPub Edition JUNE 2014 ISBN: 9780062353399

Print Edition ISBN: 9780062353412

10 9 8 7 6 5 4 3 2 1

To Neal, the sexy nerd I married.
I wouldn't want to power cycle my
modem with anyone but you.

Acknowledgments

To SAY I'M overwhelmed by the support I've received for this book is an understatement. The writing community online is amazingly supportive—from agents to editors to writers to bloggers to readers. This book would not be what it is today without them. I gained my footing and cut my teeth in online writing conferences and contests. I found beta readers and critique partners and most of all, *friends*. So this is a huge shout-out to all of you on Twitter and Facebook and Tumblr and Pinterest, sharing the love of books and reading. You all are my rock stars.

My agent, Marisa Corvisiero, is my cheerleader, fan and massive support system. Her enthusiasm for this book and my journey has been incredible.

My editor, Amanda Bergeron at HarperCollins, is an amazing force. I feel so incredibly and utterly lucky to be one of her writers. Her edits were so on point with this book that I might have cried because she *got* me and she *got* this book. She inspired me to enhance Kat and Alec's journey. Her love notes in the margins of my document were just icing on the cake of her awesomeness. Best of all, she made this book better and she made me a better writer. I owe so much to her.

I began writing MAKE IT COUNT when I was thirty-four weeks pregnant with my second child. I couldn't stop thinking about Kat. She lived in my brain for the better part of a year and frankly, I was okay with that. Hands down, I would not have made it through the querying journey without my amazing critique partners and friends Natalie Blitt, A. J. Pine and Jen Meils. I think we lived on Facebook chat for months, sharing the highs and lows of our journeys. Their support and writing prowess is really unparalleled. Sometimes I think I can't write without them. And I'm okay with that.

My husband, Neal, and two kids suffered through the writing and editing of this book. They survived burned meals and a dirty house. But I couldn't ask for a better support system at home. Neal, a large part of you inspired Alec. He's a great character and man because *you* are the best man I know. I love you with everything that I am.

My family—my parents and my brother, aunts, uncles and cousins, grandparents, in-laws, etc.: I appreciated every single text message, e-mail, and word said to me in support of this crazy author journey. Especially my parents—my mom and dad have always been my biggest fans. I love you guys so much. And I think I can write great love stories because I grew up witnessing your amazing, everlasting love.

Thank you to the people who read MAKE IT COUNT in its infancy—Sheena Baker, Jamie Farrell, Katie Bailey and Beth Vrabel—and encouraged me to keep working on it. And thank you to Danielle Lorello for letting me pick your brain about dyslexia so I could portray it as accurately as possible.

Too many authors to name have been instrumental in this journey, but I'm going to shout out a few anyway. Thank you to Jen McLaughlin, Rachel Harris, Christina Lee and Stina Lindenblatt among others for reading MAKE IT COUNT and lending your names in support. I can't express how much it means to me to even be mentioned in your company. Thank you to Juliana Haygert for answering my many messages about Brazilian culture and language. I want to make feijoada now!

Thank you to my spirit animal Lucas Hargis for being the recipient of my flailing with nerves. You are a saint, sir. A shout-out to the Cool Kids Mafia, NAAU, and the Debut 2014 NA authors. I love you all. Thanks for the support and amazing discussions.

Thank you to all of the bloggers/reviewers/readers who reached out to me in anticipation of this book. I appreciated every word, every tweet, just *everything*. Thank you a million times for the support.

And I can't forget all my friends, who have been with me since before I wrote my first book. First—my BUB girls—you mean the world to me. You've understood my radio silence and still supported me in this whole thing. And my Ship girls—you know who you are—all of you. I love you. Because of the insanely awesome time we had in college, I have so much fodder for writing New Adult romance. And Andi, I'm going to say it again, you still aren't one of the "little people."

Chapter One

KAT CHEWED ON her pen and studied her tutor's bent head. Ashley's shiny black hair was pulled back into a ponytail, held in place by a . . . scrunchie.

Seriously? Was that really a sparkly teal scrunchie? Kat bit down harder on her pen in concentration. Did they even sell those anymore? The last time she'd seen one, she'd been six and wrapped it around her side ponytail, pretending to be Kelly Kapowski while watching *Saved by the Bell* reruns.

Ashley droned on about something, and Kat yawned. She looked down at her notes but some of the words blurred, increasing her headache, so she gazed around the library. Through the windows, the late-January wind rattled the bare trees.

"Kat? Did you hear me?" Ashley's voice needled into her ear.

Kat snapped her head back. "Um . . . yeah?"

Ashley slumped her shoulders with a sigh. "Look, I'm going to be honest here. I like you, okay? But I don't think you're getting anything out of these sessions. I think my time would be better spent with someone else."

Kat opened her mouth but then snapped her jaw shut. It wasn't like she hadn't heard it before. Her inability to stay focused had annoyed plenty of tutors. Not to mention just about everyone else in her life. She jutted out her chin with as much confidence as she could muster. She'd find another tutor.

"I think that's a good idea, Ashley. I'd planned to say the same thing." The lie came easily. "I'm doing better in statistics anyway, so I don't need the help anymore."

Ashley raised an eyebrow while gathering her papers. "Okay, well, it was . . . nice to meet you." She winced, as if it was painful to say, then waved meekly and left.

Kat groaned softly. She was in the second semester of her sophomore year at Bowler University and already on academic probation. If she failed another course, she would be kicked out. This semester's bane of her existence—statistics.

She hated her brain. Absolutely hated the way it could never make sense of words and numbers on the page in front of her. How it wandered and couldn't focus on one thing for very long. How it was to blame for the dumb blonde jokes that had followed her like an unfunny comedian her whole life.

She wasn't even blonde. Not really. She held up a wavy curl and picked at the ends. It was more like a light brown. Caramel. Or whiskey. With blonde highlights.

Were those split ends? She needed a haircut, stat. And a root touch-up because her highlights were growing out. And maybe an eyebrow wax. There was that place over on Lexington that took walk-ins ...

Her cell phone vibrated on the table, announcing an incoming text message from her boyfriend. She swiped her thumb across the screen, automatically launching the text-to-speech app she'd downloaded after repeatedly reading her text messages incorrectly. She'd thought downloading it was genius at the time, until a clearly audible *Your ass looks hot today* text read in a sexy male Australian accent scandalized an unfortunate seventy-year-old at the drugstore.

Luckily, this message was tame.

Come over tonight.

She muttered to herself, "And that's an order, Private." Would it kill him to type *please*? It was only an extra six letters.

Max Payton didn't know she had a tutor. He didn't know much about her at all, really. But he was hot—really hot—and fun and as a junior, lived in a house off campus with his own room. And he liked to bake. Seriously, the man baked her chocolate-chip cookies. They were really good, too. When she asked him about the secret ingredient, he'd laughed and said *flour*. She was pretty sure he was making fun of her. But she'd learned at an early age to pretend mocking was just teasing.

She gathered her books and stuffed them into her plaid Burberry messenger bag, then headed toward the front doors, smoothie from the library snack shop in hand. Head bent, fiddling with the clasp of her bag, she stumbled into a wall of human on the pavement outside.

"Oh, I'm sorry—" Her voice dropped out when she realized the solid flesh belonged to Alec, Max's best friend.

She'd only met him once or twice before he'd moved in with Max this semester and every time, he cocked his eyebrow with a half frown like he knew something she didn't. Which he actually did, since he had brainy superpowers. Smarter than a speeding Einstein. Able to leap over C-minus students like her in a single bound.

She didn't trust people that smart. And she didn't trust a guy who didn't ogle her ass or leer at her boobs like every other member of the straight male species on the planet.

She once asked Max if Alec was gay, and Max had laughed so hard, she feared he'd pop a blood vessel in his forehead. Then he assured her his friend was in fact, very straight.

She'd believe it when she saw it.

Right now, that raised-eyebrow frown pinned her where she stood. His pale green eyes behind thick black frames roamed over her shoulder to the library and then back to her. With his pin-stripe button-down, dark jeans with Converse shoes and hair styled in a short, messy pompadour, he looked like a nerdy Elvis.

His frown morphed into a smile when he spotted the smoothie in her hand, and she *definitely* didn't notice his full lips. "You know, you don't have to venture into the forbidden zone just to get a smoothie."

Oooh. The jerk. She glanced around surreptitiously,

then leaned in and spoke in a low voice. "Just play it cool. Don't let it slip someone like me snuck in the library." She gripped his forearm and whispered. "Password today is *rosebud*."

His face blanked and he looked at her like he'd never seen her before. Kat debated whether or not that was an improvement over his other look.

But then those intelligent eyes narrowed and a smirk curled his lips. "I know. We nerds get an e-mail every morning."

See? He always needed the last word. She propped a hand on her hip and leaned in. "Well, sounds like you have a mole. Might want to look into that."

He opened his mouth but she cut him off. "Just looking out for you guys. Anyway, see ya around!"

Before he could shoot back a snarky comeback, Kat skirted around him and bounded down the stairs. She chalked that up as Kat 1, Alec 0.

She pulled out her phone and texted Max.

Come get me. At campus entrance in 10.

Kat stuffed her hands in the pockets of her fabulous— bought for a total steal—red peacoat, and took the long walk to the head of campus. The air was cold, that damp chill typical for Maryland. She glared sullenly at the bare trees on campus, wishing for spring, when they'd bloom again. She'd visited the campus in the spring of her junior year of high school with her parents, and everything about the university and nearby town of Bowler felt right. During her first year as a student, she'd built friendships and kept a decent reputation.

This second year was proving to be a huge pain.

Kat arrived at the large stones marking the entrance of the campus, BOWLER carved into them and painted red. She began to worry about the condition of her frozen toes until Max pulled up to the sidewalk in his old truck.

"Babe, get in."

She didn't need the invitation as she wrenched open the rusted door and hopped inside, smiling at him.

The first time she saw Max, he was standing on a table in the middle of a raging house party in October, fist at his mouth as he belted the chorus to "Don't Stop Believin'." He was gorgeous in that confident, cocky way. And he looked like he belonged on the cover of a romance novel, wearing nothing but unlaced football pants and artistically placed eye black, the right amount of sweat running down the middle of his tanned pecs.

Their gazes had met and when he winked those big brown eyes at her, flashing a wide easy smile, she was a goner.

And one of the things she liked most about him was he didn't ask her too many questions about herself. So she didn't pry into his life.

She wasn't going to marry the guy. But she liked his kisses and his cookies.

"Your roommates around?" She buckled her seat belt.

"Uh, I think Cam went home for the weekend. Alec is around, I guess." He squeezed her thigh. "You know, he'll be busy studying like always. Should be quiet if you want to spend the night."

She sighed and wondered if Max was fed up with her

evasion of sex. It wasn't that she didn't like sex. She loved it, actually. And while she was attracted to Max, something was holding her back.

"Maybe," she said.

Max sighed, and she absorbed the sting of his disappointment.

Kat gingerly placed her feet on crumpled fast food bags. Something oozed out of a damp corner and she hoped it was ketchup. The color suggested otherwise.

"I thought we agreed you were going to clean out your car." She eyed the suspicious substance and wished she had one of those hazardous-waste trash cans from a doctor's office.

Max snickered and nodded toward the bags. "I'm saving that for later."

Kat wrinkled her nose and he laughed harder. Organization was key to her life. She could control that—her bedroom tidy and her calendar neatly filled out with color-coded highlighter. Of course, it was a stark contrast to the riot of chaos that was her mind. But fake it 'til you make it, right?

Max parked along the sidewalk outside of his townhome off campus and as they crossed the street, Kat tried to grab his hand. He evaded it like always and wrapped a beefy arm around her neck. She huffed under her breath. For once, she wished he didn't act too cool to hold her hand.

Max's place was on the end of a row of four townhomes. The high ceilings made the already large living room feel even bigger. The kitchen was a decent size but outdated, with old appliances, a crumbling tile floor and a ceiling-fan light you had to tug just so if you wanted to see your hand in front of your face.

The staircase leading to the bedrooms upstairs was ornate, with a thick, solid railing Max often straddled and slid down with a whoop. There was one bathroom on the second floor, which for a guys' place was relatively clean.

When they walked inside the front door, Max headed right to the kitchen while Kat settled on the couch in the living room, running her hands over the ugly, fuchsia-flowered fabric. Max and his roommate Cam had found it by a Dumpster before they moved in. Kat was still unsure if sitting on it would give her a rash.

Minutes later, Max plopped down beside her with a can of beer and promptly turned on the TV to a hockey game.

Kat yawned. Hockey was boring to watch. The guys didn't wear tight clothes and lot of them were missing teeth. Playoff hockey was even worse because the players didn't shave and had scraggly neck beards. *Gross.*

When she'd had enough of trying to find the tiny puck on the screen, she said, "I'm going to make a sandwich. You want one?"

"Yeah, I think we have some peanut butter and jelly."

As she walked into the kitchen, he called to her back, "Hey, I made some cookies for my brothers earlier today, bring us in a couple, yeah?"

Kat gave a thumbs-up over her shoulder. Max worked at his dad's auto mechanics shop almost every weekend along with his older brothers. And they always demanded Max's treats.

In the kitchen, she searched through the thin plywood cabinets until she found the peanut butter, then pulled the jelly and the bread out of the puke green-colored refrigerator.

The front door opened and closed and low voices carried in from the living room. She shifted to the edge of the counter to grab a towel and ran smack into someone.

"Ouch!" She whirled around to face her opponent and met Alec's eyes. She frowned at him, rubbing her shoulder. "Seriously? Twice in one day?"

He rolled his eyes and held his hands up. "Yep, I'm following you around so I can get poked in the ribs by your bony elbows."

Her mouth dropped open. "Bony?! You think my elbows are bony?" She bent her arm and eyed the joint. "I think my elbows are quite attractive, thank you very much."

He looked at her as if she were one of those bugs you tolerate only because it eats worse bugs. Then his lips twitched into a grin and he leaned down, his lips near her elbow like it was a microphone. "I'm sorry, Kat's Elbow. You're the sexiest elbow on campus," he said in a deep, sexy voice. Wait, what? When did she start attributing Alec with anything sexy?

With him stooped for his elbow apology, their eyes met. His green irises studied her, making her feel naked. Not clothes naked but brain naked. Like he pried off the top off her head to look inside.

She didn't want anyone to peek inside the top of her head. Her brain was probably all weird colored and deformed. It looked better covered by her skull, scalp and in-need-of-a-dye-job hair.

She steeled herself against the rush of heat flooding her face, because it was really wrong to be a creeper about her boyfriend's best friend.

Didn't mean she couldn't look at his nice eyes. And big hands. And good profile with one of those Roman or Greek noses or whatever they were called. And thick dark hair she wanted to run her hands through, grip and pull. Just to see if it turned him on.

Oh sugar-snacks, now she was having dirty thoughts about her boyfriend's nerdy roommate.

Clearly, her brain was deformed.

She huffed in annoyance and backed away from him to resume her task, spreading four slices of bread on the counter and digging in the tub of peanut butter.

A hand crept into view and grabbed a banana off the counter while she slathered peanut butter on two slices of bread and reached for the jelly.

A throat cleared behind her. "If you put peanut butter on both sides of the bread, then the jelly doesn't make it soggy."

He apparently didn't even think she was capable of making a flipping peanut-butter-and-jelly sandwich.

She stuck a peanut-butter-covered finger in her mouth turned to face him. When his eyes tracked her finger and lingered on her lips, she felt as if she won this small battle of the sexes. Kat 2, Alec 0.

She smirked. "I'm so glad you're around to show me the error of my sandwich-making ways. What would I do without you, Alec?"

He took a bite of banana, chewed and swallowed. "I guess you'd have a soggy sandwich."

She rolled her eyes and turned back to her task.

He finished his banana and threw the peel in the trash.

"Do you want me to make you one, too?" she asked.

He paused with his hand on the door. "Sure. Thanks."

When he walked out of the kitchen, she pulled two more slices of bread and spread peanut butter on all the slices before squeezing on the jelly.

She carried the finished sandwiches and cookies out to the guys, then sat down beside Max. The hockey game was still on and even though she didn't give two flips about it, she pretended to care since Max did. That was pretty much Good Girlfriend 101.

She took a bite of her sandwich and squinted at the TV. "So, what quarter is this? What teams are playing?"

"Babe, this is hockey. There are no quarters. There are periods and—*What the fuck, ref! That was tripping!*—anyway, I think you ask me that question every game. Either remember or stop asking." His focus returned to the game. "That should have been a damn penalty," he muttered.

Well then. Apparently she had to retake Good Girlfriend 101.

She thought about telling him she didn't remember because she really only half listened to his answer. She cared about hockey about as much as she cared about what an absolute risk was in statistics. But it wasn't worth it, and she was hungry. Kat focused on her sandwich because the double-peanut-butter trick was pretty dang good . . .

Alec cleared this throat and she looked up. "Kat, there are three twenty-minute periods in hockey. This is the first period. The Ducks are playing the Redhawks. Ducks are green jerseys; Redhawks are black. Ducks are winning." His tone was light and almost cautious. Like he thought she was going to take off his head. It was one of the few times he had spoken to her and his attention—those intelligent eyes fixed on her—caused a rush of heat to flare in her face.

"Thanks, Alec," she mumbled, eyes down on her sandwich to hide the color in her cheeks.

But she raised her head when her spine prickled, and they locked gazes for a moment. Kat was very aware of the air growing hot and heavy around her. Alec's lips twitched slightly, and her eyes were drawn to their fullness.

Max murmured at the TV, drawing her attention before a *bow chicka-bow-wow* soundtrack could play in her head.

She was so screwed.

Alec rose stiffly. He grabbed his book bag off the couch and said, "I have some studying to do. I'll be in my room."

"Later." Max waved him off, his attention unwavering from the game. Alec walked up the stairs, and Kat willed herself not to watch him. But her willpower was only so strong. At the top of the stairs, he turned around and immediately met her eyes.

Shoot! She quickly whirled her head around and stared blindly at the TV.

"Game's getting good, huh, babe?" Max grabbed the rest of her abandoned sandwich.

"Yep," she muttered. "Great game."

Chapter Two

ALEC'S FEET THUDDED on the rubber strip of the treadmill in an unsatisfying rhythm. He'd rather run outside, but the ground was coated in ice and he didn't want to break his ankle. So he had to settle for staring at the concrete block wall of the campus gym. He'd been running for as long as he could remember, and if he went a couple of days without it, he was like a junkie—needing his fix.

He'd already run several miles, so he slowed the machine and jogged easily for a few minutes to cool down. The invisible cloud of stress and worry and responsibility that always dogged his heels was gone. As long as he kept running, he could stay ahead of it, never getting caught in the downpour.

Once he had his breath back, he stepped off the machine and wandered over to where Max was using the leg press.

"Nice gams." Alec propped his elbow on the top of the machine and wiped his brow.

"This is not *Mad Men*. If you refer to my legs as gams ever again, I'll take a crowbar to your kneecap."

Alec tsked. "I'm calling the cable company to complain about that *Sopranos* marathon."

Max lowered the bar and grinned at Alec. He kissed the scrunched fingers of one hand and then spread them wide. "Bada Bing! Gotta get in touch with my roots."

Alec rolled his eyes. "Dude, your ancestors are French Canadian."

Max harumphed and completed another leg press. "That's what I get for asking for your help on my ninth-grade genealogy project."

"You had the best project in the class, and the teacher bought you a Big Mac. Don't even whine."

Max didn't answer, but the press of his lips showed he was holding back a smile.

"I gotta go. Try not to get whacked while I'm gone." Alec walked away as Max yelled. "They won't, Vinnie. I'm a made man!"

Alec laughed while he headed toward the showers. It was good to see Max acting normal—or as normal as Max could be. He'd seemed tense and stressed since the fall, and Alec didn't know why. All he knew was that Max seemed to be taking it out on Kat, which set Alec's teeth on edge. The slump of her shoulders when Max had snapped at her about the game ...

Alec shook his head, trying to forget the feel of those

wide blue eyes on him. He stripped and showered, careful not to touch the walls because God knows what was crawling around on the cracked pink tile. He'd rather go home, but he had to grab lunch before his tutoring session. This was his first student of the semester, and he didn't want to be late because he really needed the money.

It was always about money.

But it was a good job. His boss told him what subject and where to be and he showed up at the appointed time and got paid by the university. It wasn't a bad gig and a lot of the time, he could get his own studying in. Fortunately, most of his tuition was covered. His rent had been cheaper before moving in with Max, but when his mom found out his landlord hadn't fixed the heat for a month, she'd hounded him until he moved out. His last roommate was most likely a drug dealer, so it was for the best anyway.

After his shower, he dressed quickly and dried off and arranged his hair into his usual pompadour. He'd first styled it that way when he dressed up as Danny Zuko from *Grease* for Halloween in ninth grade—his mom's idea—and he'd received so much attention for it that he'd kept up the hairstyle. It also had earned him the nickname "Zuk."

He headed toward the Thrasher Union Building named after a previous university president. The TUB, as everyone called it, rose three stories, with a large bowed glass window front. Alec had always thought it was a good thing Maryland wasn't in Tornado Alley, because those windows would have been blown out in a heartbeat. The TUB held the university bookstore, a cafeteria/

dining area and coffee shop on the first floor. The second floor was full of conference rooms and study lounges, while the third floor held offices for campus groups such as the newspaper and television station.

He didn't have a meal plan anymore, since he lived off campus, so it was easier and cheaper to grab the à la carte food choices at the TUB. Once he had paid for his pre-made cheeseburger, chips and chocolate milk, he managed to find an empty table, despite it being Monday afternoon.

After he finished eating, he sat and spun his chocolate milk bottle on the table, trying to concentrate on that rather than his best friend's girlfriend.

When he'd first met Kat, he'd chalked her up as another one of Max's vapid flings. But now all he could feel was the warmth of her fingers on his arm, hear her low, sultry voice when she'd whispered *rosebud*. That saucy wink and sarcastic wit. That smooth, shiny caramel-colored skin she'd inherited from her Brazilian parents, he'd learned from Max.

And Kat had this way about her, a semi-flighty quality, as if she constantly wobbled on the edge of a wave and could fall off at any moment. He felt the urge to reach out and steady her, just to keep her stable.

Shit.

A hand with black-painted fingernails reached down and plucked the bottle from his hands.

"Hey—" he began and leaned his head back. Danica Owens stood above him, eyebrows raised, his milk bottle between a thumb and middle finger. "Oh, hey, Dan."

She tossed the bottle in the nearby recycling bin and sat down across from him, resting her heeled black boots on another chair. "Hey there, Stone."

He'd met Danica freshman year. She was one of the few females in his criminal justice major and got a lot of shit from ignorant guys. He'd been paired with her on a project freshman year, and her smarts had blown him away. They'd been friends and study partners since.

"What's going on?" she asked, her purple eyes narrowed. He swore she changed eye color as often as she changed clothes. Her appearance morphed every day. Today, her hair was black and straight, down to about mid-neck, with thick bangs. She kind of looked like a modern-day Cleopatra.

A Cleopatra who slept with Mary Antony instead of Marc Antony.

He shrugged. "Just tired."

Danica kept her eyes narrowed. She knew him too well to let him get off with a lame excuse. "Come on, what's up? I mean, other than your normal grumpiness."

"I'm not grumpy," he mumbled.

Danica cocked her head, as if to say, *Really?*

He tapped his fingers on the table. "Okay, so as long as I don't actually *act* on it, it's okay to . . . kinda sorta . . . covet thy roommate's girlfriend, right?"

Danica's eyes widened into purple saucers. "Oh shit."

He groaned and leaned back in his chair, rubbing his hands up through his hair and down over his face. When he faced Danica again, a small smirk tugged at her lips. "This is about Kat, right?"

Alec nodded miserably.

"She's really cute," Danica nodded in approval. "Blue eyes, nice ass."

"What, did you check her out?"

"Hey, I can look." Danica shrugged, then leaned forward. "Anyway, I'm pretty sure there's nothing wrong with covetous thoughts. You can't help that."

"Max can be a real ass to her, too. He's never been the most . . . uh . . . chivalrous, but for some reason, it bothers me when he's a jerk to her."

Danica made a sour face. "I know he's your best friend, but I don't really like Max. You two are nothing alike."

Alex sighed. It wasn't the first time he'd had to defend Max from people who didn't know him. Or the real him, hidden underneath the brash party guy. "We met in elementary school when both of us had cracked Transformers lunch boxes. And when every other kid waltzes into school in brand-new clothes and you are the two wearing high-water pants, hearing 'where's the flood?' jokes, it's easy to bond. We've always had each other's backs."

He didn't go into all the ways Max drew him out of his shell, never letting him retreat into the shy, nerdy kid he would have been without their friendship. It would reveal too much and no matter how close he was to Danica, she didn't know his life story. And he didn't want to tell it while the clatter of trays and chatter of students surrounded them in the TUB.

Danica didn't say anything for a minute. "Oh."

Alec tapped his fingers on the table, wishing he had his milk bottle back, when a familiar laugh rang across the room. The part of his brain telling him not to look didn't reach his body in time, and he turned his head.

Carrie Matthews walked toward him with a group of her friends. Her head was bent, dark brown curls bouncing around her face. When she looked up, their eyes locked. Her steps faltered a little, and she gave him a half-hearted wave. He didn't have the energy to fake anything more than a half smile.

The sight of Carrie was a reminder that Kat wasn't his type.

His type had been Carrie Matthews. She'd been his type since sophomore year of high school. She'd been his type as they'd applied to Bowler University together. She'd been his type right up until she confessed last summer she'd cheated on him.

So . . . his type was a cheating high-school sweetheart. Awesome.

He turned back to Danica, whose jaw was tight, glaring at Carrie.

"Calm down, warrior princess," Alec said.

She whipped her head to face him, eyes still beaming like purple lasers. "Can I go call her a cheater and throw my soda on her?"

Alec laughed. "No. It's not worth it to get worked up. I don't anymore." When Alec saw Carrie now, he only felt a small twinge of sadness at the loss of what he had hoped to be their future. She'd been his first girlfriend, and she was the only girl he'd slept with. Like an idiot, he believed he'd marry her. Just like his parents, who'd fallen in love at eighteen and never fell out of it. But it hadn't worked out that way. That was that. Time to move on.

The normally harsh lines of Danica's face softened. "I'm sorry."

He did *not* want to have a conversation about his pitiful love life. "Dan, seriously—"

She dropped her feet from the chair and stomped them on the ground. "Okay, okay. Just trying to be . . . comforting or something."

He snorted. "How about we talk about your love life?"

She wrinkled her nose. "Ew. No. You always get this gleam in your eye. I'm not giving you fodder for your spank bank."

He threw back his head and burst out laughing.

Danica grinned at him. "There's that rare, deep Alec laughter I know and love."

"Hey, I laugh."

She shrugged. "Not enough."

"You bring it out in me, I guess."

Danica shruggd. "We'd be so good together. Why can't you be a girl?"

"Why can't you like dick?"

She made a retching sound as she rose from the table. He slung an arm around her shoulders as they headed out of the TUB.

"We get our Mock Trial case soon," Danica reminded him.

Mock Trial was a self-explanatory class that prepared students for a live courtroom. Since Alec wanted to be a lawyer, he'd been looking forward to this class since he was a freshman.

Although no one had told him they would have to sing a cappella on the first day of class. Professor Grim said they had to get over their fear of public speaking. Alec had sung "Twinkle, Twinkle, Little Star," because it was the only song he could think of that he wouldn't blank and forget the words. It sounded so awful, the professor cut him off and told him to take a seat, mentioning that he'd now "made everyone uncomfortable." Oh well, he'd completed the assignment.

Danica had sung "I Kissed a Girl" in perfect pitch, and Alec loved her for it.

"Yeah, I wonder what our trial will be about."

"Hopefully it's something cool."

"What do you consider cool?"

"I dunno. I'll know it when I hear it."

As they neared the door, Carrie stepped in front of them, eyeing Alec's arm around Danica's shoulders. "Hey." Her hands tapped an irregular beat on her thigh. "You . . . um . . . have a minute to talk?"

"Sure," Danica said innocently. "What do you want to talk about?"

Carrie's eyes darted to her face, and Alec bit back a laugh. He bumped Danica with his hip and unwound his arm. "I'll catch you later."

"But—"

"Bye, Danica."

She shot him a purple-lasered glare and stomped out of the front doors of the TUB.

Alec stepped off to the side and leaned against the wall, waiting for Carrie to speak. She followed him and stood a foot away, her eyes roaming everywhere but on his face.

He checked his watch, just to be an asshole. "Did you want something?"

"How are you?" she blurted quickly, finally looking at him.

"Uh . . . good," he said slowly.

She jerked her head up and down. "Great, great."

Silence fell again.

"Look, Carrie—"

"I miss you."

Alec had spent almost five years as Carrie's boyfriend, but now he couldn't remember *who* that Alec Stone was. Eight months of heartbreak seemed like ten years.

"I don't . . . okay. I'm not sure what you want me to say here. I'm sorry things didn't work out, but you broke up with me."

Carrie's eyes widened, those big brown eyes he used to love, but now didn't stir one ounce of interest. She stepped forward, her arms out, as if to touch him, and he stepped back. She stopped abruptly and dropped her hands, her lip quivering.

"I didn't break up with you. You broke up with me." Her voice cracked, but the words overrode his sympathy.

"No." He ground his teeth. "In my mind, the day you cheated on me was the day you broke up with me. And that's on *you*, Carrie. I'll take responsibility for our relationship stalling out, but that's it."

She opened her mouth, but he was done. "I gotta go." He brushed past her and shoved the door open, slamming it back on its hinges.

Fuck. And now he needed another run.

Chapter Three

KAT SAT AT a table in the library, her statistics syllabus in front of her, along with her student planner. With a blue marker, she highlighted each test and quiz date on her syllabus, then marked down the corresponding date in her planner as a test day in blue pen. A pink highlighter showed her paper due dates, matching the pink pen marks in her planner.

She'd never understood her friends and roommates who made jokes about pulling all-nighters to cram for a test or crank out a fifteen-page paper in one day. She needed this organization and planning, she thought, as she noted on her planner the dates she'd need to start her papers—breaking it down into when she'd complete her research, outline and type up her first draft.

Same went for studying—when she'd go over her notes and make flash cards.

Her parents had moved from São Paulo, Brazil, when

she was three and her brother, Marcelo, seven. School had always been rough for her, but in sixth grade, it had come close to unbearable. She'd no longer been able to hide how poorly she could read when forced to read out loud or how numbers were never as they appeared to everyone else. Kat-land bloomed, the magical place in her head where she retreated when everything around her didn't make sense. She'd been on the verge of giving up, to wallow in the D-list for the rest of her life.

But her guardian angel came in the form of her teacher, Mrs. Ross, the first teacher to see she wasn't a lazy student.

Mrs. Ross had been the one to show her how to her break down her assignments into steps, how to plan ahead and become rigidly organized.

In high school, she managed to squeak by, encouraging smitten boys to help with—er . . . more like *do*—her homework.

But college was harder. There weren't any smitten boys who were happy with a smile and some attention. In college, she was one pretty girl among many.

As far as the SATs, she'd never worked harder in her life. Outlines, flash cards, note cards covered her bedroom floor. She lived and breathed SAT-prep for two years. And still the test stumped her, the words on the page shifting in front of her. Her score was barely high enough for Bowler's minimum requirement. She'd hoped once she got to campus, she could start over. But sometimes she felt like that low SAT score was stamped on her forehead and everyone was whispering behind her back, telling their friends how she didn't belong.

When she was feeling low, she resented the extra work she had to do compared to other students. But no one wanted to join her pity party, so she kept her thoughts to herself and plastered on the smile.

She sighed and checked the clock on the wall above the FICTION shelf D–F and snorted to herself. Lovely reminder of her current grade situation.

Her advisor had agreed to assign her another tutor, although he all but threatened she get along with this one or she'd be on her own.

She focused back on her syllabus, drawing her name at the top in colorful bubble letters, when someone dropped a bag on the table in front of her. "Hey, Kat."

She looked up, into Alec's eyes. *You've got to be kidding me.*

"Hey," she said with forced politeness.

He raised his eyebrows. "You're really making this a thing. Studying and all."

She rolled her eyes and hoped he didn't know this was a designated tutor-student table. "Yep, just studying."

He sank into a chair and propped his folded hands on the table. "Oh yeah? What's the password today?"

"Redrum."

He snorted a laugh. "Okay, Jack Nicholson, good for you. But I need this table."

She narrowed her eyes. "No, I need this table."

"Oh?"

"I'm meeting someone, and this was our prearranged spot."

He paused for a moment and then his eyes widened. She watched in horror as his face lit up with recognition. "Are you waiting for a tutor?"

Oh no. Oh no no no. She would not be tutored by smug Alec SuperBrain Stone. The last thing he needed was more ammunition to make fun of her.

Kat moved haltingly, gathering her papers in such a rush a pen went skittering across the table. She'd sacrifice her carefully color-matched pens to the library gods if it meant getting out of there as quick as possible. Alec picked it up from where it had landed on a chair. He handed it to her as she rose from her seat. She didn't look at him. "I'll . . . uh . . . let you have the table—"

"Kat—"

"Oh my! I didn't realize the time. My . . . meeting . . . person . . . didn't show up I guess, so—"

"Kat—"

"Have fun with your . . . table . . . or whatever—"

"Kat!" he shouted, earning him some pointed stares.

She finally looked at him, cursing her brain ten thousand ways for needing a flipping tutor. For not easily being able to do what it seemed everyone else on campus could.

He pointed to her seat. "So, statistics, right?"

She rolled her jaw and kneaded her fingers into the strap of her bag. He was her last shot at passing this stupid class she needed as her math general education requirement. She couldn't fail out of school, or she would be her parents' assistant at their financial-planning company for the rest of her life, answering mundane stock questions and ordering the correct variety of flavored K-cups for the office break room.

"Sit down, Kat."

Her body jerked at his words, wanting to run out of the library as fast as she could, but she gave in to gravity and collapsed ungracefully into her chair.

Alec took a deep breath. "It's no big deal. You need a tutor. I'm a tutor. And a good one. I actually like statistics."

Of course he did.

"Kat, if you're really uncomfortable, I'm sure you can find another—"

"No!" she said a little loudly and then glanced around the library sheepishly.

"No," she said, quieter. "This is fine." She opened her bag and pulled out her notebook and textbook. "So, let's get this over with."

He blinked at her dog-eared statistics book "What happened to it? It looks like it's been through a war."

She eyed the book as if it were a live rattlesnake. "I bought it used. But I tell you what, after this semester, I'm going all *Office Space* on it. It has no idea what war is."

He chuckled, but she glared at him.

"Okay, so, it's probably better to start at the beginning to get the concepts down. You wanna show me your notes?"

She never showed her notes. Her planner might have been color coded, but her attempts at taking notes off a board or from a lecture were a whole other ball game. Because they were an extension of her brain. All jumbled, with words and symbols scribbled into the margins, half-finished thoughts floating off the page. She flipped open her notebook, shoved it at him and then leaned back in her chair, arms over her chest. A glance at the window showed a heavy downpour, and she seriously pondered whether she'd rather be in here with him or out there getting a cold shower.

Part of her resentment stemmed from her secret desire to be in his chair—the tutor chair. Teach other students who struggled like she did. But that was impossible. How could she help anyone else when she couldn't help herself?

Alec cleared his throat. "Uh . . . so, what do you expect here? I'm just going to read your notes at you? I don't think that's very effective. You could at least look at me."

Kat whipped her head around to look at him. She knew she was being a turd on a stick, but didn't he realize how much this sucked for her? "You're the tutor, so . . . tutor."

He clenched and unclenched his fists, and his nostrils flared. She definitely didn't notice how hot he looked all pissed off. "Look, princess, I'm not really sure what you expect here—"

Did he just— "Did you call me 'princess'?"

He narrowed his eyes. "Uh, yeah, I did, because right now you're acting a little entitled."

"Entitled?" she hissed.

"Are you going to repeat everything I say?"

"Are you going to call me 'princess' again?"

"Okay, how about 'brat'?"

"Ugh!" She threw herself back in her chair and looked away from him.

" 'Princess Brat,' " he muttered.

She clenched her jaw, but didn't say anything.

"Look, this isn't going to work if you aren't an active participant—"

"Sounds good." She began gathering her notebook and book *again*. She'd rather fail. Enough was enough. "I'll ask for another tutor. No biggie."

He smacked his hand down on top of her notebook, and she froze. "No way are you getting out of this."

She glared at him, wishing she had superpowers of her own so she could incinerate him on the spot. Or better yet, steal his brain so she didn't need a tutor. She concentrated really, really hard on stealing his brain, but unfortunately, she wasn't an intelligence-stealing mutant.

He sighed. "Look, let's end this for today. Next session, on Thursday, make a list ahead of time of all the concepts you're having trouble with and we'll go over those. Okay?"

A future of hearing the acronym NASDAQ every day, multiple times a day, with her parents breathing down her neck were the only reasons her mouth opened and she said reluctantly, "Okay. And can we keep this . . . you know . . . between us?"

The name *Max* lay unspoken between them.

Alec nodded. "No problem."

Kat wanted to vomit.

Well, she didn't *want* to vomit. Because vomiting was gross, and it was bad for her teeth, but she *felt* like she was going to vomit.

Of all the tutors, why did she have to be assigned to Alec? Scrunchie-wearing Ashley looked mighty great right about now.

Kat walked up the flight of stairs to her suite in McCoy Hall. As a sophomore, she had the option to move out of the dorms and into the on-campus apartments. She shared a bedroom with her friend Tara, and they shared a common room separating them from the other bedroom in the apartment, where their friends Casey and Shanna lived.

She opened the front door of her suite and stomped her booted feet to get the feeling back into her frozen toes.

"Hey," Shanna said from a beanbag chair on the floor, where she was playing some fantasy video game with swords and guys in dented armor and women in cleavage-baring dresses. Kat sometimes wondered if the controller was permanently attached to her hand. It was Kat's idea for all the roommates to pitch in to buy the beanbag for Shanna for her birthday so she would stop squinting at the TV from the couch.

"Hey," Kat mumbled. Shanna gave her a look underneath her dark fringed bangs and nodded in greeting. Kat trudged into her bedroom and threw her book bag onto her bed, then flounced onto the mattress on her back. The toilet flushed and Tara bounced out of the bathroom. "Hey, Kitty-Kat."

"Hey, Tare-Bear." She stared up at the waffled ceiling,

thinking it looked a lot like an inverted egg carton. The bed dipped and Tara's scent, minty from the gum she always chewed, tickled her nose.

"How was the new tutor?"

Kat opened her eyes at Tara, her friend since freshman year, when they lived on the same dorm floor and had horrid, shower-averse roommates.

"Guess who it is."

Tara scrunched up her nose in thought, accentuating the freckles splattered across the bridge of her nose, and toyed with a strand of her pixie-cut blonde hair over her ear. "Um . . . Theresa Spalding?"

Theresa was in their speech class freshman year and did a totally creepy presentation on Jack the Ripper. Kat still had nightmares about it. "No."

Tara shifted her lips from side to side. "Okay, how about . . . Bryan Coulter?"

Kat had gone on one date with Bryan Coulter. Turned out his job was to dress as a giant mouse at the local kids' arcade. They'd made out in his car for a little, but when she later found a game ticket down her pants from the many that littered his car, she declined a second date.

"Damn, I haven't thought about him . . ." She shook her head. "Anyway, no. But thanks for the reminder."

"How about . . ."

Kat bolted upright. "Seriously, Tara? When I told you to guess who it was, I was being rhetorical!"

Tara looked affronted. "You don't have to get all huffy."

Kat blew out a breath. "I'm sorry, okay? I'm stressed. My tutor is Alec."

Tara stared at her blankly.

"Alec?" Kat said. "You know . . . Max—"

"Oh!" Tara's eyes were wide. "*That* Alec."

"Yeah, *that* Alec. Nerdy Alec."

Tara waggled a finger. "You know, nerd is the new black. I read that in *Cosmo*."

Kat fell onto her back again and stared back at the egg-carton ceiling. "Deliver me. Please. Just put me out of my misery."

Tara laughed and smacked Kat on the thigh. "You're so dramatic, you know that?"

"Yep." Kat rolled her head to face Tara and grinned. "It's my schtick."

"So what's the big deal?" Tara shrugged. "I mean, I know you're kinda private about your studying and all of that. Is it because you don't want Max to know?"

Kat laced her fingers on her stomach and twiddled her thumbs. "I guess that's part of it. I don't know. There's something about Alec that gets me all defensive. I don't want him to think I'm . . . stupid."

Tara's face fell. "Kat, you're not—"

"I know! I know. I just . . . I don't know."

"Do you . . . are you attracted to him?"

"Have you seen him?"

"Yeah."

"What do you think?"

"Well, I think he's hot, but he's not your type."

Kat sat upright again and braced herself with her hands behind her. "What's my type?"

"Are we seriously having this discussion?"

"Clearly, we are."

Tara ran her tongue over her upper teeth. "Your type is Max. Muscled jocks who have no intentions of a long-term relationship."

"What? That's not true. There was . . ." she trailed off as she tried to remember one guy who wasn't a shallow jock. Names and faces drifted through her mind. "Wait, what about . . . ?" She frowned when she couldn't find an example to contradict Tara's statement. "Shoot," she muttered.

Tara stood up and walked to her desk. "Your relationship with Max is getting close to its expiration date anyway."

"Expiration date?"

Tara turned around and laughed. "What's it been, like two or three months? That's about the shelf life of a Kat Caruso boyfriend."

Kat shook her head and opened her mouth to deny that, too. But she snapped it shut when she couldn't think of one boyfriend she'd had for longer than three months.

"Shoot," she said again.

Tara picked up her book bag and shrugged on her heavy ski jacket. "Why is that?"

Kat hated lying to people. But sometimes it couldn't be avoided and this was one of those times. This was something she didn't want to admit out loud, so she turned away from Tara. "I don't know."

Tara heaved a sigh. "Well, I gotta get to class. We'll talk later?"

"Yep," said Kat, not really paying attention. "Oh wait!"

she called after her friend. Tara stopped in the doorway and looked over her shoulder expectantly.

Kat hopped off of the bed and grabbed a notepad from her desk. She ripped off the top paper and handed it to Tara.

She looked up and raised her head questioningly. "Alisa Dombrovski?"

"You said Amy wanted to take dance, right?"

Tara, the oldest of five, had told Kat her youngest sister wouldn't stop talking about ballet after seeing *The Nutcracker* last year. But her parents couldn't afford it and Tara had been saving money from her retail job for lessons.

"Alisa is the sister of the ballet instructor I took lessons from when I was a kid. I called Irina the other day and told her your sister really shows talent but . . . um . . . funds are tight. So she called *her* sister, whose studio is about a half hour from your parents' house, and Alisa agreed to take on your sister. No cost."

Tara blinked at the paper and then at Kat. She opened her mouth, but Kat cut her off.

"I know it's a half hour and that's a strain on your parents, but I'm sure one of your brothers can drive her. Also, don't give me crap about how you won't take charity. Alisa said if you demand to pay something, she needs her studio painted and maybe Greg can do that, too, if he's already driving her."

Tara's throat worked and she finally found her voice. "You seriously got my sister free ballet lessons."

Kat waved a hand. "I didn't do anything. I just called Irina."

"Kat, I . . ." Tara flicked the paper in her hand, then folded it carefully and tucked in into her pocket. "I'm not too proud to take charity. Not for my sister. Thank you so much. She's going to scream when I call her and tell her."

"A good scream?" Kat squinted.

Tara laughed. "Yeah, a good one." She glanced at her clock. "I gotta go, but we'll talk more, yeah?"

Kat waved as Tara walked out, but her friend poked her head back inside. "Think what I said about Max?"

Kat nodded and Tara smiled, then left.

Kat flopped back down on her bed. Max was the perfect guy for her—loud in a way that he didn't hear much other than his own voice in his ears. He didn't look closely at her other than her physical attributes and that's how she liked it.

There wasn't a commitment with Max and guys like him. She knew when they made fun of her for her scatterbrain or got tired of her and left, she could let it roll off of her back.

She was careful to stick to guys like that. Guys who would never have her heart or mean much to her. She didn't like being alone, which was the reason she even kept them around.

The problem with Alec—the reason she needed to keep her distance—was he wasn't like Max. Alec already made her feel brain-naked; with those intelligent eyes on her and a few kind words, he'd have her heart-naked, too.

She couldn't afford that. Because once he found out what she was really like, there was no way he'd stick with her. And she shuddered to think what marks he'd leave on her naked heart.

Good thing she had a boyfriend. Good thing Alec would never see her as more than a dumb girl who needed a tutor. Good thing she thought Alec was a jerk and wasn't at all attracted to him or grateful to him for sticking with tutoring her.

Oh, crap on a cracker.

Chapter Four

ALEC PLUNKED THE smoothie down on the table in front of an empty seat and sat down opposite. Hopefully the spinach concoction would be like a peace offering to Kat. He debated whether he should have spiked it with rum when booted heels clicked on the tile, and Kat's shadow fell on the table.

She stared at the smoothie questioningly, then raised her eyes to his without moving her head.

He cleared his throat. "Uh, you had a green smoothie the other day, and this was the only one the guy at the counter said was green so . . ." He gestured lamely at it with his hand.

"You remembered I had a green smoothie?"

He didn't want to tell her he remembered the smoothie was green because it matched her green sweater she was wearing that day. Because that would definitely be weird. So he shrugged. "Yeah."

She blinked at it and sat down, then wrapped her lips around the straw and sucked. While drinking, she looked up at him with those big blue eyes and his chest constricted. A bead of sweat trickled down the back of his neck as she hollowed her cheeks and— *Shit, did someone turn the heat up in this damn library?*

He exhaled roughly and looked away. When he turned back to her, she had finally stopped with her sex-act simulation and folded her hands primly on the table in mock innocence, smiling sweetly.

And that made him swell in his jeans, because damn, she was good. He didn't want to think about the fact that this was the first time in a long time he'd been so strongly attracted to someone. Getting cheated on tended to dull the libido.

A subject change was necessary. "You ready to get started?"

The innocent sex kitten look rapidly faded, replaced by tension in her body. He wanted to cringe at her obvious discomfort. She nodded curtly, then dug into her book bag for her textbook and notes.

He glanced at the syllabus she had among her class materials in the center of the table. It was covered with different colors of highlighter, and he made a note to look more closely later, to study her system. "Oh, Dr. Alzahabi? I had him for macroeconomics. He's tough but fair."

"Yeah, well, my professor could be, like, the inventor of statistics or whatever and I'd still be failing." She blushed a little and bit her lip at the admission.

Alec decided it was best to move on. "Okay, well, let's go over your notes on the class so far. Start at the beginning."

For the next forty-five minutes, they read over her notes. The pages were covered in scribbles and sometimes her notes would end mid-sentence, as if she hadn't caught the words or hadn't been paying attention. Her notes were like a dozen half-started mazes, and he hoped he had the correct map to help her finish them.

During the session, it started to rain, and he caught her several times staring out the window near their table, her eyes trailing the rivulets of water. He knew he should try to redraw her attention, but she was so beautiful in profile, all long lashes and full lips and smooth skin. She ran her hands through her hair and his fingers itched, wondering what it would be like to sift his own fingers through the dark golden strands, or see them spread out on his pillow, clear blue eyes staring up at him.

Whiffs of citrus from her shampoo or body wash hit him each time she turned her head, and it was fucking distracting. He spent most of the session uncomfortably half hard and wondered how he was going to be able to do this twice a week.

And he felt guilty as fuck. A total hypocrite. Was this how it started with Carrie? Did she start looking at some guy—he didn't know who it was—and think about touching him? Shit, he didn't want to think about it.

And here he was, turning around and thinking of doing almost the same thing to Max.

He was such an asshole.

At the end of the hour, Kat's self-consciousness had faded, and he hoped she hadn't noticed his completely over-the-top reaction to her presence.

"So, do you feel better about some of the material?" he asked.

She smiled and it was nice to see Kat relaxed, without tension or the straw-sucking sex kitten act. "Yeah, you're good at this stuff. Thanks."

"No problem." He reached for her notebook and as he handed it to her, a piece of paper fluttered to the floor.

"Let me get that!" Kat said urgently, jolting from her seat as he picked it up. He wasn't paying attention to her though, his eyes on the piece of paper. It was a quiz, dated that Tuesday.

In red print and surrounded by a broken circle was 2/10. Her score.

She snatched it out of his hand before he could look any further. "That's mine," she snapped, crumpling it and stuffing it into her book bag.

"Kat, what's the big deal—"

"Great, so we're done for now, right? See ya next week."

Her face was pinched, and her voice was shaky. She was riding the edge of that wave right now, and he really, really wanted to help steady her.

"Kat." He kept his voice calm. Her hands, fumbling with the clasp on her bag, slowed. "That was a quiz from statistics?"

She swallowed and sighed, looking out the window again. Finally, she nodded.

"Okay . . ." he said slowly. "Why didn't you show it to me? We can go over it and see where you went wrong—"

She whipped her head to the side, hair cascading around her shoulders. "I failed it. I'm not really sure what point there is in rehashing it."

Alec felt like a horse trainer trying to calm a wild mustang. "Yeah, you did fail it. But that's why you have a tutor. So we can bring your grades up, but we need to see where you struggle before we can fix it."

She still wouldn't meet his eyes, so he decided to take a chance. "I don't understand why you get so defensive—"

"I don't want you to think I'm stupid!" she yelled, then froze, biting her lips furiously, her eyes wet.

Oh shit, he didn't know what to do with tears.

"I don't think you're stupid—"

She snorted under her breath, her head turned away again.

"Okay," he hedged. "At first I might have assumed you were one of Max's typical girlfriends, but I know that you aren't. I don't think you're stupid. I think you aren't good at statistics, and you're not the best note-taker. None of that means you're stupid."

She blinked rapidly and then turned to face him, hunching over her folded arms. This self-conscious Kat made his chest hurt.

"I don't like feeling stupid," she said quietly.

Damn. "I don't think anyone likes feeling stupid."

She stared at her hands, picking her nails. "I tend to feel that way a lot and I hate it." Her eyes rose to meet his. "I've never really admitted that to anyone before."

She was killing him. All he wanted to do was wrap her in his arms and smooth her hair and never let anyone again make her feel less than brilliant.

But he couldn't control anyone else.

"If I ever do anything to make you feel like that, you tell me, all right?" Those blue eyes stared into his, and he felt lost in the whirlpool, like the rain had flooded the library and they were all actually underwater.

Something worked behind her eyes as she watched him, and he wanted to kick his own ass for ever thinking she was just another girl.

She licked her lips. "Okay, Alec."

His name on her lips, said without snark, coated his skin like a hot towel. Guess he hadn't drowned.

"So, is this kind of like a truce?" she asked.

Apparently confessional time was over. "Yeah, sure. Something like that."

"Pinky swear?" She held out her hand, little finger extended.

"Uh . . ."

She wiggled it, along with her eyebrows. "Come on. Don't be too cool to pinky swear."

"I'm twenty-one years old. I'm not going to pinky swear."

She stuck out her lower lip in a pout and widened those eyes.

He huffed out a breath, slammed his elbow on the table and linked little fingers with her. "Note I'm doing this under duress."

She raised their hands up and down. "Noted."

He released his finger from hers before he did something stupid like haul her across the table and kiss her.

She turned her head toward the window and sighed. He followed her gaze and watched as an icy rain beat against the windows. "Ugh," she groaned. "No way am I walking out in that."

"Yeah, looks like we're stuck here for a little." He shifted in his seat, conflicted over being in her presence for longer. *She has a boyfriend, man. Your best friend!*

"I don't feel like studying anymore," Kat said.

"Want to come with me to get a smoothie? I heard they have a protein one. I've been meaning to check it out. The line was long when I got here, so I just ordered yours, and I had a run before I came."

"Oh really? You run?" They rose from their seats and skirted the tables on their way to the snack counter.

"Yeah, I was on the cross-country team in high school."

"Wow. I admired those guys. I hate running."

"Oh yeah?" He nudged her with his elbow as they stood in line. "I bet you were a cheerleader."

Kat scrunched her nose. "No, I wasn't, actually. My friends tried to get me to join the team, but I didn't like the uniforms. I look bad in yellow."

He didn't know what to say to that.

"But," she continued. "I was a football manager."

"A football manager? What is . . . what did you manage?"

She looked at him, all wide-eyed innocence. "Tight ends." Then she bent over in peals of laughter, her whole little body shaking, undignified snorts drawing side-eyes from other students.

He groaned. "Kat, that was awful and seriously not funny."

She straightened, wiping her eyes. "Yes, it was totally funny."

"No, it wasn't."

"If it wasn't funny, then why are you laughing?"

He hadn't even realized he'd *been* laughing. What was it about her that he found himself smiling whenever she was around? He rubbed his mouth to cover the rest of his chuckles. "Because watching you laugh makes me laugh." *Shit, did I say that out loud?*

Kat sobered quickly, her eyes rising to meet his. All flirting sex kitten gone as she absorbed his words. Finally, she spoke. "No one has ever said that to me before."

He looked away and shrugged, unwilling to continue the conversation further because he didn't trust himself. But he mentally kicked himself, because he would have loved to hear her laugh like that all day.

He ordered his smoothie, and they returned to their table. Alec kept telling himself he should leave and brave the icy rain, but Kat's draw was powerful. He shifted in his chair and cleared his throat. "So, what's your major again?"

A faint blush crept into her cheeks. "Um, I'm actually undecided."

"Oh? Well, do you know what you want to do?"

The blush didn't fade and Kat shifted in her seat. "I'm not . . . I'm not sure yet. I just . . ." She straightened her spine and looked him in the eye, her voice strengthening.

"I know that I want a degree. I know that I don't want to be a secretary for my parents' company, which is where I would be without graduating from college."

"Why's that? There are other jobs you can do without a degree."

She shook her head. "I know myself. I'd give into the pressure of my dad—I love him, but he's kind of a battle ax—and I'd take the easy way out. And then I'd be miserable." She took a deep breath. "I believe I have some sort of purpose. Something I haven't realized yet. I have to find it." She peeked at him from under her lashes and threaded her fingers through her hair. "Does that sound stupid? I mean, I know you might not get it because I'm sure school was always easy for you, but—".

"Don't do that," he cut her off.

"What?"

"Don't compare me to you. We're totally different people and we each have our own strengths and weaknesses. And I think that's great that you're doing something for yourself. It doesn't matter if you aren't sure what you want to do yet for the rest of your life. You're only twenty. But you're going for your goal, and I think that's awesome. I'm proud of you."

She stared at him, her fingers motionless and tangled in her hair. Then she smiled that rare, genuine smile. "Thanks." She released her hair and drained her smoothie, the straw gasping in the empty cup. "But I have to pass statistics first."

He winked. "Good thing you have me."

Her snort sounded sort of ironic. "Yeah. Good thing."

Chapter Five

ALEC COULDN'T TAKE his eyes off Max's arm draped around Kat's shoulders. He had to be some sort of masochist, agreeing to come out to the bar with them, Tara, Shanna and Cam.

And he was *pissed off* that twenty-year-old Kat had a fake ID. It was stupid and risky. When the bouncer studied it, flicking it in his fingers, Alec had glared at Kat. But she had pointed her finger at him and whispered "pinky swear truce" so he shut his mouth. Plus, she wasn't his girlfriend. What say did he have in her life?

So now he alternated between seething with anger and seething with jealousy. With a cherry of guilt on top of that sundae. He was the life of the party.

His other roommate, Camilo "Cam" Ruiz, scanned the room like a predator as usual. He'd started school a semester late because he was in boot camp, having joined the Air National Guard right out of high school.

He was in Alec's major, angling to be a detective or something. On the weekends he wasn't reporting for his monthly drill, he was on the prowl. He hooked 'em with his dimples, reeled 'em in with his charm and then let 'em go. And they all loved him for it. Alec couldn't figure out how he did it without girls going *Fatal Attraction* on his ass.

Kat's friend, Tara, sat beside him, the strobe lights catching on the white blonde of her short hair. Shanna was on the other side, quiet as always, sneaking glances at Cam from under her bangs, full lips pressed tight together.

Bodies writhed and wriggled on the dance floor at Caps, and the house music pounded a throbbing pain into Alec's temples, the bright lights blinding him. He would have rather been at Craig's Place across town, a laid-back bar with classic rock on the jukebox and scratched pool tables.

"You want another drink?" Max asked Kat, rising from the table. Alec noted Kat had barely touched the rum and coke in front of her. She shook her head, and Max tugged a lock of her hair before heading to the bar.

Kat smoothed her hair down and raised her eyes to him, quickly looking away when their gazes locked.

"Kitty-Kat, Shan, let's dance," Tara shouted over the booming house music. Kat looked at her friend, her eyes skittering right over Alec, and he really wanted to know why she avoided looking at him.

Her face was blank, like she was trying to process her friend's words, or make a decision, and then her crimson-

tinted lips split into that sexy smile. "Sure." He now recognized her mask, the confident, sexy girl she portrayed
in public.

"Didn't you go out on a date with this DJ? Maybe
you can make a request," Tara said as the three of them
walked away, already starting to sway their hips to the
beat. Kat's ass looked phenomenal in her tight jeans and
red high heels. *Damn it.* That cherry of guilt was turning
into a huge, gross, rotten tomato. And he couldn't talk to
his best friend about it, because *he* was the reason Alec
currently had said rotten tomato in his gut.

"Stone."

Alec turned to Cam.

His black wavy hair shone in the light and his dark
eyes were assessing. "What's Shanna's deal?"

"I don't know what you mean by *deal*."

Cam took a gulp of his beer and waved his hand while
swallowing. "You know, like, does she have a boyfriend
or whatever."

"I don't know, why the fuck are you asking me? Ask
Max."

Cam paused and then placed his bottle gently on the
table. "What's up your ass?"

"Nothing."

"You sound like a girl right now."

"You sound like a chauvinist right now."

Cam's mouth dropped open. "Dude."

Alec inhaled, the air tangy with stale beer and sweaty
college students. He let out his breath and rubbed his
face. "I'm sorry. I'm in a bad mood."

"Yeah, Captain Obvious. Thanks for the heads up. And what else is new?"

Alec snorted a laugh and kicked out Max's chair for him as he returned to the table. "Where are the girls?"

"Dancing." Cam answered. "And Zuk's being a prick."

"What's new?" Max said. Was Alec really that awful all the time that both his friends had the same response to his bad mood? Max grinned at him and this time Alec aimed his kick at his friend's knee. Max took the hit without a wince, then shifted his chair for a better view of the dance floor. "If Kat's dancing, I'm watching. Man, that's why I asked her out in the first place."

Alec let his eyes drift to the dance floor, and there was Kat, doing some sort of grinding dance move with Tara, their bodies plastered together—*Jesus Christ*—Kat's long, shiny hair whipping around her neck, slender arms over her head.

Max elbowed him. "She can dance, right?" like Kat was some piece of meat.

The beat pounded into Alec's head and the beer fuzzed his brain. Kat's moves had him in a trance, but he was ever aware of her boyfriend's presence beside him, like a big bucket of cold water down his pants.

Alec jumped five inches off of his seat when Max stood up. "I need to run to the john. Can you watch Kat and make sure no jackass puts his hands on her?"

So now he was a babysitter? This night was getting better and better. He nodded and didn't take his eyes off of the dance floor. The guilt of watching her eased slightly. Max told him to, so it was okay, right?

Of course a minute after Max left, some guy walked up behind Kat, his eyes glued to her wiggling ass. Kat's back was turned so she didn't see him. The dude was huge, too, like six-five easy, and he was looking back at his friends, giving them a thumbs-up.

This was not Alec's night.

He stood, knowing his own height of six feet was going to look puny. He motioned to Cam, hoping he knew some sort of black ops trick to bring Big Dude to his knees with a strategic finger poke. "We gotta get the girls. Some guy is trying to get all over them."

Cam's eyes swept the dance floor, and his face hardened. "I got Tara and Shanna, you get Kat."

Course.

Alec pushed his way through the writhing bodies on the dance floor, eyes on Kat. By now, the big dude had started grinding his crotch against her ass, his hands clamped on her hips.

When Alec was five feet away, Kat dislodged the guy's hands and whirled around to face him, all of five-three with her heels, her face only coming up to his pecs. She put a hand up, right in the guy's face, and Alec saw her lips say, "No."

His heart started beating five times harder, and if he were a sap, he would have said he fell in love with her right then. Babysit Kat? She could take care of herself.

Big Dude didn't want to take no for an answer. He grabbed her hips again and leaned in, pressing his face against her neck. Kat recoiled, yelled "Ew!" which Alec heard clearly over the blasting music, and then she shoved Big Dude's shoulders.

Big Dude wasn't amused.

Alec took three more strides and was by her side. Kat whirled on him, the fight still in her eyes, as if she expected him to be Big Dude's backup. When she saw it was him, her face lit up.

"Alec!" she yelled, flinging her arms around his neck. She nuzzled her face into his chest, then leaned back. "Pretend to be my boyfriend," she whispered.

Did Kat realize that was like a death sentence when Big Dude was rolling his cannonball shoulders and fisting his fingered hammers? But he couldn't say no, not with Kat's scent in his nostrils, the warmth of her still-dancing body pressing against his.

Out of the corner of his eye, Cam led Tara and Shanna off the dance floor and that spurred his brain into working again.

"Uh ..." Yeah, that was all he had. He never claimed to be an actor. So he gripped her waist and turned around, walking side-by-side, ignoring Big Dude.

Big Dude didn't like to be ignored.

"Yo!" He grabbed Alec's shoulder and wrenched it around. Alec didn't have time to unwrap from Kat, so she came with him.

Alec didn't like to fight. When they were younger, Max fought all the rich assholes for both of them. Alec liked to sit down and talk it out. Like adults. Or as Max called it, a "pussy pacifist."

"You need to keep a better leash on your girl," Big Dude said. Kat stiffened beside him, about to launch into a tirade. Was she afraid of anyone? Guys weren't supposed to hit girls, but that didn't mean none did.

Alec grimaced at the guy's mention of a leash. "Sorry, her collar is getting dry-cleaned."

Big Dude looked like he was contemplating stomping the life out of Alec. Kat snorted a laugh beside him, seemingly unconcerned about Alec's imminent pounding.

Before he could determine the best way to diffuse the situation, a body stepped in front of him. Max had finally stopped pissing and graced them with his presence. How generous. "Fuck off, Brant."

That was Max. No mincing words.

Alec didn't stay to hear the rest. He pulled Kat along with him off of the dance floor while she craned her neck around, shooting death glares at Big Dude the whole time.

When they got to their table, she sat down in her chair and shivered. "What a jerk." She smoothed her shirt over her hips. "Ugh, he had big, gross sweaty hands."

Alec didn't say anything, watching Kat put herself together and glad it hadn't escalated into him getting his nose broken.

"Thanks for that," she said, all traces of sexy Kat gone, her blue eyes earnest.

Anytime, anywhere, just say the word, Alec wanted to say. Instead he shrugged. "Max asked me to watch out for you."

Then he wanted to break his own nose as Kat's face

fell. She recovered quickly, though. "Right. Max asked you. Well, thanks."

Max returned a couple of minutes later and sat down beside Kat.

"Everything okay?" Alec asked.

"Yeah, Brant's drunk. He's an asshole sober, so he's just brimming with it when plastered." He took a sip of beer and looked around, bobbing his head to the music. Kat fidgeted beside him, twisting her shirt in her fingers. The adrenaline of the near fight seemed to have left her, and now she looked drained.

Ask Kat if she's okay, ask Kat if she's okay, Alec tried to tell Max through telepathy. It didn't work.

Alec leaned across the table to Kat. "You okay?"

She looked up, startled. Then she took a deep breath. "Yeah, I'm fine."

Her eyes shifted away. *Liar.*

KAT SIPPED HER drink. The same drink she'd had for the past hour. Max kept offering to buy her another one, not even bothering to notice she barely drank the one she had.

She didn't really like alcohol. She had enough trouble staying focused. Being intoxicated only made that worse. Plus, she felt all worked up from that big muscle head pawing her.

When she'd seen Alec walk through the crowd, she'd been relieved, knowing he'd have her back. It wasn't until Max actually showed up that she realized she hadn't even thought of *him.* Her boyfriend.

Things were complicated.

Max was everything safe. The devil she knew.

And now Alec sat across from her, quiet and studious, his eyes on her like he was trying to figure her out. She wished she could figure herself out. Alec was a six-foot, pompadoured temptation. She loved how he made a joke rather than threw his weight around at the big guy, not that his weight would have mattered, since her unwanted dancing companion could have tossed Alec into the second-floor DJ booth. But when she thought about it, she liked that he didn't try to flex his muscles and get all arrogant. She could take care of herself, provided she had someone at her back.

And having Alec at her back had made her feel as big as the meathead.

"You want to dance?" Max said, taking her out of her super-strength contemplation.

"Um, sure." She rose and reached for his hand.

"Nah, not with me. I hate dancing." Max screwed up his lips. "Go dance with Stone."

Seriously? Was this really happening? Alec made a strangled noise from across the table. When she didn't answer, Max looked at his friend. "Go dance with Kat. You're good at it."

Alec's jaw was tight when he stood up. He reached down and took a shot that was on the table, then washed it down with beer. His steps seemed a little unsteady when he grabbed Kat's arm and snarled at his friend. "Fine."

As they walked onto the dance floor, Kat said, "If you don't want to, we don't have to dance—"

"It's not a matter of not wanting to," Alec muttered, cutting her off.

They dissolved into the crowd on the dance floor, Alec taking her to the far corner, as far away from Max as they could get. Kat didn't protest.

Once they reached an empty spot among the writhing bodies, Alec grabbed her around the waist and pulled her to him. Thigh to thigh. Hip to hip. Chest to chest. They'd never been this close before.

His eyes, normally such a pale green, sparked in the club lighting, and there was a sexy smirk to his mouth. His fingers on her lower back were insistent, pressing, and conveying a message that her foggy brain didn't want to analyze.

He leaned down so his lips were at her ear and whispered, "Show me what you got."

Now *that*, she could do. The deep bass of the song was a thudding pulse down her spine and each horn blast was like a shot of adrenaline right into her veins. She'd loved dancing ever since her mom had given Kat her first tutu before ballet class.

She closed her eyes and let the beat of the song tap into her bones. She bent her knees and rolled her hips and shoulders, her fingers tangling into Alec's hair, like she'd imagined many times, while he kept his face pressed into her neck. He let her lead at first, and then his hips began to churn. He followed her movement, anticipating every shift of her body.

And she was lost. She was lost to the music, lost to the lust roaring through her veins and most of all lost to

Alec—to the feel of the muscles in his arms and shoulders rippling under her hands, a strong thigh pressed between her legs and his hips grinding into hers.

He lifted his head and when they locked gazes, she couldn't look away. Something shifted behind his eyes, and his pupils dilated. Kat saw the desire in them—the red-blooded male look that said he wanted to rip her clothes off. His hands, which had migrated to her ass, squeezed, and she wondered if her look echoed his.

He blinked and jerked his gaze away before gripping her waist and spinning her around roughly so her back was to his front. She took a step back in her heels until they were locked in an embrace and she continued to follow the beat, grinding her butt back into him.

Alec held her tightly with a strong grip on her hips. She'd thought she'd felt his arousal before, but now she was definitely sure, the thick ridge pressing against her. His breath rushed hot along her temple, and she reached back with one hand, curling a finger into a belt-loop on his jeans, pressing him closer. Her entire body felt slick from sweat, from the press of bodies on the dance floor and most of all, because of the roaring attraction between her and Alec.

A hand brushed her hair over one shoulder and a gust of cool breath wafted over the damp skin at the back of her neck. Closing her eyes, she groaned low in her throat, and Alec rumbled a groan in response before he pressed his hot lips to the spot he had cooled. The contact sent a jolt straight down her spine, and she stiffened in surprise, shock and lust.

Alec's movements stopped behind her and then his lips returned to her ear, and he whispered in a low, raspy voice, "Kat, we need to stop."

His words were like an ice pick to her skull. This whole thing had been out of line. If Max saw them . . .

She slowed her hips and took a step forward, glancing over her shoulder. Alec stood motionless, hands fisted at his sides, hair damp with sweat and hooded eyes on her. She reached back and held her hand out. He waited a beat before slipping his hand in hers and she led him off the dance floor.

Kat pushed her way through the crowd back toward their table, constantly aware of Alec's damp hand in hers, the heat of his body at her back. When they reached the table, she let go of his hand and hauled herself into a seat. Alec did the same across from her, his face flushed. Gathering her hair off of her neck, she fanned herself and looked across the table. "Where's Max?"

Cam stared at them, his face hard. "At the bar." He whipped his head to Alec. "What the fuck was that?"

Alec flipped a beer cap between his fingers. "What?"

"What?" Cam said incredulously. "You do that little performance on the dance floor and you say what?"

Kat's stomach churned.

Cam laughed bitterly. "Geez, after that grinding, you might be pregnant, Kat. In fact, every girl within five feet might be pregnant."

Alec raised his head and fixed Cam with a glare. "Shut the fuck up."

Cam shrugged and Kat debated on what to say. *Don't*

tell Max. Tell Max so he'll break up with me because I don't have the guts to do it. Tell Alec I'll be his if he'll love me and not discard me after a month like every other guy.

But when Max returned to the table, he was all smiles, and Cam accepted his beer from him.

"How was dancing, babe? Alec keep his hands to himself?" Max winked at her.

She swallowed. "Yeah, we had fun." Understatement of the year.

"Stone can dance, huh?"

Alec hadn't looked up from his beer cap flipping. "Yeah," she murmured.

Max slung an arm around her shoulder, leaned back in his chair and Kat steeled herself to get through the rest of the night.

Chapter Six

KAT WALKED SLOWLY down the hall toward the bathroom, yawning. Her ponytail had slipped to the side of her head overnight so she whipped out the elastic band and began arranging it again. Max was still in bed, snoring. When they'd stumbled home from the bar last night, she had feigned drunkenness and Max had promptly passed out beside her in bed. One class she could pass—Sex Evasion 501.

And mostly, she couldn't think about Max touching her when Alec's scent clung to her hair and her neck burned where he pressed his lips to her skin.

It was not lost on her how wrong that whole thought process sounded.

She bent her head, her hands fixing her ponytail. A bedroom door creaked open ahead of her and she slowed her pace, remembering belatedly she was only wearing a tank top and pair of panties.

She raised her eyes and froze.

Alec stood before her wearing only a pair of black boxer briefs. *Only black boxer briefs.* And for the love of all that was holy, she couldn't stop staring. He wasn't bulky like Max, but he had a runner's body, with sinewy arms and a thin waist trimmed with that delicious V muscle leading down into his waistband. His legs were muscular and she had to bite her tongue when all she wanted to do was bite his thigh. Yes, she wanted to bite his thigh. And then that muscle at his hip. And then maybe peek down those boxers to see if his big hands meant other things were big. She could still feel the imprint of those muscles against her own, shifting to the beat on the dance floor.

And oh mylanta, his abs. Those delicious ridges were perfect, bulging under thin skin, highlighting a nice little trail of hair that started below his belly button and disappeared into his waistband. She licked her lips, wishing she could trace those ridges with her tongue.

Yep, she'd officially gone off the deep end. Just right over it. *Plop!* Into the water. She wasn't even flailing. She sank like a happy little ball of lead. Horny lead.

Alec cleared his throat and she snapped her eyes from his general crotch area back to his face. His eyes were on her general stomach area, where a strip of skin showed below her tank top.

She lowered her hands, letting her hair spill down her back and tugged her shirt down. "Um . . . hey."

Clearly, eloquent was her middle name.

"Hey," he rasped out. His hair was adorably ruffled, the part usually smoothed back in a bump now hung in a dark floppy bang on his forehead. It was odd to see him without his glasses. Odd and definitely . . . nice.

She wondered if he thought of biting or licking any parts of her. Instead of dwelling on that, she gestured toward the bathroom. "I was heading there."

"Me too. But ladies first."

She wanted to laugh. In an inappropriately hysterical way. Because who said that other than her father when he went to the country club?

"Thanks," she mumbled. She stepped gingerly toward the bathroom, which was directly in front of him. As she brushed past him to enter, he grabbed her arm gently.

His touch startled her, and she looked up. His eyes were heavy lidded, and the pale green of his irises was darker in the early morning light. She imagined this would be an amazing scene in a movie, where he whispered in a tortured voice, *Kat, I want you. I've always wanted you. Let's retreat to my boudoir and consummate our mutual attraction . . .*

His lips were moving, and she snapped back to attention.

". . . It was acting up, so flush twice."

Yep, while she dreamed of writhing naked and sweaty in his sheets, he was telling her to flush the toilet twice. Awesome. Amazing. Not embarrassing at all.

She mumbled something in the affirmative and slipped from his grasp, then shut the bathroom door quickly behind her.

She gripped the sink and bent her head. This was crazy. She should break up with Max, but she hated breakups. And Max was safe. Sure it wasn't anything deep, but she didn't especially feel as if she wanted something deep—or that she deserved it.

Max had been irritated with her lately, but really, he'd lasted longer than most guys. And every time she thought about breaking up with him, she remembered the safety of their easy, light relationship and backed off.

When she finished using the bathroom, she opened the door to the sight of Alec standing outside, his arms crossed over his *still* bare chest, a shoulder propped against the wall. And he *still* hadn't put on pants. He also looked impatient.

He uncrossed his arms and raised an eyebrow. "Any trouble in there?"

She clutched her hand to her throat in mock helplessness. "It was so scary in there without you, Alec. I didn't know which knob on the sink was for hot water, and I couldn't remember if I was supposed to pee sitting down or standing up."

He stared at her for a minute, and then his entire face cracked. His lips split into a huge grin which deepened the creases alongside his mouth and accentuated his cheekbones. A couple of his bottom teeth were slightly crooked and for some reason she found that incredibly endearing.

And then he began to chuckle. Like the male version of a giggle. His shoulders shook and his eyes twinkled. He was like Santa, but Alec most certainly didn't have a belly like a bowl full of jelly. It was a belly full of hard things that came in sixes. Or maybe eights. She wouldn't mind unlimited access to his body for further examination.

Kat pulled her eyes away from his abdomen and raised them to his face. He had stopped chuckling now, but hadn't wiped the grin off of his face.

He gave her a wink as he walked past her into the bathroom. "Next time, I'll hold your hand and we'll get through it together, Kat."

As the bathroom door shut behind him, Kat frowned at her hands, because yeah, it might make her thirteen, but she loved when a boyfriend held her hand.

She sighed and walked back to Max's bedroom. He was still asleep, but woke up as she dressed.

"What're ya doin'?" he mumbled sleepily.

"I'm headed back to my place. I have some things I need to get done today."

He rubbed his eyes. "You okay walking back?"

"Yep, I'm fine."

"Good. Call me later." The bed creaked as he rolled over. By the time she closed his door behind her, he was asleep again.

She trotted down the stairs and pulled on her coat as Alec emerged from the kitchen, a piece of toast stuck between his teeth. His hair was damp and he wore his glasses.

Maybe he *was* hotter with his glasses on. They were kind of stylish, with thick, rectangular frames. They framed his face well. She needed to see comparison pictures or something. Maybe she could take pictures on her cell phone and then put it to vote among her roommates . . .

"Kat?"

How long had she been staring at his face? *Ooops*. "Uh . . . yeah?"

Alec gave her a strange look and shoved the rest of his toast in his mouth. "I asked if you were heading home?"

"Oh, yeah, I am."

He gestured toward the door and pulled his car keys from his pocket. "I can give you a ride."

"You don't have to do that."

He shrugged and opened up the door, waving her out. "I'm heading there anyway. I have a meeting."

"Well okay. Thanks."

Alec's car was the definition of a junker. There were splotches of rust among the brown paint, and the whole vehicle vibrated violently while they idled at a stop sign. When Kat pointed questioningly at a notepad with scrawled numbers on it, he explained his gas gauge didn't work, and he kept track of his mileage on paper.

She reached for the radio dial, but he waved his hand over the instrument panel. "Yeah . . . uh . . . it doesn't work."

"You can't listen to the radio?"

"No. Well, at least, not usually. Sometimes when the moon is full and the stars align and I sit at just the right angle, I can get some gospel station."

"Silence sounds like the better alternative, then."

"Listening to music while driving is overrated."

She lifted an eyebrow at him. "Really?"

The corner of his mouth lifted in a small smile. "No, not really. Driving without it sucks and it's boring."

She laughed, and they lapsed into silence. Memories

of the night before swirled in her head, but she clenched her jaw before she said something stupid like, *where'd you learn to dance like that* or *jeez, how about this weather*. She bit her lip as he pulled into a parking lot outside her apartment.

"This is it, right?" he asked, gazing up at the building.

"Yep. Thanks for the ride." She climbed out of the car.

"No problem, Kat."

She gave him a wave as she made her way into her building, aware of his car still idling in the parking lot, and the skin on the back of her neck tingling, like he'd branded her with his lips.

She rubbed the spot with a wince and opened her front door. Shanna looked up at her from her video game. Again.

Kat nodded at her and walked into her bedroom. Tara was tacking some pictures of her family on the wall. She gestured toward a box in front of Kat's closet. "That came for you today."

Kat took off her coat and checked the return address label. "Oh good, my mom found my stuff." She peeled off the packing tape and opened the flaps. On top of a pile of clothing sat a pair of almost pristine ballet shoes. She shoved the box over to Tara's side of the room with a grunt. "It's for you, actually."

"For me?" Tara said, dropping her pictures onto her bed.

"Well, for Amy. My mom shipped all my old ballet stuff. I mean, I realize it's, like, ten years old or something, but a lot of these things I never used, so . . ."

Tara was already rummaging through the box. "Kat, I can't believe you. This stuff is gorgeous." She pulled out a light pink leotard with ivory trim. "Amy is going to look adorable in this stuff."

"I thought so. Anyway, I asked Mom to ship it so you could take it home for spring break. I hope some of it fits."

Tara dropped a pair of ballet shoes she'd been ogling and launched herself at Kat. "You're the sweetest, Kitty-Kat."

Kat wrapped her arms around her friend's waist and squeezed. Tara was the best big sister she'd ever met, sacrificing so much to help her family. If Kat could help in any way, she would in a heartbeat. "Anytime, Tare-bear."

Tara released her and tilted her head toward her wall. "You busy? Can you help me with these pictures on my wall? I think they look stupid, all up in a row. You have your side of the bedroom decorated so cool. Arrange mine for me."

Kat cast an eye over to her side of the room. Her comforter was a lavender with light yellow piping and she'd incorporated those colors around her space, finding different shades of purple and yellow frames to display her pictures. She had even managed to save up from her summer job filing paperwork for her dad to buy a purple laptop.

Now comparing her side of the room to Tara's, hers did look more organized. But that's how she needed things to be.

"Okay," she said, taking the pictures from Tara she'd ripped off the wall. She leaned back, treating the wall as a

canvas, and started layering the pictures into a big group-
ing on the wall. Tara's family was beautiful, all blond
and happy. Kat smiled at a picture of Amy, clutching a
Nutcracker doll last Christmas. Beside it, Kat tacked up
a picture of Tara crossing a 5K finish line. "So, are you
nervous about your race?" she asked. Tara planned to run
her first marathon over spring break in March.

"Yes!" Tara said. "I'm excited but freaking out at the
same time. Did I tell you that I ordered one of those 26.2
stickers for my car already so I can slap it on right after I
cross the finish line?"

"When I see those stickers on cars when I'm driving, I
think, 'Oh, there's a completely insane person,'" Kat said.

Tara laughed. "Yeah, I know I'm crazy. Actually, after
we're finished here, I'd planned to go for a run. Wanna
come?"

Kat shot her a look out of the corner of her eye. "You
know that question gets a perma-no from me."

"I know, but I think you'd like it. Clears your head.
Just flushes everything out and refreshes it."

"Sounds like a plumbing problem."

"Kat—"

"Thanks for asking, honest. But I'm gonna say no."

Tara sighed. "Fine."

Kat smoothed a corner of a photo with Amy and her
twin, Natalie. "Alec likes to run."

"Oh?" Tara said, her tone a little too smug for Kat's
taste.

She shot her friend a glare. "Just making conversation."

"I think you're talking about what's on your mind."

Kat ignored the comment and stepped back, eyeing the collage of pictures on Tara's wall. "What do you think?" She overlapped the photos so they looked like one massive shiny heart.

"It looks awesome!" Tara clapped her hands. "You're so good at this stuff."

"I'll take care of the decorating for the two of us, and you take care of the amazing physical achievements," Kat said, walking back to her side of the room to unload her book bag. Tara followed her. "So, are we going to discuss last night?"

"What's there to discuss?"

"Um . . . you grinding your ass on Alec."

Kat turned a glare onto her friend. "There was no ass grinding. I don't know what you're talking about."

Tara folded her arms over her chest. "Really."

"Yes, really."

"You both looked pretty flushed when you came back—"

"Well, it's only normal for a guy to get hard while dancing with a girl—"

"A-ha!" Tara shouted. "You had to be close enough to feel that! Unless he's got a foot-long shlong, which I highly doubt—"

"Oh my God, we're not discussing Alec's anything." Kat pointed a finger at Tara, who remained silent. Then Kat groaned. "Who am I kidding? I saw him in his underwear this morning and that image is going to be ingrained in my brain forever. Along with you saying the word *shlong*. What's with that word?"

Tara shrugged. "It rhymed with foot-long."

"Whatever, if he can get me to pass this statistics class, I'll do anything with his foot-long that he wants."

Tara snorted. "I'll be sure to tell him that."

Chapter Seven

Kat skipped—yep, she was skipping like a giddy ten-year-old—out of her statistics class, a quiz paper clutched in her fist. She barely felt the cold as she made her way to the library for her second study session with Alec. When she reached their table, he was already there, head bent over a book. She slammed the paper down on top of his book, startling him.

"Ooooh yeah, read that Mr. Smart Alec! Who's the genius now?" She placed her fists on her hips, elbows out, and grinned triumphantly down at him.

Circled at the top of the paper in red ink, was 7/10. Yeah, it was a 70 percent, technically a C. And there were only ten questions. But it was a heck of an improvement over 2/10.

Alec looked at the paper and then up at her, a prideful smile splitting his face. "Way to go. See, I told you we could bring these grades up."

Kat squealed and clapped her hands, again reverting back to her ten-year-old self, knowing Alec wouldn't mock her. She wasn't used to this—this whole idea of being proud of herself for grades. She hadn't realized what a high it was to work hard and see the benefits. She could get addicted to this. And to those prideful smiles on Alec's face.

"Yeah, yeah," she said, plopping down in the seat across from him. "I got this tutor. He actually doesn't help me at all. I can do statistics blindfolded. But I feel bad for him and I want to make sure he feels important."

Alec rolled his eyes. "What a sucker."

Kat reached into her backpack, pulled out a candy bar, and handed it to Alec, knowing it was his favorite. "Yep, he is." Then she winked.

His answering wink and the small moan he made as he bit into his chocolate-caramel goodness made her gut lurch. First in a positive way because she liked both. A lot. Then in a negative way because she had no business flirting with Alec.

Why did he have to be so charming and nice? Right now, a stray lock of hair grazed his forehead, having escaped from its pomade pompadour prison. Her hands twitched to reach out and smooth it back.

"So, I know your major is criminal justice, but what do you want to do?" Kat asked.

Alec stuffed the rest of the candy bar in his mouth, chewed and swallowed. "Lawyer, and possibly judge."

"Is that something you always wanted to do?"

He paused. "Yeah. Pretty much. And it's a job that

pays well. Mom and I never had a lot of money so . . ." his voice trailed off and he waved his hand as if to push the conversation away. "Anyway, so you have a test coming up, right?"

Kat blinked at the change in subject. "Um . . . yeah. I have the midterm in a month."

He smiled softly. "I say let's make a bet. If you get a B or above, I buy you dinner."

Kat wiggled in her seat and grinned wickedly, rubbing her hands together. "You're on."

They broke out their notebooks and began to go over the notes from that morning's class. Kat yawned. She had been up late the night before, and was coming down from the high of her improved quiz score.

She was finding it hard to pay attention.

"So, in this problem, we first need to find the mean difference in the population between the male student absences and female students absences." Alec explained. "How do we do that?"

Kat stared at her notes, but her handwriting wasn't neat and the numbers on the page kept jumping around. She knew if she stayed silent long enough, Alec would answer for her.

But he didn't this time.

She cringed because sometimes the letters on the page in front of her looked disjointed and the numbers didn't match up. Add in the words from this statistic problem and the whole thing was a jumble. She couldn't remember what the mean was. Or the difference. And the mean difference just sounded cruel.

Alec paused, his finger on the paper. He looked at her and furrowed his brow. Cripes, she felt stupid.

"Um . . ." she said.

Alec squinted his eyes, studying her face.

"Um . . ." she repeated.

He had mercy on her. Finally. "Right here," he tapped the page. "We subtract the boys' absences—fifteen—from the girls' absences—ten. So it's five."

So, she couldn't subtract ten from fifteen? How embarrassing. But as always, she was a master at the coverup. "Right!" she laughed, but it was fake, and Alec didn't even crack a smile. "Yep. Sorry. Long day."

He slowly leaned back. "Okay, you want to take a break from studying and get a coffee or something?"

"Yeah, that would be great."

Alec seemed lost in thought as they gathered their bags and headed out of the library. He glanced at her several times out of the corner of his eye. Kat ignored the looks and focused on her second biggest gripe—after her brain—which was the cold. The icy rain had dulled to a bone-chilling mist.

But at least it took her mind off of the failed library study session.

"We should be able to use something for transportation around campus. Like little enclosed golf carts or those Zipcars. Something with heat." Kat wrapped her peacoat tighter around her body. "Ah! I know. Segways with umbrellas. Then we would be protected from rain and sun. Dual purpose." She hummed thoughtfully to herself. "Covered Segways. Gosh, I'm a genius."

Alec seemed to jerk out of his thoughts and raised an eyebrow at her.

"It's necessary," she explained. "This misting rain or whatever is making my hair frizz."

Alec's eyes roamed her head and then returned to her face. "I don't think it looks any different."

"What? Are you blind? My hair is all kinky from the humidity. And these little whispies of hair around my temples look awful and drive me nuts."

"Whispies? Are we speaking the same language?"

Kat shrugged. "Um, probably not. This is Kat-speak." She rolled her eyes dramatically and waved her hand in a circle. "I thought you were supposed to be smart. Keep up, Alec."

He stared at her for a minute and then started laughing. That wasn't the first time she'd surprised him into laughter. She liked it. It made her feel clever. She'd never felt clever in her life.

"Hey, since when are you two friends?" The familiar voice of Max—oh right, she needed the reminder she had a *boyfriend*—reached her as Alec held open the door to the campus coffee shop.

She turned around to see Max grinning, striding toward them. "And making Zuk laugh? Wow, Kat, that's a tough thing to do." When he reached them, he slung his arm around her shoulders and guided her inside. He turned to wink at Alec, who still held open the door. "Thanks, buddy."

Kat tried to crane her neck to watch if Alec followed them inside, but she couldn't see over Max's massive shoulder. She faced ahead and bit her lip, letting Max lead her to a table. He took her bag from her shoulder and looped the strap over her chair for her, then gave her a swift kiss on her cheek. "I'll get your mocha for you, babe," he said, then left to stand in line at the counter. Alec appeared at his side, and their heads bent as they talked.

Sometimes Max could be so nice. Sure, he made comments every once in a while that made her feel dumb. But nowhere near the level previous boyfriends did. And there were times he treated her like a queen.

But Alec never made her feel dumb . . .

No. *No.* She could not do this. She would not be sucked into some weird love triangle like some teenage rom com. She was twenty years old, for goodness sakes, and Alec was her tutor. At most, a friend. That's it. She smacked her palm on the table for emphasis, and then looked around, hoping no one noticed her lips moving like a crazy person.

"Hey, you okay?" Max appeared over her shoulder and nodded toward her palm. "Did you smack the table?"

"Um . . . yeah. I did. There was a fly. Black one. Wicked huge," Kat made up, reaching for her coffee as Max took the seat next to her. "I missed it though."

Max twisted his head from side to side, front and back. "I don't see it. Let me know if you do. I'm a pretty good fly swatter."

Kat had no idea why that was such a stunning claim to fame. She pictured Max armed in a beekeeper outfit, but skintight of course, since he liked to show off his muscles.

He had a fly-swatter extension in each hand and several cans of insect killer in a handy-dandy tool belt around his waist. He flailed wildly with his swatter hands, yelling, "*Vanquish!*" as flies the size of bats swarmed him, breathing fire-

"Hey." Alec appeared at her other side and sat down, breaking her out of her dragon/fly hybrid-infested fantasy.

"Kat said there's flies buzzing around," Max said.

Alec blinked at Max and then looked at Kat. She widened her eyes at him.

Alec's lips twitched and he took a sip of his chocolate milk, probably to cover his grin. "I'll be on the lookout."

Max nodded and then scanned the room again. The laughter bubbled up in Kat's throat and she sighed loudly to stuff it down. Max ignored her, intent on his fly-hunting mission and Alec was doing the opposite, staring at her intently.

Yep, despite her best intentions, she was in a romcom.

Kat zoned out while they were talking, and eventually, Alec left for class, his gaze lingering on her as he said his good-byes.

Once he left, Max pulled out his phone, tapping away. Kat continued her musings, bestowing Max with the title Maggot Manager. She choked on a laugh and Max looked up, quirking an eyebrow at her.

"Hairball," she explained.

He did that head-shaking thing he always did when she said something weird. Which was a lot.

"Hey Max," a female voice called from over her shoulder.

Kat turned around. A fairly pretty girl, her face a little on the long side, with brown curly hair, stood behind her, eyes darting between Max and Kat.

"Oh, hey, Carrie." Max put down his phone—a miracle—and smiled at her.

"How are you?" she asked.

Max nodded. "Good, you?"

"Good."

Stimulating conversation, really.

"Hi, I'm Kat," she said brightly.

Carrie sent Max another searching look before meeting Kat's eyes. "Oh hey. I'm Carrie. I went to high school with Max . . . and Alec."

"Oh cool! I didn't." Kat quipped and Carrie stared at her like she was on another planet.

"Is Alec with you guys?" Carrie asked, returning her gaze to Max.

"No, he just left," Max answered.

Carrie nodded. "Okay, well, just wanted to say hi. Talk to you later." She turned to walk away and Kat waved at her back.

"Super friendly," Kat said. "She have a crush on Alec or something?"

Max tapped the table. "Uh, no. She and Alec were together. In high school. They broke up last summer, before junior year."

"Ooooh," Kat drawled, turning around to catch another sight of *the* ex-girlfriend, but she was already out of sight. That was Alec's type? "What's her major?" she asked, still craning her neck for a glimpse of Carrie.

"Um . . . biology, I think. She wants to be a physical therapist."

Kat turned back around and huffed, glaring at her coffee. That's the kind of girl Alec chose. Smarties like Carrie, who would fit into his life.

She looked over at Max. He wasn't perfect, far from it. But there was no danger of falling for him and so no danger of getting her heart broken.

But Alec was different. In the way he looked at her, in the way he treated her, in the way he made her feel like she was something special. Not just another pretty girl with mediocre intelligence.

Which was why she had to keep her chips with Max. The safe bet. If she tried playing Alec's numbers, she didn't know how she'd keep from going all in. And then losing it all.

Chapter Eight

PROFESSOR GRIM STOOD at the front of the classroom, her arm extended to draw an imaginary line down the center of the room, between the four rows of seats.

"This side," she said, pointing to Alec's section, "will be in charge of the prosecution for the cases I hand out, and the other side will be in charge of defense."

She plopped a packet of papers down on the first desk in Alec's column. "Pick a case, then a partner in the other column of seats." Then she did the same on the other side of the room.

Alec was in the last row and grabbed the last packet he was passed, then turned to Danica, beside him. "Hey, partner."

"Who said I wanted to work with you?" Today, she was some sort of angel, with a flowing cream-colored dress, white-blonde hair and impossibly blue eyes.

He ignored her and instead focused on what case

they'd have to argue. He skimmed the handout, and the words *death by vehicle* and *distracted driver* each sent a heavy brick slamming into his gut.

"Fuck," he whispered.

"What's up? Crappy case? I wanna win," Danica said, reaching her hand out. "Gimme."

He handed over the papers, keeping his eyes on his desk, not risking a look at those unnatural blue eyes.

"Okay," Professor Grim said from the front of the classroom. "I'm going to let you go for the rest of our class time. I'd prefer you take this time to work with your partners or set up future meeting times to read the material and begin your cases."

Alec was barely listening, his mind swirling with the thoughts of arguing a case similar to the one he'd seen played out when he was six years old. The case that made him want to be a lawyer.

He hadn't thought about that case in years, and he didn't want to.

Danica didn't look at him as she read out loud. "Oh, this is a good one. *Lisa Stevens was driving in a construction zone where two lanes merged into one. She ran through several cones and hit the foreman, killing him. Makeup residue was found on the steering wheel and in her car and her phone history had been deleted. But records were pulled and she'd been texting.* They are charging her with homicide by vehicle and tampering with evidence. She's claiming she was distracted by something in her eye. Wow, this is a cool case."

Her words were like more bricks in every vulnerable

part of his body. "Fuck," he said again, letting his head thunk onto his desk as the sounds of exiting students clamored around him.

"Stone?" Danica was too perceptive. A hand settled on his back, long nails curling to dig through his shirt. "Hey," she said quietly. "Come on, let's get out of here."

He took a deep breath and stood up, lifting the strap of his messenger back over his shoulder so it crossed his chest. Danica slipped her arm in his as they left the classroom. She didn't say anything as they walked down the hall and pushed out of the doors into the chilly air, leading him to some stone benches among a grove of trees.

Unlinking her arm from his, she pushed him down onto the bench. The cold of the stone seeped through his jeans and a hole in the back pocket he had meant to patch. He shifted and the skin scraped on the rough surface. The bite of pain focused him, breaking him out of his memories, so he dug his fingers into his thighs to prolong the hurt.

Danica took a gulp from her water bottle and handed it to Alec. He wasn't really thirsty, but took a drink anyway. She didn't say anything, and that was really the only reason he was able to speak, because there was no pressure.

"My dad died when I was five. He was a cop. Pulled a guy over on the side of the road. Some drunk asshole hit him while he was walking between cars."

"Oh shit," Danica whispered, "I'm so sorry."

"That's why I'm not really thrilled to be arguing this case." He rubbed his palms together, the skin red from the cold because he'd forgotten his gloves at home.

Danica stood up.

"Where are you going?"

She fiddled with the strap of her bag. "I'm going to talk to Grim. I'll get us another case—"

"No." Alec said firmly. "No."

"But—"

"Dan, when I'm practicing law, what am I going to do? Say, 'no cases involving cops and car accidents'? I can't do that. Just . . . let's do this, okay, and let's win the fucker."

Danica pressed her lips together and nodded. "Okay."

ALEC ARRIVED HOME that afternoon after the last of his classes for the day. As he trudged up the stairs, Max's voice carried through his bedroom door, increasing in volume.

He didn't hear another voice, so he figured Max was on the phone. That guess was confirmed when he heard a strained, "Dad."

Alec cringed. Jack Payton was one scary mother-fucker. He was huge, looked like he could carry an eighteen-wheeler on his shoulders and had a wicked scar on his face caused by a failed jack while he was working under a car.

But his appearance wasn't the scary part. It was the way he ruled over his three sons like a dictator. As the youngest, Max received the worst of it, since his mother had left after he was born. Alec had heard Mr. Payton lob the word "mistake" at Max more than once.

He owned Payton Auto in their hometown of Tory, and enlisted Max's help almost every weekend and every summer, despite Max's protests. Alec couldn't mention *oil change* without inducing Max's rage, but Max worked there anyway, needing the money for school.

And because no one said no to Jack Payton. Not without consequences.

As Alec reached the top of the stairs, a loud crash sounded from inside Max's room. He rushed to the door, about to throw it open, but thought better of it. He knocked. "Max?"

No answer, but he thought he heard a moan.

"Max, answer me now or I'm coming in. Are you okay?"

There was a pause, followed a muttered, "Fine."

"I'm coming in anyway." Alec turned the doorknob and swung the door open. Max sat hunched in front of his small closet, a hole punched through the thin plywood door.

Alec took a deep breath. In the past, he'd have known what to say and what to do. But Max had been volatile lately, his moods unpredictable, for a reason he hadn't divulged. Alec decided against Compassionate Alec and went with Macho Skirt-the-Issue Alec.

He nodded toward the closet door. "That's going to come out of your security deposit."

Max snorted a wry laugh, and Alec wanted to pat himself on the back for picking the right persona. He sat down on the bed and rubbed his palms together. "Ol' Jack being his charming self?"

"Of course," Max said softly. "He doesn't know how to be anything else."

Alec waited until Max spoke again.

"It's cool, whatever. I can handle it." Max shrugged and ran his hand through his hair. His knuckles were bleeding.

Alec knew Max had school loans, but he didn't know if Max's father helped him with rent and other living expenses. Max's family was the one no-go topic in their friendship.

"Look, if I can—" Alec began as Max jerked his head up, lip curled, nostrils flared.

"God, you think you can fix everything, don't you?" Max sneered, his normally warm eyes now dull and cold. "Believe it or not, some things are past the powers of Alec Stone."

The bitter tone from his best friend pierced Alec's skin like blades. His mouth dropped open. "Where the fuck did that come from?"

Max stared at him for a minute before he rolled his jaw and looked away, running a hand over his face. "Sorry, forget I said anything, okay? I'm a little worked up. Wanna go grab a beer?"

Alec had a sickening feeling he was missing something important, but he knew a peace offering when he heard one. "Sure."

Max gave him a weak smile. "Cool."

Chapter Nine

"HEY MOM." KAT lay on Max's bed on her stomach, legs bent at the knee and crossed at the ankle in the air behind her, absentmindedly picking at a pull in his navy comforter.

"Hello, Katía." Her mother always called her by her full name. "How are you?"

"Umm . . . good. Busy."

"Classes are going well?"

Kat's parents' lack of alarm over her academic probation status was disconcerting.

"Yeah, statistics is the class that's tripping me up this semester."

It had been several weeks since the start of Kat's tutoring sessions with Alec, and she hated to admit that she looked forward to them.

But she did.

Alec was patient with her, allowing her to study at her

own pace. When he saw she was getting frustrated with the material, he'd make a joke or get her a smoothie. And worse, the more she got to know him, the more she enjoyed looking at him. When she got a particularly difficult concept down, she allowed herself that mental image of him stripped down to those black boxer briefs and sleep-roughened hair. As a well-deserved reward. "I have a tutor, though, Mom. That's helping a lot."

"Well, if you don't pass the class, it's okay, sweetie. We miss you at home anyway and your father's secretary is retiring soon."

Kat clenched her jaw and bit back a scream. She loved her close-knit Brazilian family, but sometimes they were smothering. She didn't want to be a secretary. Not that there was anything wrong with that profession, but it wasn't something she wanted to do and there was no way in hell she wanted to work for her father.

It would be a nightmare. He'd constantly remark on her too-tight clothes—*All buttons must be fastened, Katía*—he'd try to hook her up with every bachelor within a fifty-mile radius, and she never would get his coffee right. Was it two creams and a sugar? Or a sugar and one regular cream and one flavored cream? Crap on a cracker, she was pretty sure—

"Kat?" Her mom said. "You still there?"

"Oh, yeah, sorry, Mom. Um, I'm working really hard not to fail out. I really want my degree."

"Okay, dear," the placating tone was like nails on a chalkboard.

"Hey, I gotta go. Tell Dad and Marcelo I said hi, all right?"

"Sure. Your brother is featured in the local newspaper as a 'Who to Watch' businessman, by the way. I'll e-mail you the link."

Flipping perfect Marc.

"Sounds good, Mom. Thanks. Love you."

"Love you, too."

Kat tossed her phone onto the bed in frustration. Of course, Marc was encouraged to go to college and get his degree, while Kat was patted on the head, told she had a pretty smile and encouraged to date.

But while it was easy for Kat to get dates, it was hard to hold on to anything long term. She told herself it was because she got bored easily and needed to move on. But really, it was because her boyfriends either found her sense of humor odd or grew tired of her wandering attention span.

She saw how Alec looked at her. But she was some novelty now. Once she zoned out during the hundredth conversation or he realized what her brain was really like, he'd boot her out like all of them.

Kat sighed and rose from the bed, then plodded her way down the stairs to the living room. Max was sitting on the couch, bent over a textbook with a highlighter. Cam was in the recliner, playing a video game with lots of explosions.

Cam was cute, with his smooth tanned skin and black hair he kept just long enough to skate by his military regulations. He nodded and grinned at her as she walked by, flashing a dimple.

"Hey," Max said, looking up. "How's your mom?"

"Good. Marcelo has some important article in the newspaper she's all excited about."

"Cool."

She reached for his glass of soda. "Can I have some of this?"

"Sure."

The door to the kitchen swung open and Alec entered the living room.

"Hey," Kat said, acknowledging Alec's nod of greeting.

Cam blew up a car onscreen and then turned away from his game. "Hey, a friend of mine from high school is coming up next weekend. Wanna have a party here Saturday. You cool with that?" He asked his roommates.

Max shrugged. "I don't care. I have to go home that weekend though, to work for my dad."

"Doesn't matter to me," Alec said. "I'm not putting down the deposit for the keg, though."

Cam waved his hand. "Yeah, no problem, I'll take care of it."

Kat finished off the soda in Max's glass. She picked up the half-full can and began to pour the rest over the remaining ice.

Shanna had a crush on Cam so she'd want to come to the party if Kat mentioned it. Kat, though, wasn't such a fan of drinking. As a freshman, she had attended a fraternity party and drunk her face off. She woke up the next morning with a wicked headache, her underwear over top of her jeans, and no recollection of the evening. She vowed never again to drink that much. She was really good at pretending to be drunk, though. It was actually a lot of fun. It was an excuse to dance like a fool and giggle hysterically at jokes that weren't really funny—

"Earth to mother-fucking Kat!" Max bellowed as cool liquid splashed onto the leg of her jeans.

Max roughly grabbed the can of soda from her hand, and she looked down to see that during her daydream, she had completely missed the glass and poured soda all over the coffee table. Oh sugar-snacks.

"Jesus Christ!" Max said, tossing the now empty can behind him and hurrying to clean up his papers off the soda-sticky coffee table. "Do you ever watch what you're doing? Shit, now my book is all wet, and the resale value is going to suck."

"I'm so sorry. I just kinda . . ." She waved her hand as she jumped up, "zoned out. I'll clean it up. I'm sorry." She bit her lip and looked at Max, but he wasn't looking at her, his brows furrowed as he studied the damage to his textbook.

Alec appeared at her side, a roll of paper towels in hand. He ripped off several sheets and began wiping up the soda.

"I'll do that, Alec. I'm the stupid one who spilled it," Kat said, taking the roll out of his hand.

He frowned at her. "It's not a big deal. It was an accident. It's soda, not acid."

"You can say that when it's not *your* textbook, asshole," Max muttered.

Alec jerked his head up and fixed his roommate with a glare. "I'm pretty sure I'm not the one being an asshole right now."

"It's not *your* girlfriend who's a flake."

Alec rose slowly, his spine straight, hands clenched at his sides. "Chill the fuck out, Max. It's a fucking book. What's with you?"

"Yeah, dude, calm down. It's not like Kat did it on purpose." Cam chimed in.

Max grumbled unintelligibly.

Kat ignored the words around her and hurriedly wiped up the rest of the soda. She carried the dripping paper towels into the kitchen, dumped them into the trash bin, and then carried the overflowing bag out the back door to the carport to toss into the can.

The door opened and closed behind her.

"Why do you let him talk to you like that?" The anger in Alec's tone was clear.

Kat froze, her back to him. She straightened and turned slowly. "Excuse me? I don't *let* him do anything."

"Yeah?" Alex shot back. "Then what the fuck was that in there? Why don't you speak up for yourself?"

Kat shrugged in what she hoped was nonchalance, but the movements felt too jerky and Alec was too observant to fall for it. "It doesn't matter. He's just teasing mostly." She brushed her hair over her shoulder and made to walk past him.

Alec stepped in front of her, blocking her way. "He just teases," he said flatly. "Seriously? Is that what you tell yourself?"

Kat clenched her jaw, but stayed silent. Because yes, as long as she told herself the words and tone were all teasing, they couldn't hurt her. Words only hurt if you let them, right? She'd keep telling herself that until she believed it.

"You stood up to that meathead dude at the bar, but you can't tell your boyfriend to treat you better? You told me you don't want me to think you're dumb, which I don't. But why do you let Max—"

"Because it's different with you!" she blurted out, and then immediately wished she'd kept her big mouth shut when Alec froze, his eyes bugged out of his head.

"What—"

"Nevermind," she snapped and tried to walk around him. But Alec wasn't satisfied with that because he flung out his hand and grabbed her arm. They stood shoulder-to-shoulder, facing opposite directions, but Alec's head was turned, his eyes boring into her temple like a pistol held to her head.

"What do you mean it's different with me?" His voice was soft and cautious, like he was talking to a trauma-tized child.

No way could she tell him how she lay awake at night thinking about him beside her, a place currently being held by his best friend. No way could she tell him no one had been this patient with her since Mrs. Ross, her sixth grade teacher. No way could she tell him that with him, she felt smart and respected.

No way could she tell him that given a chance, she'd be his. Because he would leave, like all the rest of them, and she'd be in pieces.

She turned her head slowly, so now that pistol he held was aimed right between her eyes. "Because you see me like no one else does."

He released her arm like someone sprung a trap and the rush of blood back to the constricted area was almost painful.

She was at the top of the stairs leading into the house when he called her name. She turned around.

Alec's jaw was set, his spine a steel rod. "You know I'd never treat you like that. If you were my girlfriend."

So he'd fired the gun, right in her noggin. Like it mattered. Her brain was messed up anyway. But the pain still seared with the knowledge she'd never be on his arm, and with that came the anger.

"Yeah, well, we'd never know for sure, right? I don't have the GPA to be the girlfriend of Alec Stone." Her lip was curled in a sneer and she wanted to smack herself for being so mean. But she couldn't help it.

Alec didn't skip a beat, firing back, "Right, because I always give SAT tests to all my dates. What the fuck?"

She was over this conversation, needing to get away before she said something really bad that wouldn't be forgiven. She turned around and pushed open the screen door.

"Kat, wait . . ." he began.

She paused and turned her head, shooting him a wobbly grin. "It's okay. We all know guys aren't with me because of this." She tapped her temple with a forefinger before slipping into the house, slamming the door behind her.

When she returned to the living room, Max was still mopping up his book, red-faced. Kat sank into the seat beside him, took the book from his hands and wiped it herself.

She bent her head, intent on her task.

"Babe," Max said quietly.

"Hm?" she said distractedly, turning the book in her hands for any remaining soda.

"Babe," he said again. "Look at me."

She looked into his chagrined face.

"I'm sorry for being a dick," he said, rubbing his hands nervously on his pant legs. "I was pissed about my book, but I shouldn't have said that shit."

Drained from the conversation with Alec, she sighed and gave in. "I know. It's okay."

"So, we're fine? Everything's fine?" he asked eagerly.

So many times a boyfriend had asked her that question. She always answered the same. "Yep, everything's fine."

Kat wondered when she'd actually mean it.

Chapter Ten

ALEC SAT IN his room, staring at the wall, hearing Kat's voice again and again in his head *because you see me like no one else does.* And it was killing him.

He did see Kat, all sides of her. The smart, witty side that made jokes about managing tight ends, the day-dreamer side that mumbled about covered Segways, the sex-kitten side that could make drinking a smoothie look erotic, the bighearted side that gave him his favorite candy bar every single tutoring session as a thank-you, and the honest, sensitive side that was trying to find a place in the world. And fuck if he didn't like all of her.

Well, if he couldn't be the one to treat her right, at least he could try to convince her boyfriend to be less of a shithead.

Alec rapped on the open door of Max's room later. His friend sat on the end of the bed, slipping on his shoes. It was Tuesday, two days after the Great Soda Textbook

Sabotage and he hadn't spoken to Max since their terse words.

Max turned around at the knock and Alec caught a flash of guilt over his friend's face. If only Max knew the guilt Alec was battling.

"Hey Zuk."

"Hey."

"You here to call me an asshole again?"

Alec sighed and walked over to stand in front of Max. "I'm not going to apologize. You know you were an asshole."

Max ran his tongue over his teeth. "Look, I do care about her, but I think you're blowing it out of proportion. She knows I kid around with her and I don't really mean it."

"You sure about that?"

Max clenched his jaw. "Yes."

"Well then I think you aren't paying attention. You hurt her feelings and it's a shitty thing to do."

Max waved his hand. "Kat isn't some delicate flower or damsel in stress or whatever. She's tougher than you think."

"Distress."

"Huh?" Max frowned.

"It's distress. The saying is 'damsel in distress.' "

Max rolled his eyes. "Dude. Whatever. Quit trying to be her white knight. Bet you didn't think I knew that term, did you?"

"Okay, first of all, I don't think she's a damsel in distress, and I don't think she needs a white knight. She needs a decent boyfriend. What's been with you lately? You've never treated girls badly."

Max snapped his chin into his neck. "What do you mean what's been up with me? Nothing's up." His voice was a little high, his denial forced.

Alec steeled himself. "You've been different, and then that phone call with your dad—"

A vein in Max's forehead had its own pulse. "You don't know shit."

"You're right, I don't know shit, because you don't tell me anything."

Max sucked his lips between his teeth and made a strangled sound in his throat. "Look, leave it, okay? And stay out of my relationship, all right? Kat's fine."

Alec was sure he had a death wish for continuing this conversation. "Did you ask her if she's okay?"

"Yes. I said 'Kat, is everything fine?' and she said 'yes.' She said she's fine, what else is there to say?"

Alec shook his head in bewilderment. "How you get laid is a mystery to me. Because you don't know shit about girls."

Max's face relaxed, and he puffed out his chest. "Me. Tarzan. I flex me big muscles and woman squeal."

Alec blinked slowly. "You're an idiot."

Max flashed his brilliant white-toothed grin. And Alec remembered that's how Max got girls. "I might be an idiot, but that's never hurt my love life."

"Riiigght."

"Come on, you have to admit I'm an excellent wingman, even if you've never fully utilized my skill set. Which reminds me, you need to put yourself out there, my bespectacled friend."

Alec pushed his lips out and cocked his head to the side, as if he was talking to a baby. "Aw, has little Maxi Pad been hitting the thesaurus again?"

Max rose and punched Alec in the arm. "I told you not to call me that, assface."

Alec snickered. "Okay, *Kotex*."

Max growled and reached for Alec, who ducked and dodged his friend's arm.

"Hey, watch it. Remember this?" Alec bugged out his eyes and pointed to the scar on his left eyebrow, caused by a ten-year-old Max and a broom standing in as a hockey stick.

"Look who's talking." Max raised his pant leg and pointed to a ragged red line, courtesy of sixteen-year-old Alec and a runaway golf cart.

"Damn, that was funny. I never saw you run so fast in my life."

Max growled again, and Alec laughed, managing to make it to the door unharmed. "I gotta go. My mom's meeting me at the diner for lunch."

"Tell Mrs. Stone I said hi. And watch your six, Zuk. I'll get you back."

"I *always* watch my back!" Alec said and leaped out of the door while Max groaned.

Alec made it to Hot Cakes Diner in less than ten minutes, which didn't even give his junker car time to heat up. He jogged inside, spotting his mom in a corner booth. She'd driven the forty-five minutes from his hometown of Tory on her day off.

"Mama." He exhaled softly when she rose from her seat to hug him. The warmth of her embrace seeped into his bones and the contentment only she could provide washed over him.

"Alec," she murmured, her bobbed brown hair tickling his neck. They broke apart reluctantly and sat down, grinning at each other over the scarred formica table. She wore a pair of jeans and light green sweater that matched her eyes. The telltale lump under her neckline showed she still wore her wedding bands on a chain around her neck.

"How are you?" he asked.

She smiled. "I'm good. I got a raise at work because they promoted me to manager at the day-care center."

"Really?" Alec grinned. "That's awesome. Pie for dessert to celebrate. On me."

She pursed her lips and shook her head. "Nope, on me. I'm the one who got a raise."

"Whatever, we'll see who's the quickest on the draw when the check comes."

She narrowed her eyes, so like his own. "You're on. So how you doin', baby?" she asked, taking a sip of her tea, the familiar scent of peppermint wafting across the table.

He never lied to his mom. Not even by omission. "I don't know. Kinda stressed."

She frowned. "Classes okay?"

He rolled his lips between his teeth. "Yeah. I mean, they're hard but I'm doing okay. Just . . . stuff." He mumbled the last of his sentence and looked down at the table, running a finger over a crack in the top.

A waitress approached their table and they ordered sandwiches for lunch. Grilled cheese and tomato soup for his mom, tuna melt for him. When the waitress left to fill their orders, the bell over the front door sounded, and Alec turned to see the new customers. Kat walked in with another girl he didn't recognize. Kat scanned the room with her big blue eyes. When she saw him, she smiled slowly and gave him a tentative wave. He hadn't seen her since their . . . tiff at his place.

When he turned back around, his mom's eyes were on Kat. Then she turned those intelligent pale green eyes on him.

"Who's that?"

Alec took a sip of his water and swirled the glass around in its little island of condensation.

"Alec?" She said his name slowly.

He looked up. "That's Max's girlfriend."

She shifted her eyes to where Kat sat in a booth with her friend. "Something I need to know about?"

She could read every emotion on his face. Damn her.

"It's kind of complicated. I'm actually tutoring her and . . . I think I'm starting to like her. I mean, *like her* like her. She just . . . she needs to be treated a little differently than a lot of girls and Max . . . doesn't do it. He doesn't get her and I don't think he ever will. It drives me nuts."

His mom cocked her head slightly to the side. "And you think you could treat her right?"

He shrugged. "I don't know. I'm sure I'd screw up but I'd at least try."

"She's really pretty."

"Hell yeah. I mean. I know she is. But I don't even notice that as much anymore. I notice her laugh and her wit and . . ." Alec widened his eyes in horror. "Shit. I do really like her. Fuck me."

"Stop swearing."

"Shit. I mean, shoot. Sorry."

"But Max—"

"I know, Mom. *I know.* Even if they break up, I'd be a shit—er, I mean, crappy friend if I tried to date her."

His mom sighed. "This is one area I don't have advice for you, honey."

"Yeah, I know. It's my problem to figure out. Right now, I want to help her with her grades so she passes her classes."

And that's when Kat suddenly bounced up to their table.

"Hey, Alec," she said, her smile wide, and his chest hurt at the sight of how pretty she was, having been reminded of her looks by his mom.

"Hey, Kat. This is my mom. Mom, this is Kat Caruso."

"Hi!" Kat beamed. "Nice to meet you."

"Nice to meet you, too," his mom said. "You're also a student at Bowler?"

"Yep. Your son is my statistics tutor. He's great at it."

Alec smiled. It was easy to get into his mom's good graces. Just praise him in front of her and she'd love you forever.

"Yes, by high school, he was teaching me trigonometry functions I didn't even know existed."

Kat wrinkled her nose. "Ew, trig. "

Alec's mom laughed.

"Well, I have to get back to my table. Nice to meet you Mrs. Stone. Alec, we have a session tomorrow, right?"

He nodded. "Yeah. But I can't make our meeting time. I have a group project for one of my classes. Can you meet later?"

"Yeah, um . . . do you want to come to my place when you're finished? I'll be around all night."

Red flags flashed in front of his eyes but he decided at that moment to be color-blind. "Sure."

"Great, see you then!" she turned around, light brown hair swirling around her shoulders, and walked back to her table.

His mom turned to him, her eyes sparkling. "She's adorable."

Alec groaned. "I know. Fuck me."

"Stop swearing."

Alec sighed.

"So, the real reason I came is because the victim coordinator from the district attorney's office contacted me." She fidgeted and took a deep breath. "Samuel MacEnroe is up for parole."

Alec swore his blood leaked out through his pores and was replaced by warm, fuzzy cotton. Because he didn't think his heart was beating his blood through his veins.

He hadn't heard that name for probably ten years. They didn't talk about him. They didn't talk about that cool February day when Sargent Michael Stone never came home. They didn't talk about how they hated Sam MacEnroe with every breath.

He opened his mouth but the words stuck in his throat. Could you talk without blood? He took a sip of his drink and then cleared his throat. "Okay, so . . ."

His mother shifted in her chair, the cracked pleather squeaking under her weight. "The coordinator asked if we wanted to write a letter."

"A letter?"

"To protest his parole."

Alec did the quick math in his head. MacEnroe would be in his late sixties by now. He'd been in and out of prison his whole life, and had just served a lengthy fifteen-year sentence for ruining Alec's family.

"I don't . . . Do you want to?"

His mom rolled her lips between her teeth. When she released them, Alec watched the blood rush back to the abused area. "I know this is a lot to ask, but I'm leaving it up to you."

"Mom—"

She turned away from him, and did that teeth-clench thing she always did when she was trying not to cry. He had to fight to keep his own eyes from blurring.

She spoke without looking at him. "He was the love of my life and I . . ."

Her voice trailed off and Alec leaned across the table to grab her trembling hand. "It's okay, Mom. It's okay."

She shook her head.

"I'll think about it, all right? I don't know what I want to do."

She nodded tightly and then took her hand from his to dig into her purse. She slid a business card across the table. "Here is the victim coordinator's information from the DA's office. You can speak to her directly, if you want."

He didn't even look at the card, just stuffed it in his pocket. He'd deal with it later. "Thanks, Mom."

She turned back to him now, so he could see the tears glistening on her cheeks. "If I didn't have you—"

"Yeah, well, you do have me, Mom. None of that, okay?"

A tear dripped off her smiling lips when she nodded. "All right, now let's eat some pie."

Chapter Eleven

KAT SAT CROSS-LEGGED on her bed in a tank top and sleep shorts, her notes in front of her on the comforter. Alec spun lazily on her computer chair, his eyes drifting around her room, as if avoiding landing anywhere on her person. It gave her uninterrupted Alec-admiring time, when she was supposed to be studying her notes so he could quiz her.

Alec had stripped down to a T-shirt because of the wacky heat in her campus suite, his Converse-clad feet propped up on her desk. He had a hole in his jeans and she kept staring at it, wanting to take one of those taunting white threads and pull until the whole thing unraveled in a denim pile on her floor.

"Your mom is cute," she blurted. After meeting his mom that morning, she could see where Alec got his cheekbones, eyes and mouth.

Alec finally turned his attention on her. "Thanks, she's great."

"Yeah? She seems like it. So, you said something before about it being only you and your mom growing up?"

Alec's lips shifted and his jaw worked, as if he was biting the inside of his cheek. "Yeah."

Since when was Alec not wordy? She pried, unable to help herself. "So are your parents divorced?"

Alec paused and licked his lips. His eyes shifted away before returning to her face. He shook his head. "My dad was a cop. He was killed on duty by a drunk driver when I was five."

Kat sucked in a breath. *Oh no.* "I'm so sorry." She pictured five-year-old Alec, all big green eyes and dark hair, dressed in a little suit at his hero father's funeral, holding his mom's hand as well-wishers gave their condolences in a stuffy church among foul-smelling bouquets. And . . . now her eyes were watering.

Alec's eyebrows snapped together and he leaned forward. "Are you crying?"

"No!" she protested, but her voice shook and the tears spilled over. Oh jeez, now she looked like an emotional basket case.

"Aw, Kat. It's okay. I mean, I was really young . . ." His voice died when she hiccupped a sob. He sat down beside her and put his arm around her shoulders. "Christ, if I knew you were going to cry I wouldn't have told you."

"I'm sorry," Kat blubbered. "I'm glad you told me. I feel stupid, because shouldn't you be the one crying while

I comfort you and we talk about the lasting effects of your father's death on your psyche?"

Alec paused and then laughed. *Laughed!* While she was a teary mess. The nerve.

His eyes softened as he took in her face. "You might be the only one who can make me laugh after I just talked about my father."

Alec propped a leg up on the bed, facing her. They were chest to chest, and he leaned in, his face inches from hers, his hands on either side of her head, wiping her tears. His thumbs caressed her cheeks, leaving behind streaks of heat with every touch that echoed throughout her body.

"I don't really tell people about him, or that he's the reason I want to be a lawyer."

She let the *why* hang between them unspoken until he answered. "The guy who killed him got out of a previous drunk driving conviction on a technicality because of an inexperienced defense lawyer and a lax judge." He took a deep breath. "I want to prevent other families from going through what I went through, or make sure that whatever bastard takes away their family gets put away for a long time."

"God, that's . . ." she shook her head. "That's amazing. That you took what happened and turned it into something positive, something that fuels your ambition."

His smile was slow and when she smiled back, his eyes dipped to her lips.

The heat on every inch of her skin intensified and she knew this moment had to end. She was too close to the fire. Way too flipping close, because she could barely focus through the desire to put her lips on his, to mean something to this man who lived his life with purpose.

Alec's smile dimmed and his Adam's apple bobbed in his throat as he swallowed. His thumbs lowered from her cheek and swiped her bottom lip once.

"We crossed the line five minutes ago, didn't we?" he whispered.

"I think so, because I can't see it anymore," she whispered back.

"What do we do?"

"I don't know."

The high-pitched guitar rift of *Sweet Child o' Mine* pierced the heat between them like an iceberg of *Titanic*-sinking proportions, and they both reared back. Kat fumbled on her bed for her phone and quickly answered it without looking at the caller ID. Alec stood abruptly with his back to her, and she stared at his shoulders as she answered her phone. "Hello?"

"Babe." Max's voice cut through her.

"Hey, Max," she said softly. Alec's shoulders tensed, and he quickly began to gather his things and shove them into his book bag, his back still turned to her. She closed her eyes slowly as Max talked.

"What was the name of your oral communications professor? The one who always had the white spittle on his mouth, and it made you want to gag?"

Was this really happening? She couldn't do this. She felt like a total, awful cow.

"Um . . . Worrel."

"Ah! That's it," Max said, then his voice was muffled when he yelled. "Cam, it's Worrel!"

"You couldn't have texted me to ask me that?"

"I have Cheeto dust on my fingers. I speed-dialed you with my chin." There was the distinct sound of a crowd cheering, probably coming from the TV. "Shit, Hammonds just took a puck to the face! Gotta go." The line clicked off.

Kat remained motionless, phone pressed to her ear. Alec's entire back was tense, the muscles practically quivering through the thin T-shirt. Finally, he turned around, and he looked as guilty as she felt.

Kat held his eyes, biting her lip, body exhausted from the high to low emotions coursing through her.

Alec threw his glasses on her desk and collapsed in her desk chair. He ran his hands through his hair and scrubbed his face. "What are we doing?"

"I—"

Alec looked up sharply. "Max is my best friend and has been since elementary school. I can't . . . I can't do this to him."

Kat's stomach churned and she looked away, the sting of tears threatening. "I don't cheat. Despite what this looks like."

Alec's face clouded, and he tensed his jaw. "I gotta go." He reached for his book bag and then whirled back to face her. "But, I need to tell you that you deserve better than him."

She blinked. "Why do you think that? What do you even know about me?"

His face hardened and his jaw ticked. He lunged forward, hands fisted on her bed on either side of her hips, his nose touching hers. "I know you squint your eyes when you're about to say something funny. I know you snort when you laugh, especially when you laugh at your own jokes. I know you go on crazy cute rants about your hair whispies and covered Segways. I know you're in college because you fiercely want to be your own person and decide your own future. And I know you are, without a doubt, the hottest, most interesting girl I've ever met. I know you, Kat. Don't doubt that."

She wasn't breathing. There was no way air entered and released from her lungs. Did her heart stop, too? Every word was like a sledgehammer to the meticulously crafted, carefree Kat Caruso veneer. She didn't know what Alec saw, but she knew it certainly wasn't the face she wore for everyone else.

All she could see were Alec's bottomless pupils, blown wide as they studied her face. What would it be like to be able to wake up to those eyes? For them to look at her every day with the admiration they held now?

She didn't know if she could take the leap. Max or other boyfriends put her down? She let it roll off her back. But Alec? With him, she knew he'd see the real her. Judge her without any of the protections she'd learned to keep in place. Once he really got to know her, would he be like all the rest? Would he tire of her? Because if he did, she wasn't sure she could handle it.

But none of that mattered now, because she still had a boyfriend and Alec had made it clear his loyalty was to Max.

Alec grunted in frustration and pulled back. He grabbed his book bag and started for the door.

"Alec," she called.

He turned back around.

"I'm sorry," she whispered.

His hands clenched and unclenched around the straps of his book bag at his shoulder and he rolled his jaw. "Me too." Then he walked out.

Chapter Twelve

ALEC BLEW THROUGH the common area of Kat's suite, ignoring the stares of her roommates.

When he got to his car, he turned it on, blasting the heat.

And then he sat.

What was he thinking, getting involved with Kat? He'd been loyal to Max since elementary school. He never thought of himself as a guy who tried to steal other guy's girlfriends. What did that say about him? The guilt clawed at his gut and he wanted to hurl.

He yelled in frustration, slamming his hands on the steering wheel. Other than Max, Danica, and his mom, he'd never spoken to another person about the death of his father. But with one look from Kat's big blue eyes, he'd vomited out his whole heart.

And how hypocritical to let things get this far with Kat, when he despised cheaters with every cell in his body.

Unable to think of even facing Max, he put his car in gear and drove in the opposite direction.

Danica lived in the new apartments built on the outskirts of campus. Brickside Apartments rose tall and dark in the dusky evening.

He parked outside, and ran up the steps to the second floor. He pounded on the door and continued to pound until a voice yelled. "Cool your shit! I'm coming!"

Danica flung open the door, irritation in every line of her face until she saw it was him. "Stone?"

"Can you talk?"

Danica held the door against her hip and peered over her shoulder. "Mon! You need to go. I gotta take care of something."

Something in the apartment thudded and there were sounds of shuffling. A petite Asian girl appeared behind Danica, frowning. "You're seriously kicking me out for a guy?"

Danica rolled her eyes. "Give it a rest, Monica. He's a friend. I'll call you later."

Monica huffed and Danica grabbed her around the neck, planting a rather heated kiss on her lips. It was a testament to Alec's depression that the sight did nothing for him.

Monica sighed in acquiescence, but turned an intense glare on Alec as she sidled past him out the door.

Danica flung the door open and retreated back into the apartment. "Get your ass in here and this better be an emergency."

"Was that your girlfriend? She's pretty."

"Did you come here to talk about my love life?"

"No."

Danica flopped onto her couch. "That's what I thought."

Alec sank into the corner of the couch and leaned his head against the back rest. He mulled the words in his head, unsure where to start.

"So, who pissed in your Cheerios? I thought Max was housebroken."

Alec snorted a laugh, but stayed silent.

"Stone—"

"I almost kissed Kat," he blurted cutting her off.

Silence.

He raised his head and Danica's eyes, a light gray, were wide. "Is gray your real eye color?"

"Yes. Now how did this happen?"

He gave her an abridged version of the evening's events in Kat's bedroom.

"Whoa."

"Is that all you have to say? Whoa?"

"You're a big boy, Stone. Actually, you're a twenty-one-year-old man. Grow a pair."

"Fuck you. It's not that easy. She's my best—"

"Blah blah, best friend's girlfriend, Jessie's girl, blah blah," Danica flapped her hand like a puppet.

"It's a big deal, Dan!"

"I know, Stone! Here's the question. Do you want to hook up with her or do you actually like her? Do you want to have a relationship with her?"

"I want all the things with her." He said the first thing that popped into his head.

"All the things?"

"Well, obviously, I want to . . ."

"Hit that?" Danica smirked.

Alec blinked. "Um . . . sure Miss Vocab. But yeah, I'd like to date her. I like her. She makes me laugh. And I admire her."

Danica's expression grew serious. "You like her more than you liked Carrie?"

Alec thought about that. "I don't know. I mean, I thought I loved Carrie. But looking back, I don't even know the Alec who was Carrie's boyfriend. I don't know . . . maybe the first time someone stabs you in the heart, you grow up a little. But I can look back now and see it for what it was—just high-school infatuation."

"And Kat's different?"

"I'm not just infatuated with her. I don't think of trying to get her in my backseat to screw her. I want to be with her. Plan a future . . ." The truth struck him in the gut. The last girl he'd wanted to plan a future with had cheated on him. Shit, this was getting too real and too scary.

"What does she want?"

Alec sighed. "I don't know. I feel so guilty doing all this shit behind Max's back. Doesn't this make me just like Carrie?"

Danica shook her head. "First of all, you didn't actually do anything. Second of all, from what I understand, Max and Kat do not have the kind of relationship you and Carrie did. Hadn't you planned to be with her for, like, ever?"

"At the time."

"Max and Kat?"

"I'm pretty sure they've never even talked about what they're going to do this summer."

Danica snorted. "Well, there you go. Look, nothing happened, all right? She's still your best friend's girlfriend for now."

Alec leaned his head back on the couch and closed his eyes. "My head hurts. Can I stay here tonight?"

"I have a futon in my room that pulls out into a bed. My roommate won't care."

He opened his eyes and rolled his head to the side. "Thanks, Dan."

She punched his arm. "Anytime, Stone."

Chapter Thirteen

ALEC BLINKED HIS eyes, slowly waking up. He yawned and rolled onto his back. The loud sound of breathing was somewhere above his position on the futon. He rubbed his eyes, opened them, and stared into a pair of eyes, one blue and one brown.

"Holy shit!" He bolted upright, slamming his forehead into the abomination above him.

"Ow!" howled the creature, who sounded suspiciously like Danica. She clapped her hand onto her forehead. "What the hell, Stone?"

"You're saying what the hell to me?" He rubbed his own forehead. "You are standing over me, mouth-breathing like a freak, and *what the fuck is up with your eyes*!?"

Danica pushed her hair out of her face and widened her eyes at him. "You don't like them? I decided to switch up my contacts today."

"Um, if you naturally had different-colored eyes, it would be fine. However, since you don't, you look like a Siberian husky."

Danica frowned and walked over to her mirror, cocking her head back and forth as she studied her reflection. "Really?"

"Yep. When's the Iditarod, Fido?"

"I hate you." Danica stomped into her bathroom. Grumbles and slamming drawers came from the bathroom before she emerged with two blue eyes. "Happy now?"

"I'm just being honest," he said, rising from the futon and stretching with his arms over his head. Danica took advantage of his insecure position and punched him in the kidney.

"Ow! Enough with the abuse. I slept like shit."

"Really? I think the futon's pretty comfy."

"It wasn't the futon, it was those things." He gestured toward the row of wig-wearing mannequin heads on her dresser. "I kept thinking those things were going to come alive and beg me to save them."

Danica ignored him and headed out of her bedroom door. "Put on some pants, Stone. We can get some work done before your first class."

Half an hour later, after a shower, bagels and coffee, Alec and Danica huddled over their mock trial notes.

"This case seems cut and dry. I mean, makeup residue, texting, speeding," Danica said.

"Yeah, but I'm sure the defense will easily claim she put her makeup on when the car wasn't in motion. And the texts that were made were several minutes before the accident, Alec said."

Danica narrowed her eyes. "Which side are you on?"

He laughed. "Just playing devil's advocate. I'm worried they're going to argue the construction site wasn't clearly marked. We should make sure we have all the details on where the signs and cones were set up."

Danica squinted at him, then dropped her head to scribble some notes. "Damn, you're smart."

"I try."

After finishing up her notes, Danica took a sip of her coffee. "So aside from taking advantage of your position of superiority and sexually harassing your student, how is tutoring Kat going?"

Alec flipped her the finger. Danica smirked. "Seriously."

He tapped his pen on his textbook. "It's going pretty well. There's just . . ." he trailed off, unsure how to say what was on his mind. "Never mind."

"What?"

Alec continued to tap his pen until Danica slammed her hand on top of it. "Okay, it's something about the way she studies that's bothering me. Or, I guess it's making me think something isn't quite the way it seems."

Danica took her hand off his pen. "What do you mean?"

Alec bit his lip. "She seems to avoid reading out loud to me. Is that weird? And there are a couple of times she has read out loud, and she doesn't read the correct words or numbers."

"Really," Danica said slowly.

"Yeah. And she's not dumb. When I explain things and use diagrams or graphics, she gets the concept right away. And she's crazy imaginative. The things she comes up with are hilarious."

Danica began typing on the laptop in front of her. She pulled up a website and tilted the screen in his line of vision, pointing at a bulleted listing. "Do you think she has dyslexia?"

Alec peered at the screen. "Problem in area of the brain that helps interpret language . . . specific information processing problem," he murmured, reading aloud. "Difficulty with reading comprehension . . . yeah . . . difficulty with spelling . . . oh hell yeah, her spelling is awful . . . can overlap with attention deficit disorder." He scrolled down the page to read a little more. According to the site, dyslexia varied greatly in severity and manifested itself differently in different people.

But one thing was clear—from what he knew of Kat, she fit the description.

Alec leaned back in his chair and blinked, then looked at Danica. "Yeah, but wouldn't someone have noticed this earlier? Like a teacher or her parents?"

Danica shrugged. "My dad has dyslexia, which is the reason I thought of it. There are cases of it being worse in adulthood and sometimes it's just not noticed. Teachers or parents just think the student doesn't get the concept or isn't a good reader or writer. Who knows? It's probably worth mentioning to her."

"But if she is, what does it matter? There are no medications or anything for it."

"No, but there are techniques she can use. And Bowler has a learning disability center where she can get tested. If she does have dyslexia, the university will recognize it and give her an advisor to help arrange more time on her assignments or different assignments based on her abilities."

"Oh, that would help," Alec said thoughtfully.

"And, I would think she'd like to know there is a reason she struggles a bit, don't you think?"

"I know she feels dumb sometimes. I mean, she hides it, but it bothers her."

Danica smiled softly. "You're so observant. Better than that neanderthal she's with now."

"Will you quit ragging on Max?"

"But it's so easy and fun," Danica whined.

He rolled his eyes. "Anyway, thanks for that. I think I should probably do more research before I say anything to her."

"I can ask my dad for some more info, if you want."

"Yeah, that'd be great. Thanks, Dan."

She smiled. "No problem."

A door opened in the hallway opposite Danica's bedroom door. Danica's roommate emerged, a petite girl with long, straight dark hair. As she walked closer, Alec noticed she had a slight limp, favoring her right leg. She was a thin, pretty girl, a little young-looking, with small features and wrists that looked like they would snap in half in a strong wind. She walked with her head down, paging through her student planner.

"Oh hey Lea. This is my friend Alec. Alec, this is my roommate, Lea."

"Nice to meet you," he said.

She flashed him a quick smile, all small white teeth. "You too." Then she waved that delicate hand and walked out of the door.

Alec looked at Danica questioningly.

"You haven't met Lea before?

Alec shook his head. "I don't think so. And her . . ." He waved his hand at his own leg.

"Car accident when she was a kid. They saved her leg, but she has a lot of nerve damage."

"Damn, that sucks."

Danica shrugged. "Yeah. She took the accident in stride. She can be a little quiet sometimes, so we'll have to hang out sometime so she gets used to you."

"Sounds good." He glanced at his watch. "Shit, I gotta go. I have class in a half hour. Thanks for everything." He leaned in and smooched Danica on the cheek while she fake-retched and shoved him away.

He grinned at her and headed out the door to campus.

BY THE TIME he made it back to his townhome, it was four in the afternoon and he was exhausted.

And he really needed to change his clothes.

He heard yelling from inside as he reached the front door. When he swung it open, the first thing he saw was Kat, facing off against Max. Her face was flushed, her fists were clenched at her sides, and her body vibrated with tension, but her eyes were bright and clear and she held her head up.

"Give me my book bag, Max." Each word emphasized slowly.

"No." Max shot back. Alec's eyes darted between the two of them and to Kat's book bag, clutched in Max's white fist.

"What the fuck is going on?" Alec said.

"Stay out of it, Stone." Max spoke out of the side of his mouth, his eyes never leaving Kat.

"Uh, no, don't think I will." Alec kept his voice steady but inside, his stomach rolled. All he wanted to do was rush to Kat, ease her tension and make her smile. The protectiveness surprised him. He took a step toward his friend.

Kat's eyes darted to him and then back to Max. "It's over. Now just give me my bag so I can leave."

"Babe, this is fucking stupid. We're not breaking up."

Kat screamed in frustration. "It doesn't make it true no matter how many times you say that! We're done. Finito. And it's not me, it's you!"

Max jerked his head back. "What the fuck does that mean?"

Kat took a step forward, her petite size contrasting with Max's bulky frame. "It means *you* are the reason we're breaking up. You wanted a reason. There it is." Her eyes flicked to Alec and then back to her now ex-boyfriend. "I deserve better."

Alec wondered if Max caught that glance in his direction.

Max took a step toward her, and Alec reacted instinctively. He stepped between Kat and Max, facing off against his best friend in a physical way he had never done before. They were the same height, so they stood chest to chest, eye to eye. Before this year, he would have said Max would never hit him. But now? He wasn't so sure. Max's actions had been surprising him lately.

"Don't even try to physically intimidate her."

Max's eyes flared. "She's breaking up with me."

"Yeah? Well, shit happens. Life sucks. Move on."

Max spoke through gritted teeth. "Stay out of this, Stone. Stand. Down."

Alec took a deep breath and inched closed. "I'm not the one who needs to stand down."

"This is between me and Kat."

"Fuck off, Max. You're an asshole to her the way you talk to her, and you brought this on yourself."

"I apologized for that." Max growled.

Alec huffed a laugh. "And that's supposed to make it all better? I don't know what's been with you, but you know better. Have some fucking dignity and let her leave."

Max took another step closer. "Fuck you, Alec. Mind your own business."

"I'm your best friend, aren't I? You are my business."

"Honest to God, Alec, I'm seconds away from punching you in the face."

Alec snorted. "Go ahead, asshole. Show me how much of a man you are. I'm sure Kat'll be really impressed if you break my nose."

Max opened his mouth but instead a feminine voice spoke up quietly. "Stop."

Alec turned toward Kat. She stood by the door, holding her book bag. In their showdown, Max must have dropped it.

"Come on, ignore him. We were going to see a movie—" Max started but Kat cut him off.

"I'm sorry, Max, but this isn't working out." She straightened her shoulders slightly and Alec felt a surge of pride when her voice strengthened. "I don't like how you treat me. How you make me feel."

She took one last look at Alec, opened the door and slipped out.

Alec wanted to go to her, but his friend's voice broke through the desire.

"What was that look she gave you?" Max's voice was a little too quiet.

Alec went for ignorance. "I don't know. Probably because I stuck up for her."

Max stared him down, and Alec held his gaze.

"So, you're not going to apologize to me for basically making my girlfriend break up with me?" Max said.

Alec blinked and then laughed. He couldn't help it. Max was fucking clueless. "You have to be kidding me. She broke up with you because of you, dumbass. Honestly, what's with you lately? Ever since the beginning of the year, you've been a jerk. You're not . . . This isn't my friend, Max. I don't know who the fuck you are."

Max rolled his jaw from side to side. He looked away and his chest heaved, clearly lost in some sort of inner battle.

"Well, stay away from her, all right?" Max said.

"Stay away from her?"

"Yeah. Because I'm going to try to get her back, and I don't want you fucking it up. Even if we stay broken up, I'm going to be pissed if you try to date her."

Alec stared at him. "Are you serious?"

"Dead."

Alec took a deep breath. "How pissed?"

"Like, don't fucking talk to me ever again pissed."

A sensation raced over Alec's skin, like a thousand pin pricks. "So, you're saying I stay away from her or we're no longer friends? You'll say that shit to me after all we've been through over a girl you've been with for a couple of months?"

Max tilted his head. "Would you? For a girl like Kat?"

Alec didn't want to think too hard about that. Because a tug in his chest told him he would. He stayed silent.

Max nodded and snorted sadly. "Yeah," was all he said before he walked upstairs and slammed his door.

Chapter Fourteen

TARA PLOPPED HERSELF down on Kat's bed.

"Wanna talk about it?"

"No." Kat kept her eyes on her computer screen while sitting at her desk.

"Um . . . you sure? Because you walked in, said, 'I broke up with Max,' without looking at any of us and ran into the bathroom for an hour."

"I needed to shave my legs."

"Okaaaay," Tara drawled slowly, holding her arms out like she wanted to prevent a meltdown. "Unless you're Teen Wolf, I'm pretty sure it doesn't take an hour to shave your legs."

Kat huffed. She didn't want to admit that she hadn't shaved her legs. She had sat on the toilet staring at the cracked tiles on the wall, replaying the breakup scene in her head. Except this time she was witty and funny and it ended with Alec sticking his tongue in her mouth. In a sexy way, not a creepy violating way. In her daydream, he was a fantastic kisser who tasted like a caramel *macchiato*. Extra drizzle.

"Come on, Kitty-Kat," Tara whined. "I need to pluck my eyebrows before my date tonight and you're delaying my prep."

Kat sighed and turned her chair to face her friend.

"I was over it, you know? I felt like he didn't really care much about me anymore, and he was sticking with me because he'd already put the time in and wanted to get laid for his efforts."

Tara winced. "Ew."

Kat laughed in spite of her depressive mood. "He's not that bad. Just not for me. I think he has some shit to figure out."

"Did this have anything to do with his nerdy roommate?"

Kat smacked Tara's arm lightly. "Will you quit calling him nerdy? He's not nerdy!"

Tara raised her eyebrows.

"Okay, well Alec is maybe a little nerdy but I have decided I like *nerdy*. It's the new black, remember?"

"Hey, I like nerdy too! Maybe he has some nerdy friends."

"Other than Max, I think his closest friend is a lesbian."

Tara's face fell. "Well, that's not going to work well for me."

Kat laughed. "Thanks for cheering me up, Tare. Now go deforest those brows before you can't find your eyes."

Tara playfully shoved Kat's shoulder before running to the bathroom and laughing.

"Have a good night!" Kat called after her.

She sighed and pulled out her statistics book. Maybe she could actually get some studying done with her roommates out of the apartment.

Two hours later, Kat was alone, bored and hungry. A shrimp pesto pizza from the Pizza Box sounded amazing, even though it was almost midnight. Kat grabbed her coat and began the four-block walk off campus to the best pizza shop around.

Bowler was a cute town, with uneven brick sidewalks and quaint shops somehow able to stay in business despite their patrons consisting of poor college students.

Kat kept her eyes on her feet as she trudged to her destination. Being single made her feel like a kite with the strings cut. Sure, it was fun for a little to be willy-nilly, until she took a painful nosedive into the sand. It was part of the reason she kept herself attached, usually only moving on when something better came along.

Alec would most likely be something better. Everything about him fired her up and sent off warning bells at the same time. He wouldn't be just another guy, the harmless ones she dated until they got tired of her. When Alec grew tired of her—which she assumed was inevitable—his leaving wouldn't be so harmless.

In her musings, she'd walked a hundred yards past the Pizza Box. She growled to herself and turned back around.

When she opened the door, the usual smells of dough and sauce mixed with the sounds of employees hollering orders and students chatting. She kept her head down and walked to stand in the line at the counter. The girl two people ahead of her ordered about every topping with a five second pause in between each. Kat cracked her neck and huffed with impatience.

"Hey," said a voice next to her. Kat looked up into the eyes of Danica Owens. Well, more like the face of Danica Owens, since her eyes were an unnatural bright green. She wore a red curly wig and some weird medieval lace-up-type dress. Kat wanted to ask her the direction to the nearest joust.

"Hey, Danica." She'd only met her once or twice, but wherever Danica was . . . Kat let her eyes roam the restaurant.

"Yeah, I'm here with Stone."

Kat snapped her eyes back to Danica, who looked at her with one eyebrow raised. "Oh, Alec?"

Danica snorted. "Don't play dumb with me. I know that's who you were looking for."

Kat pursed her lips and faced forward again.

Danica placed a hand on her arm. "Get your food and then come sit with us, we're in the back corner." Without waiting for a response, she turned and walked away, long skirt swishing around her legs.

Kat silently fumed. Who was Danica to give her an order? All she wanted was to get her shrimp pesto pizza, walk back to her apartment and eat in silence. Not sit with Alec and his Irish lassie.

When it was her turn at the counter, she stomped up and made her order.

"For here or to go?" The guy behind the counter asked in a monotone voice, not even looking up from the register.

But of course, her mouth did the talking for her, and apparently that mouth wanted to be with Alec. "For here," she spat out angrily. Stupid Danica.

When her pizza was ready, she collected herself and walked to the back corner. Danica saw her first and smiled. She said something to Alec and he turned around, surprise on his face. Danica hadn't told him she saw Kat? Jeez.

"Hey Kat! Glad you decided to stay and chat." Danica's face was a little smug and Kat didn't like it so much.

"Yeah, thanks for asking me. Hey, Alec."

"Hey." He scooted over in the booth so she could sit beside him. She slid into the seat and put down her plate, brimming with two slices of shrimp pesto pizza.

Alec raised his eyebrows. "That's quite a midnight snack you have there."

"Yeah, well, long day." *Dumping a boyfriend builds up an appetite*, she wanted to say. "What are you two doing here?"

"Alec needed a girl chat." Danica said, grinning at him over the rim of her soda cup. Kat thought her green eyes looked a little radioactive, and it was disconcerting. She took a bite of her pizza.

Alec glared at Danica before turning to Kat. "We were working on a project and decided to break for the night. We were hungry, so here we are."

"Titillating conversation," Danica mocked.

Alec probably would have incinerated Danica with his eyes if he were a superhero. Kat wanted to avoid any violence, so she tried to ease whatever was going on between them. "So, what's your project about?"

Alec gave a brief description of their mock trial project, with Danica interjecting where she could. When he was finished, the three of them sat in silence for a minute or two. Kat picked at the remaining shrimp on her pizza.

"So . . ." Danica said, "I wonder if they have peanuts here?"

"Peanuts? You want peanuts?" Kat asked.

Danica shrugged. "I don't know. I heard elephants like them. Pink elephants, I believe? Big pink ones."

"Dan, will you shut up?" Alec growled.

"Right, then, that's my cue to leave, so you two can discuss the big pink elephant in the room. Or at least give it peanuts." Danica rose from the booth, tossed her hair over her shoulder and left with a wink.

Kat twirled her straw in her water. "So . . ."

"So . . ." Alec tapped his fingers on the table. "You okay?"

"Yep, great." She went for cheery.

He sighed. "Seriously, Kat. It was kind of a scene. What happened?"

Kat licked her lips and shifted in the booth to face him. "Nothing really, at first. I went over there and told him that it wasn't working out and I thought we needed to end it. He got all huffy and macho and took my book bag and said I wasn't leaving until we 'talked it out.' But he didn't want to talk about anything. He wanted to glare at me until I backed down. And then you came in . . . so . . . you know the rest."

Alec snagged a crust on her plate and took a bite. He chewed and swallowed before he spoke again. "If . . . you . . . me . . . last night hadn't happened, would you still have broken up with him?"

No. "Yep."

"Kat . . ."

How did he do that? She rolled her eyes. "Maybe? Probably? Eventually? I don't know. Because last night *did* happen, okay?"

Alec stuffed the rest of the crust in his mouth and stared at the far wall as he chewed. "Look, I'm glad you guys broke up, but . . ."

The *but* cut through her and she sucked in a breath. She didn't want to hear about how last night was a mistake and he couldn't be with her. Even if she wasn't willing to take the risk, a part of her held out hope for the possibility of some sort of future with Alec. "Yep, me too. Long time coming. Welp, look at the time. I better go get some sleep."

"Kat . . ."

She couldn't have this conversation, another reminder of her failure to hold on to something lasting. She stood abruptly, picking up her plate and swiftly carrying it to the trash to dump the remains of her late-night grease fest. Footsteps sounded behind her as she walked out the door, and she figured it was Alec.

"Kat," he said again.

She stopped. He walked in front of her and after a

quick glance up and down the street, he stepped closer and cradled her cheek, rubbing his thumb along her cheekbone. "I'm sorry," he whispered and the heat of his breath coasted over her lips. She licked them, thinking that was the closest she'd ever get to tasting Alec. His eyes dipped to her lips before he spoke again, his voice a deep, strained rasp. "Max is my best friend, but for once in my life, I wish he wasn't."

She didn't say anything, her entire focus on that inch of skin on her face he caressed. She didn't know what she wanted him to say. Her sensible side told her to run, and her emotional side told her to grab his face and kiss him breathless. The two parts were fighting so hard, they shut down her whole system, so she stood mute, caught in those green eyes.

"You gotta know," he murmured, almost as if he was talking to himself. "Walking away from you right now is killing me."

She bit her lip and looked him right in the eye. "Ditto." Then she reluctantly pulled from his grasp and walked away first.

As she walked, she waited to hear her name. She wished for it so hard, she heard ghosts of whispers in her ears. But after a block, she turned around. Alec wasn't there.

MAX WAS SULKING. And when Max sulked, everyone paid the price.

But right now, Alec felt like he was paying way more than anyone else.

"Can't they get decent lettuce in this place?" Max held up brown-tinged, shredded iceberg lettuce from his sub. They were eating lunch in the TUB with Cam, but Alec would have rather been anywhere else, like pulling out his teeth. With no anesthetic. He stayed silent while Max went back to muttering. Alec rolled his eyes at Cam, who swallowed a bite of cheeseburger and shrugged.

Alec had to cancel his first tutoring session of the week with Kat Tuesday and he'd just left their Thursday session. It'd been the first time he'd seen her since outside the Pizza Box. They were both incredibly uncomfortable and spent the whole time speaking only about statistics. So yeah. Back to teeth pulling . . .

"Yo, Payton." Some big, muscled dude stood near their table. The same muscled dude who had tried to molest a dancing Kat at the bar. Alec couldn't remember his name. Brian? Brant? Something like that. From what Alec remembered, Max worked out with the guy at the gym and they did other meathead stuff together. The guy had a huge nose and a forehead that went on for days.

"Yo." Max answered.

The big dude didn't even look at Alec.

"Heard Kat Caruso dumped you. Bad news for you, man. She's a hot piece," said Mr. No Neck and Alec had the overwhelming urge to punch said neck. Fucking jackass. Kat wouldn't look twice at that dude. She'd probably make some joke about how his neckties would wrap around the Earth twice. Alec snorted to himself, and Max glared at him before turning back to the big guy.

"Fuck you, Brant. We're on a break. Keep your sweaty hands to yourself."

Alec whipped his head to the side. A break? Where did Max get that idea?

There were more words back and forth before Brant No Neck walked away but Alec was still stuck on *break*.

"A break?" Alec asked.

Max shrugged. "Yeah, she didn't mean it."

"Um . . . she sounded pretty sure, man."

Max quirked his lips. "Max is never out of the game."

"Please do not talk about yourself in the third person."

Max waved him off.

Cam crunched a chip. "Forget her, man. I mean, I like Kat, but come on. We're in college. We have hot girls in tight jeans and cleavage-baring shirts at our fingertips. Don't tie yourself down."

"I want it noted I have none of those things anywhere near my fingertips right now," Alec said.

Cam glared at him. "Because you put no effort into it."

Alec fluttered his lips. "I'm busy."

"Priorities," Cam muttered.

Alec and Cam had one big experience in common—cheating high-school sweethearts. Cam's ex-girlfriend—the She-Beast Who Shall Not Be Named—cheated on him while he was in basic training. Cam took that anger and fueled it into playing the field. Alec took that anger and just shut down.

"I'm so pissed you won't be at the party tomorrow, Max," Cam said. "It's just not the same without your karaoke stylings and tricks of hand playing President."

"I hate that fucking game," Alec muttered.

"That's because I'm always President and you're always Asshole and I can make you do shit." Max bumped him with his shoulder. Alec glared at him.

Max took a gulp of his water. "So Zuk, can you do me a favor?"

"Depends what it is."

"I'm heading home tonight to work with Dad. If Kat comes to the party tomorrow night, can you watch out for her?"

Alec dug his fingers into his thighs under the table to keep from yelling. Why? Why of all the girls on campus, the only one he'd paid attention to after Carrie was Kat? Fuck him.

"I worry some asshole is going to take advantage of her or something and I won't be there to watch out for her," Max was saying.

Alec relaxed his hands before he gave himself bruises and cleared his throat. "Yeah, yeah, man. I'll watch out for her." If Max had paid a bit of attention to her, he would have known Kat could take care of herself.

Max smiled and clapped his hand on Alec's shoulder. "Thanks, Zuk. Knew I could count on you."

Alec thought he was going to be sick.

Chapter Fifteen

"I KNEW YOU were going to drag me here," Kat grumbled.

"Have you been over there? Is Cam's friend as hot as he is?" Shanna was vibrating with excitement. She'd already detailed all the reasons Cam was, apparently, her future husband. Kat hadn't heard her talk this much since her favorite video game came out with some sort of patch so she could design her avatar's clothes.

"Max and I broke up, remember? No, I haven't been over there."

"Oh, yeah, sorry. I thought you were dating his roommate now?"

Kat looked at her incredulously. "Seriously? You think I dumped Max and hopped into his roommate's pants in, like, a week?" Never mind she wanted to. She wasn't admitting that out loud.

Shanna frowned. "If you're going to be this grumpy, I'll go to the party by myself."

Kat brightened. "Great! Sounds good. Have fun!" She waved obnoxiously and began to turn around to head back to campus.

"No!" Shanna grabbed her arm. "Just come on."

Foiled! Kat walked alongside Shanna reluctantly, plotting her next escape attempt. She needed one of those fake heads like those prisoners at Alcatraz used. Penal system history came in handy when trying to get out of parties where nerdy, attractive tutors would be in attendance.

"Quit trying to get out of this. I can hear your brain working."

Kat scowled at her friend as they mounted the stairs to Alec and Max's town house. She glanced along the street, looking for Max's truck and hoping he went out of town as he'd planned. She didn't see it.

Sighing, she opened the door and stepped inside.

College parties all smelled the same—a mix of AXE body spray, sweat and cheap beer. It was a wonder students ever had sex. Kat wrinkled her nose and tried to look like she wanted to be there. Shanna had already brushed past her to take up residence against the wall near Cam. Hopefully, she'd actually worked up the nerve to talk to him.

The living room was large and almost filled with people. She couldn't help it—her eyes scanned the room until she found Alec. He stood in a corner near the beer pong table, iPhone in hand, tapping away. His glasses had slid down his nose and his brows were furrowed. He wore his typical uniform of dark jeans, Converse shoes and plain black T-shirt, but he'd styled his hair so it stuck straight up instead of smoothed back in a pompadour.

As if sensing eyes on him, he looked up and met her gaze, tucking his phone in his back pocket. He smiled slowly and she returned it. Just the sight of him, which used to unsettle her, now balanced her.

Alec blinked and swallowed. He grabbed a cup of beer from a nearby table and walked toward her.

As his long legs ate up the distance between them, she made the decision to live a little tonight. She was here, Max was out of town, and Alec was sauntering toward her, looking like a modern James Dean, minus the cigarette breath.

Even if she only got Alec for one night, it was worth it. It was worth it to feel desired, respected, and in his league. Kat planted her feet and waited for him. He had to make the first move.

"Hey," he said when he stood in front of her. Thank God he didn't smell like AXE.

"Hi."

"You came."

"I came."

"You know Max isn't here—"

She shook her head. "The only reason I let Shanna talk me into coming is because Max wouldn't be here."

He took a sip of beer, keeping his eyes on hers over the tooth-nibbled rim of the plastic cup. "It's over for good?"

"It's over for good. Forever and ever. Amen."

Alec licked his lips, and she allowed herself to track

his tongue. She was single now. No more guilt. Well, at least not enough to stop her.

"I'm glad."

She licked her lips, a test to see if he looked at her mouth. As always, Alec aced that test, his eyes glued to her roving tongue.

He cleared his throat and jerked his head back toward a table behind him. "Want to play flip cup?"

Kat watched the table, where a line formed on each side. Each player chugged a cup of beer, placed it on the edge of the table and then used one hand to flip it onto its top. One side of the table raced the other.

"You trying to get me drunk so you can get in my pants?" She winked at Alec.

He blushed—he freaking blushed—and it was the cutest thing she'd ever seen. Max would have said *yep* and smacked her ass. But Alec blushed. Adorable.

She knew her tolerance and figured she could handle three games with her beer a third filled before she got too drunk. "Sure, let's do best out of three."

"Yeah?" he said as they walked over to the table. "Winner gets what?"

She smiled coyly. In the library, Alec was master. He called the shots. But here? Flirting at a party? The possibility for sexy times? Kat was queen. "Whatever the winner wants."

Alec paused and ran his tongue over his teeth. "You're on."

The table was already separated into the age-old battle

of the sexes. So Kat and Alec easily slid into place across from each other.

After two games of chugging and flipping, the teams were tied.

Kat and Alec were the finishers at the end of the table. Kat stood with her legs apart and back hunched, in a wrestler stance. "Remember, whatever I want," she singsonged.

The game started at the head of the table with Shanna and Cam. Cam slammed back his beer and flipped his cup in one try, while Shanna struggled. The girls fell behind until the guy right before Alec, who fumbled his cup on the floor.

As Alec and Kat raised their cups, they were even. Kat opened up her throat, slugged back the beer and with an agile index finger, flipped her cup and watched it glide easily onto its top on the table.

She raised her head and Alec stood motionless, his eyes on her, his cup in his hand.

The girls went crazy as the guys all groaned.

"What the fuck, Stone! You didn't even drink your beer!" Cam yelled. "Man, I'm never playing flip cup with you again."

Kat didn't pay attention to the noise around her. She held Alec's eyes. He stood motionless, his lips parted, cheeks flushed and chest rising and falling with deep breaths.

"Did you throw the game?" Kat tilted her head.

"What do you want?" Alec's voice was low as he stepped around the table to stand in front of her.

Kat wanted a lot of things. She wanted a pony and a house on a lake and a college degree, but none of those things were standing in front of her right now. Alec was. And what she wanted most of all, he could give her.

"A kiss," she whispered.

Alec's eyebrows shot up and his mouth dropped open. She would have laughed if she wasn't flipping out inside.

"Kat . . ." his voice trailed off and he looked away, running his hands through his hair.

"No rush," she persisted. "But by the time I leave tonight, you will give me a kiss, Alec Stone." And then she turned and walked away.

KAT WAS KILLING him. She knew it, too, the brat. Princess Brat.

It had been an hour since the end of the flip cup game and everywhere he looked, Kat was taunting him. She hadn't approached him again, but she purposefully stood in his line of sight at every turn, licking her lips, arching her back, bending over.

Reminding him he owed her a kiss.

The only thing holding him back was the echo of Max in the whole damn house. He'd told Alec to stay away from Kat, but it wasn't like she was going to go back to him. He knew it was some sort of best friend violation to do anything with Kat, but fuck, he was only human.

At least he'd appreciate her.

Shanna and Cam walked by him, and he overheard something about a controller combination and he knew they had geekily bonded over a video game. Maybe their avatars could get it on in one of their sessions

Alec knew Kat had walked upstairs, probably to use the bathroom. He'd seen her and sternly told himself to remain in the living room. He planted his feet and gripped the edge of the couch.

But as the party swirled around him, his damn feet wouldn't stay put. It was like a fishing line had hooked him through the gut and slowly reeled him toward the stairs, up each step, then let him off the hook right outside the bathroom.

Like a fish out of water, he couldn't swim away and couldn't catch his breath.

The bathroom door opened and Kat stepped out. Her head was bent so she didn't see him until she smacked into his chest.

"Oh!" She looked up and froze.

He didn't know what his face looked like. But hers was flushed and her lips were a perfect full pout, and she was so damn beautiful, he could do nothing but give in.

There was only one way to fix this, one way to swim and breathe again.

So he dove in, unable to see the bottom to know when his feet would touch.

He cupped the back of her head with one hand while his other fisted her shirt at her lower back. But what gave him breath again was his lips on hers. They were soft and wet and *Oh God*, she'd opened her mouth. Her tongue slipped between his teeth and swiped his eagerly and then he kind of lost it.

He plunged into her at the same time he stumbled forward with a growl. Her back hit the wall, but she didn't protest. In fact, she seemed to like it. She moaned and gripped his shoulders, pulling him closer, her fingernails digging through the thin fabric of his T-shirt.

She didn't accept his kiss. She fought it. That's what it felt like. A fight for power. Their teeth clacked and lips mashed and tongues clashed.

A tremor ran from the back of his neck all the way down to his heels, because this wasn't the same dynamic they shared over a statistics book. Alec was no longer the teacher and Kat the docile student. This, her tongue tangled with his, her full breasts pressed against his chest and the scent of her citrus shampoo surrounding him in a light brown curtain . . . this was Kat's world.

It was the single hottest moment of his life.

And then, somehow, he was walking backward. Hands tugged on the bottom of his shirt as they entered his bedroom. He tripped over a tear in the carpet and Kat's little teeth crunched down on his bottom lip. He grunted in pleasure-pain and Kat pulled away, ripping his shirt over the top of his head.

Her eyes hypnotized him. Swirling crystal pools of aquamarine, clear and deep as the sea. He couldn't see the bottom. He was free-falling, and it felt fucking fantastic.

She hooked her fingers in the belt loops of his jeans and hauled him closer. Her cheeks were flushed and her kiss-swollen lips were parted in a smirk, her breath rushing between them in hot pants. "Wow, you're a shit kisser." Then she wrapped her hand around the back of his neck and pulled his lips back onto hers while he chuckled into her mouth.

She surged forward and the backs of his knees hit his bed. He dropped, tugging her with him. She landed on him with a thump and their noses collided, lips connected with teeth and Alec thought he tasted blood. He broke the kiss and pulled up on the bottom of her shirt. The only word he could mumble was "off."

Kat rose from his chest and straddled his hips, looking down at him through blazing eyes, her hair framing her face in a mass of caramel. He touched his fingers to his lips and saw blood when he pulled them away.

Kat crossed her arms over her stomach and in one swift move straight out of his fantasies, pulled her shirt over her head and tossed it to the side.

Holy fuck.

He was already harder than he'd ever been in his life, but now he was in pain staring up at Kat in her black lace bra. Her round, plump breasts made his mouth water.

She cocked her head to the side. "Like what you see?" Her voice was husky.

"Nope," he growled. He gripped her hips and lifted her off of him, throwing her to the bed beside him on her back. His eyes scanned down her body and his hand followed, palming the soft curve of her belly. He ran his fingers over to her side, loving how her torso carved in at the waist and then flared out into a sexy set of full hips. "I don't like what I see at all. You are so not perfect and so not sexy."

Her belly shook as she laughed silently.

He grinned. "I'm not even turned on."

She opened her mouth and let out a booming laugh, which he quickly swallowed as he dove into her mouth again.

That's when things got frantic. Her bra landed somewhere behind his headboard. His pants ended up shoved under a pillow and her jeans blanketed the keyboard on his desk.

She lay under him, wearing only a lacy black thong. When he pulled one strap down over her hip, she took a deep breath and raised her arms over her head. Her tongue curled over her top teeth and she looked right into his eyes. He wasn't sure if it was a surrender or a dare.

He didn't care.

He tore her thong down, threw her legs over his shoulders and placed the flat of his tongue at her core, giving her one long, slow lick.

Her back arched violently. "Oh. my. *God*," she moaned.

He grinned and went back at it, swirling, sucking, licking and plunging. She ground her hips into his mouth and thrashed her head, so he held her steady with a firm hand on her stomach.

He was lost in her smell and taste and feel, barely coherent as she muttered unintelligible words mixed with moans.

She shuddered under his palm and placed a hand on his head. She gripped his hair and pulled hard, then said in a fluttery voice, "Alec."

He growled as the sweet pain lanced through his

scalp and the vibration must have been the last push she needed because she came in one, keening cry.

When her hips stopped moving and her breath quieted, he wiped his face on the sheet and raised his head.

Kat's eyes were closed and her amazing breasts rose and fell in gasping breaths. He unhooked her legs from around his shoulders, and they dropped to the bed like dead weights.

As he crawled up her body, she cracked her eyes open. He held himself above her with arms braced on either side of her head.

"That was . . . incredibly unsatisfying," she said breathlessly.

"Oh yeah?"

She nodded weakly. "Don't ever do it again."

He tried to keep his face serious, but he knew he was failing. "Okay, never again."

She smiled and grabbed his head, pulling it down until his lips met hers. She kissed him, hard, not hesitating despite the fact she could surely taste herself on him.

Her arm shifted under him and he looked up as she reached for the drawer in his nightstand. She kept her eyes on his as she pulled out the drawer and rummaged inside. He might have stopped breathing again when she thrust a condom wrapper in his face.

"Alec Stone, I do not want to have sex with you." She shook her head emphatically, pursing her lips to look irritated, but the glint in her eyes gave her away.

He couldn't help it. He laughed. "Oh yeah? Well I don't want to have sex with you either, Kat Caruso."

Her eyes crinkled and then she rolled him onto his back, straddling his hips. After tearing open the package she handed him the condom. As soon as he rolled it on, she raised up on her knees and lowered herself on top of him.

His eyes closed and rolled back into his head and he moaned. She felt so fucking good. Tight and hot and everything he'd ever wanted.

And then she began to move.

He snapped his eyes open, because he didn't want to miss this. She looked so gorgeous braced above him, with a soft, sexy smile stretching her lips, her beautiful hair draped over one shoulder, curled around a breast.

He dug his fingers into her hips, then let his hands drift back. He cupped her ass and squeezed, something he'd never thought he'd be able to do.

Her smile got bigger, more seductive. "Like my ass, huh?"

"No. It's definitely not the best ass on campus."

Her eyes flashed, the blue a churning whirlpool he never wanted to escape. She parted her lips, licked them and rode him harder.

He matched her, thrusting hard with every slam of her hips. She dug her nails into his shoulders, repeating "Fuck, yes" over and over again. He would have chanted it along with her if he had remembered how to talk.

He lasted an embarrassingly short amount of time. At least, he thought so. He actually lost track of time, in a Kat-induced time warp. So when he came, he had no idea how long it'd been. But he knew Kat lay on top of him, her skin covered in a sheen of sweat, her head tucked under his chin, breath gusting over his chest.

Eventually he moved, shifting her so he could roll off the condom and toss it in his trash can. She snuggled into his side as he lay on his back, and he grazed his fingers down her spine, feeling each little bump, then palmed one perfectly formed ass cheek.

She traced patterns on his stomach with soft fingers. Finally, she broke the silence. "Yeah, that"— her voice caught and she cleared it—"that didn't go well at all."

He cupped her chin so she'd raise her head to look at him, then he rolled onto his side so they faced each other.

Kat looked beautiful, with her hands folded under her head, her blue eyes clear, wide and relaxed. He ran his thumb over her cheekbone. "The last thing in the world I want to do right now is fall asleep with you."

She shifted closer to him and wrapped a hand around his neck. "Ditto," she said, before placing a soft kiss on his lips.

He tucked her head under his chin. In five minutes, her breaths had deepened with sleep and he knew he wouldn't be far behind.

Chapter Sixteen

KAT WOKE, SAW an unfamiliar wall and strange sheets under her hand and waited for the panic.

But none came. Instead, the warmth of a hand at her naked hip spread throughout her body.

Alec.

The steady rhythm of his breath tickled the hairs at the back of her neck and the strong *tha-thump* of his heart tapped a beat down her spine. She rubbed her eyes and Alec's fingers flexed at her hip.

"Hey," his voice rasped.

She shifted onto her back and rolled her head to the side to face him. He lay on his side, his features sleep-softened.

"Hey," she whispered.

Alec raised his hand and cupped her cheek, his thumb swiping her cheekbone. The possessiveness of the gesture pierced her in the heart like a harpoon and she knew already, no matter how hard she tugged, she wasn't going to be able to pull Alec out without a whole lot of pain.

"What are you thinking about?" he said softly.

Like she could tell him the truth. "I'm thinking about how you need a pillow-top mattress, because I think I feel a spring in my butt."

Alec threw back his head and laughed, his face unguarded in a way she'd never seen before. He bent his head back to her, pressed a kiss to her lips, and murmured. "You are such a princess."

And then he tickled her.

The big, major jerk.

She fought back, using all the dirty tricks she'd learned as an undersized female with an older brother. She pulled hair and an earlobe. Scratched with her manicured nails and aimed a knee right at the spot between his legs that she had come to really love the night before.

Before she could hit any of the goods, Alec tucked and rolled, protecting himself—she wouldn't have actually hit him there, how cruel did he think she was?—but she took the advantage, rolling him onto his stomach and straddling his upper thighs.

She pinned his arms on either side of his head. He was still laughing, his face turned to the side so he could peer at her out of the corner of his eyes.

"Don't ever call me princess." With each word, she bounced, eliciting a groan with each descent.

"Fine, you win."

She took her hands off of his wrists and leaned back on her haunches, admiring the muscles of his upper back. "I like the view up here. I think I'm going to stay awhile."

Kat's eyes strayed down to admire the cheeks of his ass, which was when she noticed his tattoo.

"Oh. My. God. You have a tramp stamp." She ran her hands over the justice scales on his lower back.

Alec surged up, toppling her onto her back with a squeal. The tickling began again, a vicious attack on her rib cage. "Uncle! Uncle!" she cried.

Alec stopped immediately and wrinkled his nose. "Please do not cry 'uncle' while we are in bed naked together. That feels creepy."

"Well it got you to stop, so it's effective."

Alec's eyes narrowed.

"Okay, so can we discuss your tramp stamp? Or . . ."

He let out a long-suffering sigh "Please, don't call it a tramp stamp."

"I'm calling it like I see it."

"You're mean."

"I want the story, Stone."

Alec rolled his eyes. "I got really drunk one night last summer after something shitty happened. I woke up with that. All I can say is, I'm glad I chose something I actually like rather than . . . I don't know . . . a butterfly or something."

"Tinkerbell would look fantastic on your ass."

Alec's fingers curled, a clear warning that she was in a vulnerable tickle position.

"I like your tattoo!" Kat protested. "But it's in an unfortunate location."

"I can't disagree with you."

"So, what crappy thing happened?"

Alec's amusement faded. He bit his lip and rubbed his eyes. "Um, I had a girlfriend all through high school and into college. Last summer, she cheated on me. We broke up."

Cheat on Alec? Who would . . . *Oh.* "Was your girlfriend's name Carrie?"

He frowned. "Yeah, how do you know that?"

"I was in the coffee shop with Max and some girl named Carrie talked to him. She asked where you were and after she left, I asked Max who she was. He said she was an old girlfriend of yours."

Alec nodded, and the melancholy in his eyes made her stomach hurt. "I'm sorry," she said, running her fingers through her hair. "But I'm not completely sorry because then I wouldn't be here, in this uncomfortable bed, right now."

Alec's smile came back, full force. "For the first time since Carrie broke up with me, I'm not sorry about it either."

A knock at his door rattled the hollow wood. "Yo, Alec?" Cam's voice was muffled.

Kat and Alec froze. "Yeah?" he said.

"I gotta run Trevor home and I'm gonna stay there tonight. Be back later tomorrow."

" 'Kay!" Alec called.

They stayed silent until double sets of footsteps drifted down the stairs and the front door opened and shut.

That knock and a third voice was like a gas, seeping under the door, surrounding them with the reminder there was a real world. Kat didn't want to bring it up. She wanted to stay in this moment forever where it was she and Alec in a little room in a crappy apartment and no one else existed. Especially ex-boyfriends.

"Do you feel guilty?" she said slowly, wanting to know the answer but hating herself because she already knew it.

Alec rolled onto his back and dug his palms into his eyes. "Yeah."

"I don't want to come between you and Max."

"Honestly, I'm not sure how that's not going to happen, seeing as Max told me if I didn't stay away from you, he wouldn't talk to me again."

Kat's stomach dropped and the harpoon in her chest pulsed painfully. "He didn't."

Alec rolled his head on his pillow. "He did."

She squeezed her eyes shut, and then peeled the covers back, crawling to the end of the bed and searching for her bra and underwear.

"I can't come between you," she said. "I just can't. I'd feel guilty and then you'd resent me and that would drive a wedge between us—"

"Whoa, whoa, slow down." Alec wrapped his arms around her where she sat on the edge of the bed, trying to hook her bra. " 'Drive a wedge between us?' You sound like a movie trailer."

She smacked his hand. "This isn't funny."

His sigh gusted a hot breath over her shoulder. "I know. I just . . . don't leave, okay? Can we be together today and worry about everything else tomorrow?"

She clipped her bra and placed her hands over his.

"You know, with Max—"

Alec's arms tightened, and he choked on a breath. "I don't want to know."

"No, but I want to tell you—"

"Kat, seriously—"

"We never slept together," she confessed in a rush. And then waited. The tension in his arms didn't ease and the heat of his chest on her back was making her sweat.

"What?" he said quietly.

"I wanted you to know. That Max and I never had sex." Something told her this was really important for him to know. "And even if we did, it wouldn't have been anything close to what we did."

His chest rose and fell against her back. His nose nudged along her neck and his lips touched on her ear. "I've only ever been with Carrie," his voice was pained, as if he had pulled the information out of himself with a rusted fish hook. "And it was never like it was with you."

"I guess that tells us something. About this. About us."

His arms finally loosened, and he exhaled slowly. "Yeah, I think it does."

They sat in silence, both staring ahead of them out the window in Alec's bedroom, which had a view of the brick wall of a nearby building. She was sure neither of them paid much attention to the view.

Finally, he pressed a kiss to her temple. "Let's get some breakfast."

Kat rose and pulled on her underwear, grabbed a T-shirt of Alec's and slipped it over her head. "Are you going to make me breakfast?"

Alec tugged on a pair of sweatpants and paused while pulling on a shirt. "Uh, sure. I make a mean omelet."

"Really?"

"Yep. Cooked a lot when I was a kid because my mom worked weird hours."

She smiled and headed toward the bathroom. "Great, I like double cheese and bacon."

"Princess," he muttered behind her back.

She whirled around to give him a much-deserved smack, but he was already halfway down the stairs, laughing.

ALEC WHISTLED TO himself while he poured the whisked eggs into the pan. He took a sip of his glass of chocolate milk as Kat walked into the kitchen. She yawned. "Coffee?"

"I think it's in the fridge."

Her brows puckered. "You drink cold coffee?"

He tilted the pan so the egg could cook evenly. "Kat. The grounds are in the fridge. I didn't make any coffee."

"You didn't make coffee."

"No." He took another sip of his chocolate milk.

"What's that?"

"What does it look like?"

"Chocolate milk."

"Great detective work, Kat."

"What are you, six?"

He pointed his spatula at her. "Don't insult the cook."

Kat took a step closer, walking right into the spatula, one corner of her lips quirked up. "You drink chocolate milk. That's so cute."

He glared at her. "No bacon for you."

She laughed and turned away, heading to the fridge. "Fine. I'll have to make my own coffee."

Instead of eating in the kitchen, they took their plates upstairs. Alec sat on his desk chair, legs propped up and crossed at the ankle on his desk. Kat sat on his bed, one leg tucked under her.

Wearing his T-shirt, her tangled hair spilled around her shoulders and face fresh of makeup *in his bed*, Alec was so far past gone for her, he didn't know if he'd ever come back. She moaned around a forkful of omelet, which now became his absolute favorite food.

"This is so good," she said.

"Thanks."

She picked at her food. "So, what did your mom do that she worked weird hours?"

"She's a day-care worker. So, she was out of the house super early and sometimes she got home late if parents didn't pick their kids up on time."

"You two get together at the diner a lot?"

"Um, not really. She . . . well, she had some news for me."

Kat cocked her head. "Yeah?"

He put down his fork and rubbed his face. "Uh, the guy . . ." he blew out a breath. "The guy that killed my dad is up for parole. Mom wanted to know if I wanted to write a letter to protest his release for his parole hearing."

Kat pushed her plate aside and leaned forward on the bed, her attention on him. All her energy focused on him was soothing and exhilarating at the same time. "What do you want to do?"

Alec twitched his lips back and forth and tapped his fingers on his desk. "I don't know."

"Well, what would you get out of writing the letter? If he was released, how would that make you feel?"

He squirmed, because this was territory he'd made a major effort in his life never to visit. It was like Alec's Area 51.

"Well, if he was released, I'm not really sure how I'd feel. I mean, he served his time and he'd be almost seventy now. I don't really think about him anymore."

Kat nudged his leg with her bare foot, her eyes wide with sincerity. "I think you need to do what's best for you now. Don't do what you feel like you should do, to honor your father or something. You've honored your father by being who you are."

She was beautiful, all big eyes and open heart and her words tore at that trap in his heart where he housed all his bitterness, begging to be let free.

"Come here," he said, and held out a hand. Kat unfolded herself from the bed and took a step toward him. He tugged her onto his lap and she came willingly, knees on either side of his hips, arms around his neck.

"You're incredible, you know that?" he said, running his thumb over her cheekbone.

Her eyes blinked slowly, once. She cocked her head and gave him a smirk, a look he was starting to recognize as an act, a defense mechanism when she was feeling too much. "I thought I was here because I was hot."

He grabbed her face with both hands. "Don't do that, Kat. Don't make jokes when I'm trying to be honest with you."

Her smirk immediately dropped and a cautious hope shone over her face.

"I want you here with me, first, because you're fucking incredible." He smiled then. "And second, because you're hot."

Kat chuckled and tightened her arms around his neck. She bent her forehead to his. "Ditto," she said softly.

Chapter Seventeen

THEY SPENT THE day in his room, wrapped up in each other on Alec's bed, watching movies on his computer, talking and eating. And definitely not bringing up a certain best friend/ex-boyfriend.

Even though they were in the same room, Alec touched her a lot. Just a brush of her hair over her shoulder that made her gasp or twining his fingers with hers that raised goose bumps on her arms.

He lay on his back on his bed in a pair of gym shorts and she lay on her side in her underwear, bra and one of his T-shirts. They were watching a movie, her legs tangled with his, head on his shoulder. Their joined hands lay on his chest and Alec idly played with them, rubbing her palm or stroking her fingers. She raised her head and met Alec's eyes. "Are you watching the movie?"

He paused. "No."

"What are you doing?"

"Watching you."

"I'm just laying here. It's really not anything exciting."

Alec chuckled and paused for a minute before speaking. "I'm trying to imprint this day, waking up next to you, you in my bed, in my mind. Don't wanna forget it."

It was on the tip of her tongue to suggest it could be like this tomorrow and the next day, but she didn't want to spoil the moment to talk about the future. Who knew what was going to happen when the real world intruded into their safe haven?

Instead she rose up and pressed her lips to his, taking control of the kiss. He let her for a little before pushing back, surging his tongue into her mouth. She smiled into the kiss. She'd always been a take-charge girl in bed. But with Alec, the duel for control was exciting.

She straddled him and lightly ground her hips into him. He groaned into her mouth and the deep vibration went right through her, flushing her body with heat. She ground down harder, and Alec growled while easily flipping her onto her back. He braced himself on his elbows and ran his lips along her jaw, behind her ear, and down her neck, leaving small nips. Kat had a momentary thought that she hoped he'd leave marks.

His hips settled over hers and she instantly spread her legs, accepting him into the cradle of her body. He cupped a breast, thumb swiping her nipple, and she felt the echo of it on her cheekbone.

"Kat," he whispered, pressing kisses along her collarbone, a place she never thought before could be an erogenous zone. But Alec took his time, skimming his hands over her rib cage and stomach, while his tongue had a mind of its own, doing crazy things to the swells of her breasts and nipples.

"God," she moaned. "Right there. Yep, there."

He chuckled, his breath gusting over her wet skin. "Who's on top here?"

"You," she said grudgingly.

He grinned. A wicked, sexy, Alec grin that pronounced the curve in his top lip. "Yeah. Yeah, I am," he murmured. And then he went back to his task of touching lips to every inch of her skin.

She shut up, because she sure as heck didn't want him to stop.

When he reached her belly button, she'd had enough though. She grabbed a condom from the drawer beside his bed and shoved it under his nose. "Please. Now."

He peered up at her, eyes darkened with lust, and snatched the condom out of her hand. "Don't think you're winning this. I was heading for the drawer myself," he muttered, rising on his knees to slip on the condom.

"Less talky, more fucky," she said, grabbing his shoulders.

He came down on top of her in a heap, laughing. "You only swear when you're turned on. It's like screwing a sailor." He kissed her long and deep, and at the same time, he positioned himself at her entrance and slid in.

She arched her neck, enjoying the hot slide of him inside of her. He began to move, slowly rocking his hips while placing soft, moist kisses all over her face and neck.

She felt beautiful and adored and she wanted this to last forever.

She began to feel it building inside of her, as Alec found her spot and hit it over and over again, speeding up, and she met each of his thrusts.

Kat came on a shout, the orgasm rocketing through her, curling her toes and digging her nails into his back. Alec buried his face in her neck, moaning her name and several other choice words as he finished.

He kept his head there as they both took in air, his breath ghosting over her sweat-slick skin. Everything in her body pulsed with a satisfied ache. The weight of Alec's body on top of hers was hot and an elbow dug into her side, but she didn't care. She didn't want to untangle from him, to feel the cool of the air when his skin no longer touched hers.

"Christ," he whispered.

Kat bit her lip, unsure what to say.

Alec finally raised his head, their noses almost touching, and stroked her face with his fingers, starting at the hair of her temple and ending on the hinge of her jaw. His brow was set in silent contemplation, as if he was memorizing the bone structure of her face. He gave her another peck on the lips and then slowly rose.

As predicted, the loss of him was unwelcome.

"I'm going to go to the bathroom and then head downstairs and make us some dinner." He pulled off the condom and threw it in the trash, then pulled on a pair of jeans. "Peanut butter and jelly sandwiches?"

She smiled and nodded.

He grinned at her, leaned in for another peck, and then walked out.

She lay there for another minute, listening to the screech of the old pipes in the house as Alec used the sink in the bathroom. When his footsteps descended the stairs, she rose and pulled on her clothes.

Thinking they could go see a movie, she opened up his laptop and pulled up a web browser. The home page was his e-mail and although she hadn't meant to snoop, the subject line of one of the e-mails struck her—*Talk to Kat yet?*

Hovering over the touchpad, Kat's fingers began to shake. The email was from Danica. Maybe she wondered how their talk at the pizza shop went. Kat didn't mean to click on the e-mail. She really, truly didn't, but her finger did and when she opened it up and began to read, she wished to all heck she'd stayed as far away from the computer as possible.

Just checking if you mentioned to Kat about how she might have dyslexia. Like we talked about, here are a bunch of links I researched for you. Let me know what she says! Glad you mentioned her struggling to me.

    Love, Dan

Kat sat, frozen. She couldn't feel her limbs and she wondered if they were even attached anymore.

Dyslexia? A learning disability? She remembered overhearing a conversation between her parents about her neighbor, an elementary school classmate of hers.

Did you hear about Elijah? her father had said.

That must be so rough on him and his parents, her mother had answered, clucking her tongue. *He's going to be labeled as* on the spectrum *for the rest of his life, in special classes and nonsense.*

Kat remembered the cruelty of kids whispering behind his back, mocking his hand gestures and facial tics.

All this time, she'd studied her butt off, believing that if she just worked harder, studied more, she could be like all the other kids. But if this were true, if she had a learning disability, then she'd never get better.

Well, that was it. Screw this stupid plan and stupid school and stupid everything. Maybe she would be better off answering phones and ordering K-cups.

And Alec . . . God, what had she been thinking? She'd been dreaming of some sort of future with him, and meanwhile he'd been talking to Danica about her like she was just another dumb tutoring student. Who'd always be a dumb student, if this e-mail was anywhere near the truth. Because she knew enough about learning disabilities to know they couldn't be cured.

The numbness slowly dissipated and in its place was a bone-chilling cold, which steadily warmed into anger directed at the one source in close range.

Alec Stone.

She didn't belong with him. He'd never put up with her for long, and *damn him* for thinking she could be in his league.

Before the tears could fall, she quickly rose from the desk and searched the room frantically for her purse. She had to get out of here, get home and wallow in self-pity alone. The last thing she wanted was for Alec to see—

"Kat?" She whipped around and Alec stood in the doorway, two plates in hand, his expression confused. "What are you doing?"

At the sight of him, her objective wasn't to get home anymore. All the hurt, embarrassment and feelings of inadequacy during the last twenty years bubbled up in a rush. She had to release this poison, because right now it was racing through her veins. She had to get it out if she had to scratch herself to death to do it.

"I can't believe you." She squared her shoulders to face him.

He took one step inside the door and placed the plates on the bed. "What are you talking about?"

She pointed to the computer. "I went online to search for a movie and instead saw an e-mail from Danica."

He still looked confused, and she wanted to scream.

"Did you think about me, or my feelings, at all when you were talking to Danica and speculating on whether or not I have a *learning disability*?" She spat out the last two words as if they were the poison-tipped arrows that were slowly sickening her bloodstream.

Alec closed his eyes and ducked his head. When he met her eyes again, his were in a pained squint. "It wasn't like that—"

She cut him off, not wanting to hear what it was like, because she knew what she felt right now, and that's what mattered. "Did you think about how I would feel?" she repeated.

His breaths sounded uneven and he tucked his elbows close to his sides. "I guess I didn't, or I would have done things differently," he said quietly.

She would have given him some points for honesty, if she could muddle through the anger dragging her down. He could take his good intentions and shove 'em.

"Why couldn't you come to me first when you had these suspicions? Because I wouldn't understand?"

His teeth clenched. "It didn't happen that way. If you'd let me explain—"

"Who do you think you are?" She snarled, on a rant now, only recognizing Alec as a dartboard for her insecurities. "Just because you're some university tutor doesn't give you the qualifications to . . . diagnose me or whatever. Your job was to tutor me, not analyze me."

His jaw clenched. "I wasn't trying to analyze you, I was trying to help—"

"You should have come to me first." She swiped at the tears beading on her lower lashes. "All my life, people have talked about me behind my back." The tears ran down her cheeks now and she couldn't get them to stop. "You think I don't know what people think about me? *Kat is so dumb, look at her grades, she's so flaky, thank God she's pretty.* I know what people say. *I know*," she thumped her chest. "And I've become really good at ignoring it and not caring. But I thought you were different. I thought . . ." she laughed maniacally and ignored Alec's stricken features. "I thought this was different.

"Kat." He stepped forward as she finally spied her purse on the floor near his closet and rushed to it. When she slung it over her shoulder and faced him again, she didn't like the determined look in his eye as he spoke. "Do not stand there and say you thought it was different, as if you now think it wasn't. Last night, this morning, *us*," he gestured between them with a waved hand, "*happened*."

She nodded emphatically. "Yep, it did. Past tense. *Happened*. With a big, fat ED."

Now he looked sick and when he spoke, his voice was tortured. "Kat—"

The front door slamming open cut him off. "Hello? Stone?"

Max. Because life wasn't complicated enough. Alec stood frozen, five feet from her, his eyes widened in horror that would have been comical any other day when she wasn't furious at him and heartbroken. She considered opening up his bedroom window and taking her chances on jumping two stories to the ground. A fractured ankle might be preferable to whatever crap-show was about to go down.

Footsteps sounded on the stairs now and each thump was like the theme from *Jaws*.

Ba dum. Ba dum. Ba dum ba dum ba dum.

I think we need a bigger boat. . . .

Max stopped in the doorway, frowning, his eyes roaming Alec's bare chest and Kat's flushed face. She was vaguely aware that the room smelled like sex, and she hoped to all that was holy that Max had a cold or something.

"Uh . . . what's going on?" Max propped his hands on his hips.

No matter how mad Kat was, she wasn't going to do anything to hurt their friendship without Alec's consent. She cleared her throat. "Nothing. I . . . uh . . . forgot my purse. Alec let me keep it in his room last night so no one would steal anything and I forgot it. Just came back now to get it."

Alec hadn't taken his eyes off her and his color still hadn't returned.

Max looked skeptical.

"Right, Alec?" she prompted.

Part of her still wished Alec would speak up. Right then and there. Declare his intentions like this was the 1800s and lay claim to her. Tell Max the truth. Then hold her in his arms while he told her he loved her and respected her and that e-mail was a mistake . . .

But instead, he hauled that harpoon out of her heart, taking a bloody chunk along the way, when he said quietly, "Yep. She just came to get her purse."

She hid a sob behind her hand, murmured some goodbyes through a film of tears and ran down the stairs.

On the way home, she cleared her mind enough to focus on the e-mail. All she knew about dyslexia was that it was a type of learning disability. No one had ever mentioned it before. What did Alec think he was, some kind of teaching expert now?

This sucked. She was tired of feeling out of place at school where everyone seemed to understand things she couldn't. Where others aced tests without studying and wrote ten-page papers in one night.

She was tired of being different.

And the knowledge that she truly might be different. That she truly might not get better with extra studying was a punch she didn't have the ability to block.

And of all people, *Alec* had to be the one to see it. In what world would someone like him be with someone like her? Kat-land, that's where. And unfortunately Kat-land was a mystical, fantastical place where she rode a unicorn through fields of golden wheat while eating chocolate that was somehow delicious and still fat free and cute little pheasants lined her path, blowing bubbles on her—*because who didn't like bubbles?*—while telling her how brilliant and smart she was.

Kat-land was *awesome*.

Too bad it wasn't real.

Chapter Eighteen

ALEC STOOD IN the shower, the water sluicing through his hair and down his back. He wondered how long he could shower without turning into a prune or Max invading his sanctuary. He could still hear his friend banging around in his room on the other side of the bathroom.

After Kat ran down the stairs, Alec had mumbled about getting in the shower and bolted.

What Alec really wanted was to melt into a pile of goo and be washed down the drain. That's what he deserved. Because it was obvious he had hurt Kat. Twice. Not only for talking about her to Danica, but for turning coward and denying everything to Max. Because as soon as he had agreed with her, Kat had looked even more devastated than before. Which he hadn't thought possible.

With Max standing there, he couldn't admit what he and Kat had. He thought that was the right decision, to stay loyal to his best friend. But as soon as Kat turned her back, he thought about never being able to laugh at her silly jokes, or run his hands over those soft hips, or smell that citrus shampoo on his pillow.

And now he wasn't so sure about his choice.

He slammed his hand on the faucet, turning off the shower, and stepped out. He dried off hastily and wrapped a towel around his waist. As soon as he stepped outside of the bathroom, Max raised his head from where he was leaning against the wall, arms crossed over his chest.

"Hey." Max didn't sound as mad as Alec thought he would.

"Hey. What are you doing home?"

"Needed to get a book for an assignment I need to work on tonight. I'm heading back home because I have to get up early to work at the garage."

"Oh." Alec brushed by him and went to his room. Hopefully alone.

Unfortunately, Max followed him.

"So . . . Kat?"

Facing away from Max, Alec slipped his boxer briefs on under his towel and then took it off to dry his hair. "What about her?"

Max was silent, and Alec turned around. It felt like a face-off, and Alec really wished he was wearing more clothes.

Max didn't say anything, just squinted his eyes at Alec and shifted his weight from foot to foot. It was unnerving to see Max so uncertain, so lacking in confidence.

"What's going on with you, man?" Alec asked. "You

ever going to tell me why you've been so fucking weird this whole year?"

Max took a deep breath, puffed out his cheeks and exhaled. He opened his mouth, but then winced and turned his head to look out the window. A prickly feeling crept up Alec's spine. "Max?"

"So, Kat was okay last night? You kept an eye on her?" Max kept his eyes trained out the window.

"Kat was fine," Alec said slowly, unwilling to lie anymore. And conveniently pretending there was no lying by omission.

Max nodded and then turned to leave, avoiding all contact with Alec. "Great, thanks. See ya tomorrow."

When Alec heard the front door slam shut, he released the tension in his shoulders, then yelled in frustration. What the fuck was going on with Max? And most important, why wouldn't he talk to Alec? Since they'd become best friends in first grade and shared lunches out of their Transformers lunch boxes, Max had always been transparent. He didn't hold back, which actually resulted in many detentions and missed recesses when they were kids. And the weirdest thing was, he'd never been a bully, which was why his behavior toward Kat was confusing.

Alec was a small kid with glasses. His mom called him a late bloomer, which was a nice way of saying it took for-fucking-ever for his voice to deepen. But Max had always been a stocky kid, friendly, unless you pissed him off, and then he had a face like thunder.

An easy target for bullies, Alec was on his third pair of glasses that his mother could barely afford during first-grade recess. Some big kid named Kevin had been holding said glasses, twisting them in his pudgy fingers.

And then, like some sort of Old West movie—minus the tumbleweed—a shadow fell over Kevin. The kid looked up, but he didn't have a chance. Max grabbed Kevin's wrist, wrenched it painfully and said "Drop 'em." Like Kevin was a dog.

Kevin dropped the glasses, no one ever bothered Alec again, and Max and Alec had been at each other's side ever since.

Alec flopped back onto his bed, sheets still rumpled and smelling like Kat. He missed her. He missed the old Max. He missed his life when it wasn't complicated.

And he would bet a million bucks things were about to get worse.

THE WOODEN CHAIR was uncomfortable, the smoothie tasted like grass and Alec was prepared to punch the next person who glared at him for tapping his pen on his book.

Kat was half an hour late for their study session. He told himself she was late. He didn't want to believe she wasn't coming. He hadn't seen her since Saturday and he knew she had her midterm in an hour.

He wanted to see her, but he also wanted to make sure she did well on her test. Was she nervous? Did she study well? His mind was consumed with Kat, and he wanted to scream.

He took a gulp of his smoothie and cringed, wishing it was chocolate milk.

He stared blankly at his mock trial notes and then checked his watch again. Only five minutes had passed? This was torture.

Half an hour later, he was still alone. And an hour after that.

The room was too quiet, dull and dark. It took the shadow of Kat's absence for him to realize how much he'd grown addicted to her light.

He stayed until her midterm time was over, hoping she'd stop in at the library afterward.

But she never did.

Chapter Nineteen

KAT WALKED OUT of the statistics classroom, head held high despite her certainty she had bombed the midterm about five minutes earlier.

Glass half full, she was not.

But her studying during the past week had taken a nosedive. Every page of her notes, every highlighted section in her textbook reminded her of Alec. And then she wanted to cry. So she would cry. Then she'd have to clean her face. She'd do that and then sit on the toilet for half an hour staring at the walls. Then she'd return to her books, start studying and it would start all over again until she decided to sleep.

Clearly, none of that was productive.

Her stomach churned at the thought of Alec dismissing her in front of Max. And her head pounded when she thought about the fallout if Max found out what happened. She'd never want to come between two friends.

It made her want to stomp her feet and pull her hair and wail, "It isn't fair!"

Shame on her for thinking she could get and keep a guy like Alec Stone.

Kat trudged through campus, her windbreaker no match for the March breeze. When she reached her suite, she let herself inside and headed straight to her bed. She fell into it—jacket, shoes and all.

"Uh-oh," Tara's voice came from somewhere behind her. "Test didn't go well?"

Kat shook her head, face planted into her pillow.

"Aw, Kat." The bed dipped and Kat rolled to her side to see her friend sitting on the edge of the mattress

"I need to get out of here." Kat brushed her hair out of her face.

Tara frowned. "What do you mean?"

"I'm going home. This was my last midterm. I was going to go home for spring break anyway, and now I'm going to go a day early. I can't . . . I can't deal with any of this right now." Kat hopped off the bed and dragged out her suitcase, throwing random clothes into it.

"I think that's a good idea," Tara said. "Get away, gather yourself, then come back and kick some school butt."

Kat gave her a suffering look. "Please don't go all motivational poster on me."

"What? I'm trying to be encouraging. Isn't that what friends do?"

Kat smiled. "Yeah, thanks."

It was another hour before she finally managed to

make it out the door, dragging her heavy suitcase behind her and wondering why she packed for five million years when she planned to come back to school in a week.

Oh well, a girl still needed to coordinate her casually chic sweatshirts with her yoga pants. Even though Kat hadn't done a day of yoga in her life.

It took another fifteen minutes to reach the underclassmen parking lot on the outskirts of campus.

By the time she made it to her car, she was sweating under her coat and her shoulder ached from her suitcase. This was why she never drove anywhere, because her car was parked in flipping Siberia.

Then she got in her cute little red convertible Volkswagen Beetle—wishing it was summer and she could put the top down—and pulled out of the parking lot and drove.

As the miles stretched behind her, she purposefully didn't think about midterms or learning disabilities or smart guys with glasses who could kiss *really* well. She blanked her mind into Kat-land, where everything was perfect.

That lasted for a whole five minutes before her mind reverted right back to where it wanted to—thoughts of Alec.

Stupid brain.

She wanted him. She didn't want him with the teenage-like hormones that she had wanted all her other boyfriends—Max included. She wanted Alec because he laughed at her jokes and made her feel witty and looked at her like she hung the flipping moon in the sky. Because she dared to think they could be partners in this crazy thing called life.

It was an abrupt change from her norm of adolescent relationships. Sure, lust played a part in how she felt about him, but there was also a stronger emotion, another one that started with an L . . . and it hit her.

It hit her at the same time as a flash of tan and white fur skittered across the road in front of her. She tightened her hands on the wheel, swerved while screaming, and the car fishtailed before stopping with a jolt on the side of the road.

"Oh. my. goodness gracious," she breathed. "I almost killed a rodent, and I'm in love with Alec Stone."

She wasn't sure which was more depressing.

After sitting on the side of the road for who knows how long, still gripping the steering wheel with white knuckles, she took her foot off the brake and continued home. Now, her mind was actually blank, as if the realization had given it some sort of electrical shock. She didn't plan to defibrillate it for a while. Poor, tired brain needed to rest.

She finally made it home an hour later. Her house was three stories, made of contrasting brown and white stone, with a large, white wraparound porch and a wide staircase leading to a double front door.

She pulled into the circular driveway and parked, then lugged her bag out of the trunk.

"Mom! Dad! Hello!" She said as she stood in the foyer, determined not to take another step. They could come to her.

Footsteps clicked down the stairs and then her mom appeared in the hallway ahead of her. She wore kitten heels and a light blue knit dress, which matched her eyes. The eyes Kat had inherited, along with her mother's hair. "Katía? Why are you home at"—her mom checked the grandfather clock at the entrance—"eight at night on a Thursday?"

"I needed a break, and so I came home a day early."

"A break?" her mother asked, but Kat didn't have a chance to answer before her father's voice boomed from the entrance to his office farther down the hall.

"*Minha flor*," he said softly, using the Portuguese term of endearment meaning "my flower," his pet name for her for as long as she could remember. Kat wasn't bilingual anymore, but knew a couple words of her parents' mother language.

He walked toward her, arms outstretched, his skin and dark hair a handsome combination as always.

"Hey Daddy," she said, falling into his arms and wishing for a moment that she was nine years old and her biggest problem was what hair bow matched her outfit.

"We never get visits from you, and on a Thursday?" he said, leaning back to study her face.

She shrugged, unwilling to start listing the many reasons she had returned home. "Like I told Mom, I needed a break."

"Hmm," her father said, still studying her face and she knew she wouldn't get out of an explanation before the end of the weekend. He released her, giving her a reprieve for now. "Are you hungry? We can heat you some dinner."

"What did you have?"

"I made roasted chicken with mashed potatoes and asparagus," her mother said.

Kat's mouth watered, reminding her she skipped dinner. "Oh, yes, please. Sounds delish."

She followed her parents into the kitchen, thinking only of filling her belly and sleeping in her queen-sized bed with a pillow-top mattress.

The rest of her worries could wait.

THE MORNING LIGHT creeping through her pink lace curtains woke up Kat, and she snuggled down further into her comforter. She'd slept like the dead last night, and now today, she had to drag her ass out of bed and do something.

She wanted to wallow for a week, stomping her feet about boys and school and the injustice of her life. Okay, so she was a little dramatic. She'd never claimed not to be.

Since Saturday, she'd typed *dyslexia* into Google several times, but never once had she hit ENTER. She'd avoided learning more, worried about being different, worried about Alec being right.

She emerged from her cocoon of bed covers and grabbed her laptop off of her nightstand, where she'd placed it after hastily unpacking last night.

This time, when she typed *dyslexia*, she actually hit ENTER.

And her world was *blown. up.*

These sites spoke her language. These blogs were people who were like her. Troubles with reading comprehension and writing. Words disjointed on the page in front of her. Some inability to focus. She read about famous people—including Albert Einstein—who were dyslexic. When she read "dyslexia is not a sign of poor intelligence or laziness," she had to press her fist to her mouth to stop the tears.

After a quick trip to the kitchen for some coffee and toast, she returned to her bed and took a short online test to identify dyslexia. Most of her answers showed a moderate to severe rating, which identified strongly with dyslexia.

Her parents had already left for work, and she was glad. Because she didn't know how she was going to tell them.

There was only one person she wanted to speak to.

She took a shower, slipped into her gray sweater dress with a black belt and black knee-high boots over leggings, and grabbed her keys. She was heading back to school.

Chapter Twenty

CROSS KEYS MIDDLE School, for grades six through eight, was a squat brick building that bustled with pimple-ridden, brace-faced preteens.

Was there anything worse than middle school? Kat thought not, as she stood in the lobby, watching students whispering to one another as they hustled to class. It was such an awkward age, where most of the girls had hit puberty, their boobs stuffed in ill-fitting training bras. And the boys were an odd mix, some still stuck in prepubescent bodies and others with cracking voices, full of the lovely raging hormones that afflicted men worldwide.

Kat smoothed her skirt and headed into the attendance office.

"One moment," the woman at the counter said without looking up as the bell over the door sounded.

"No problem. Take your time." Kat glanced around the office, full of inspirational posters, like that kitten hanging from a tree with the caption "Hang in there!" She always wondered about that poster. Obviously, they didn't throw a cat up in a real tree. So did they hold a twig over a pillow in case the cat fell? What kind of person volunteered their cat for that? Poor thing. She hoped its owner gave it lots of treats afterward—

"Kat Caruso?"

Kat snapped her eyes back to the attendance desk and smiled. Mrs. Gandy, her neighbor, was still the attendance officer. Which was unfortunate if you wanted to call in sick to lay out in your backyard to get a base tan for the eighth-grade sock hop. Hypothetically.

"Hello, Mrs. Gandy," Kat said in greeting stepping up to the desk.

"Well I'll be. Look at you, all grown up. Are you in college now?" Mrs. Gandy wore a pale pink sweater set and her glasses sat on the tip of her nose, the frames attached to a beaded string around her neck. Her graying hair was pulled back in a tight bun.

"I am, at Bowler."

"Major?"

Kat tried not to cringe. "Oh, um, I'm undecided."

Mrs. Gandy's smile dimmed. "Well, you have time to decide. What can I help you with today?"

"Well . . . ah . . . I was hoping to see Mrs. Ross. Is that possible?"

Mrs. Gandy pursed her lips and then relayed some instructions to the other attendance officer. After some typing, she told Kat Mrs. Ross happened to be free with a planning period. They supplied Kat with a visitor's badge and sent her on her way to Mrs. Ross's classroom.

When Kat reached the closed, glass-paneled door, she peered inside. Mrs. Ross looked the same as Kat remembered her. She walked around the room straightening up, a tall, black woman with hair shorn close to the scalp. Kat could still hear her voice in her head, a slight Ghanian accent left over from when she moved as a child. She married an American man, hence the last name.

Kat knocked on the door, and Mrs. Ross glanced up. She blinked, then her eyes widened in surprise, and she gestured Kat inside with a large smile. Kat returned the smile and stepped into the classroom.

"Kat Caruso? Live and in the flesh." Mrs. Ross pulled her in for a hug and Kat breathed deeply, loving the warm, familiar scent of cocoa butter.

"Hello." She pulled back and took the seat to which Mrs. Ross gestured. The teacher took the seat across the small desk from her.

"So, please, tell me how you've been." Mrs. Ross said.

Kat took a couple of minutes to catch her up with her life since sixth grade.

"And you like Bowler?" Mrs. Ross asked.

"Yeah, I do. I mean, I like college. It's just . . ." she blew out a breath and gave a sad laugh while looking at her hands twisting on the desk. "It's really hard."

She looked up, expecting to see disappointment or pity, but Mrs. Ross looked thoughtful. "College is challenging," she said generically.

Kat bit her lip. "Yeah, well that's part of why I came today. I wanted to ask you about something. I have this tutor and he . . . he mentioned I might have dyslexia. Does that make sense to you?"

Mrs. Ross cocked her head and frowned slightly. "Weren't you tested for that in middle school?"

"Um, not that I remember."

Confusion passed over Mrs. Ross's face. She opened her mouth, then closed it and looked away.

"Mrs. Ross?"

Her teacher sighed and then turned back to her. "When I had you as a student in sixth grade, I saw some signs of a learning disability. I suspected dyslexia, but I wasn't sure. I mentioned to your parents that the district could test you or they could take you to a private psychologist."

Kat's jaw was close to hitting the desk, it was so low. "I never knew about that."

Mrs. Ross shook her head, her voice heavy. "They declined."

Kat wasn't sure she heard that right. "Excuse me?"

Mrs. Ross sucked her lips between her teeth and spoke again. "They declined to get you tested. And they are your parents, they got the final say. Not me and not the school."

Kat squeezed her thighs so hard, she thought she'd leave bruises, so she shoved her hands under her butt and sat on them. Her parents were told and did nothing? She struggled all this time on her own? She wanted to ask Mrs. Ross why her parents declined to test her, but she thought that question was better directed at the source.

She looked away and bit her lip. "So, this makes sense to you?"

"Kat, you were an incredibly bright student. Very creative, full of imagination. But you had trouble with reading comprehension, spelling and writing that didn't seem to match up."

"Is that why you took all that time with me? To show me how to organize and plan? Kat asked.

Mrs. Ross nodded. "And that helped?"

"Oh God, yes, I'm not sure where I'd be without all your help back then."

Mrs. Ross placed a the desk between them. "Honestly, I'm so impressed you made it into college with no help for your possible learning disability."

"Would you believe I got by on good looks? Feminine wiles?"

Mrs. Ross laughed. "I do think your charm has most likely saved you more than you think."

Kat sobered. "What do I do now? I mean, now I have this . . . thing . . . this word *disability* hanging over my head and—"

Mrs. Ross reached out and took Kat's hands, rubbing them softly, cutting her off. "Kat, dear, this is a good thing. Most colleges have learning support centers. You go and you speak to them. If they determine you do have dyslexia, there are ways for them to help you with your classes. You can get altered assignments to suit your abilities and extra help or time. I think you'll be relieved to know you have struggled for a reason."

Kat hadn't thought of it that way. All the times she labored over assignments that other kids breezed through had only made her feel frustratingly lacking in intelligence.

Mrs. Ross leaned back. "And don't let anyone make you feel bad about this. There shouldn't be a stigma about learning disabilities. They can't be helped, just like any other type of congenital disability."

Tell that to my parents, Kat wanted to say. Instead, she shifted in her seat, releasing her hands from their confinement. "Can I hang out here for a little this afternoon?" Kat asked. She wanted to delay going home to tell her parents their child was just like neighbor Elijah and could have greatly benefited from "special classes and nonsense."

Mrs. Ross patted Kat's arm. "Of course."

Kat spent a good portion of her morning learning about Native-American tribes and the multitude of uses for a bison carcass. She didn't remember learning in sixth grade that the scrotum was used for baby rattles. Mrs. Ross muttered that fact was the result of letting the students pick their own research topics.

The last class before lunch was language arts and Kat migrated to perch on the heater to watch the students write. Their assignment involved picking a Greek god or goddess, writing about his or her attributes and then citing the source from their textbook.

One girl, a little freckled thing with red curly hair, scowled at her page as if she wanted to light it on fire. Mrs. Ross hovered near her and began speaking softly.

"Rachel, what's wrong?"

"I don't understand." The girl huffed.

Mrs. Ross knelt down, her knees brushing the girl's denim skirt. "What are you having problems with?"

Rachel peered at her teacher under bronze eyelashes. "I know Poseidon holds something but I can't find in the book what it's called and I'm getting really frustrated." She threw her pen onto her desk for emphasis, in a little redheaded snit.

Mrs. Ross jerked her head back in surprise but kept her face neutral and kind. "Rachel, honey, remember what we talked about? What to do when you get frustrated?"

Rachel looked chagrined. "Close my eyes and count to ten. Start again when I'm calm."

"Right, and did you do that?"

Rachel shook her head.

Mrs. Ross patted her hand. "That's okay, now try again. Read the paragraphs on Poseidon slower and I'm sure you'll find the name of the object he carries."

"Thank you, Mrs. Ross," the little girl said.

Mrs. Ross smiled and walked slowly away, her eyes scanning the classroom. Rachel took a deep breath and focused back on her book, reading with her finger moving on each line. Then she gasped, her face lit up with a smile and she scribbled quickly onto her paper. Kat could only guess she'd found *trident*.

And in a weird snapshot of her life, Kat pictured herself sitting at that same desk in sixth grade, in a perfectly matched outfit and hair in a French braid, feeling frustrated like Rachel. Although her problem was the inability to express her creative ideas on paper and parents who didn't understand her.

But she had Mrs. Ross. And Mrs. Ross was still there for her.

She remembered something her teacher had told her all those years ago.

I care about every single student. Not just the ones who always get A's, she had said, when Kat needed extra help on a writing assignment.

And for once, something actually clicked into place in Kat's brain. She'd been floundering for so long, she almost missed the feeling of fitting. Of things being right.

She glanced around the classroom, taking in all the posters on the wall and the vocabulary words on the chalkboard. What if this is where she belonged, but on the other side of the classroom. As a teacher and not a student. All her life, she thought she wouldn't be capable but she had a reason for her problems now. What if she was able to be the inspiration for struggling students like herself?

AFTER SHE SAID good-bye to Mrs. Ross, she left the school and stopped for a celebration caramel *macchiato*. Extra drizzle. Because nothing said "I might have finally realized my calling" like a thousand-calorie caffeine jolt.

Although, she still had to get her statistics grade back on track before she could declare a major and get a degree. Details.

When she got home, she changed into a pair of yoga

pants and a tank top under a dolman-sleeved sweatshirt. Then she dug out a notebook, sat at her laptop and began her research.

She made all the notes on dyslexia she could and visited the website for Bowler's learning support department. She e-mailed the director to schedule a meeting after spring break. And then she composed an e-mail to Alec, but didn't send it.

After lunch, she walked to the curb to get the mail. She'd flipped through three credit-card offers and a magazine when she heard, "Kat!"

Her neighbor, Mrs. Carter, Elijah's mom, walked toward her, wearing a blue tracksuit and holding pink hand weights. She was doing that weird, puckered-mouth exercise breathing.

"Hi Mrs. Carter."

"Hello." Her neighbor stopped in front of her, walking in place, swinging her arms. Kat instantly felt lazy. "How's Bowler?"

"Uh, good. Great."

Mrs. Carter nodded as Kat was talking and almost cut her off to speak. "Elijah is doing great! He has an internship this summer with a software developer and is going to graduate a semester early."

On the spectrum, special classes and nonsense. Kat heard her mother's voice in her head. Would Kat be graduating early if she had that? If her parents hadn't brushed her teacher's concerns aside? She clenched her fist until the envelopes in her hand crinkled.

She smiled politely, happy for Elijah, who had always

been a nice, albeit quiet, kid. "That's great. Please tell him I said congratulations."

Mrs. Carter beamed, clearly proud of her son. *As she should be*, Kat thought.

"I will. You home for spring break?"

Kat nodded. Mrs. Carter was still walking in place, and it was giving her a headache.

"Elijah is participating in a programming competition in Las Vegas," Mrs. Carter said. "He was really excited."

Kat thought it sounded like torture, but maybe he could get to hit a fun strip club or something. "Well, I wish him luck."

"Thanks, honey. I'm off on my workout since it's not too cool outside. See you soon!" And Mrs. Carter pranced off, pink-weighted hands pumping.

Kat sighed and walked back inside her house. In the kitchen, she poured herself a glass of water and stared into her backyard. Good for Elijah. His label wasn't holding him back. He had been in some special classes, from what she could remember, but other than that, he'd been in the general school population. He was smart and generally well liked.

Kat recognized her life wasn't horrible. Her parents were well off, she had plenty of friends and she'd managed to get into college. But she'd still spent her formative years insecure about her intelligence. Her confidence in her grades and ability to function in a professional job hadn't just taken a hit. It'd been knocked out. For a decade.

She couldn't have said how she would have reacted if she'd found out she had dyslexia in sixth grade. She'd been eleven. But her parents had been adults.

And they hadn't done a thing.

She glanced at her watch. They'd be home from work soon, and they were going to have a conversation.

And after that, she needed to make a call to Alec. She was still hurt that he talked to Danica about her, but she saw now he had meant well. And denying her in front of Max? Well, she'd pushed him to do that, hadn't she? Either way, they needed to talk, because despite it all, she still wanted his arms around her, his hand holding hers, his voice in her ear cheering her on.

Chapter Twenty-One

ALEC YAWNED AND rubbed his eyes as he walked out of his mock trial midterm. He and Danica had argued the fuck out of the case. As predicted, the defense tried to blame the foreman, which made Alec seethe, claiming the site was improperly marked. But he was prepared with documentation that it had been. In the end, the jury—Professor Grim—had declared the prosecution the winner. Danica had jumped up and down and yelled "suck it!" at the defense.

Alec wasn't as excited as he thought he was going to be. He was happy for the good grade, but he didn't feel vindicated at all, like he should have been. The case had been personal, but when it was over, even if it was all fictional, there was no winner. There was a dead foreman and a woman with two teenagers sentenced to probably seven years in prison.

The part of him that wanted justice was vindicated.

The personal side of him didn't have the energy to be angry anymore. Not at drunk drivers and not at Sam MacEnroe. It was a feeling he never thought he'd have, the bitterness that had clung to his heart like a barnacle now cut off. With a Kat-hot knife.

He heard voices around the corner of the building in a shaded area but didn't take notice until he heard that familiar voice say, "Max, please."

His feet stopped of their own accord and his skin prickled. He closed his eyes as his best friend answered in a low deep tone, then Alec slowly turned his head and opened his eyes.

Carrie leaned with her back against the wall of the classroom building, while Max loomed over her, his forearm pressed to the faded brick above her head. Their heads were close, too fucking close, and Alec blinked, concerned in his sleep-deprived state that he was seeing a mirage.

But he wasn't dehydrated, and this wasn't a desert.

Nope, he was definitely witnessing some type of intimate contact between his ex-girlfriend and his *best fucking friend*.

"I can't, Carrie. I'm sorry," Max was saying in that soothing voice. Carrie's face was blotchy and tear-streaked. When she raised her hand and cupped Max's cheek, Alec felt the echo of the touch on his own skin.

And then he lost it.

"Please. Please, tell me there's a really good explanation for this." Alec stepped closer to them and waved his hand in their general direction.

Max leapt back from Carrie, his face white and his eyes wide. "Um . . ." he stammered while Carrie said, "Oh no."

Alec wanted to roll his eyes, because she wasn't even trying to find an excuse.

She wiped her eyes and stepped closer. "Alec, I'm sorry—"

He sliced his hand in the air, cutting her off. "No offense, Carrie. Actually, no, I take that back. I do mean offense and frankly, I don't care what you have to say. This isn't about you."

As the words were out of his mouth, he realized they were true. As his bitterness over Sam MacEnroe had faded, so had his bitterness to Carrie. He was over her and being cheated on. It was time to grow up.

Dismissing her and ignoring her gasp of outrage, he turned to Max. Because what Max was doing? No, that could not be forgiven.

"What the fuck, Max?" Alec took another step closer.

Max swallowed and licked his lips. "Alec . . ."

Alec waited. And waited some more. Max gaped like a fish but no sound came out.

"Are you kidding me? You gave me all that shit about Kat, meanwhile you are clearly doing *something* with my ex-girlfriend?"

An odd shadow passed over Max's face and his eyes shifted behind Alec's shoulder, where Carrie stood.

And that look was like a kick in the balls and a punch to the temple at the same time. Knockout. But he didn't land on a mat or grass, he landed in quicksand that was slowly pulling him under, suffocating him.

"Oh my God." He took a step back, lacing his fingers behind his head and closing his elbows to hide his face. Bent at the waist, he gasped for air. "Oh my God." He dropped his hands to his knees and looked up at Max. "It was you."

Max's face had gone beyond pale and was now one step away from corpse. And he was frozen like a corpse, all rigor mortis. But his eyes, they were alive, bugged out and red.

"I'm sorry." Max's voice was a croaked whisper.

Alec stood, one hand wrapped around his stomach because he was sure his aching, sick guts would fall out if he didn't. "You're sorry?" he whispered. "You're sorry?" He took a deep breath and shouted, "You're fucking sorry!"

Alec heard sobbing and wiped his eyes, thinking it was him breaking down like a crazy person in the middle of campus. But when his fingers came away dry, he realized it was Carrie.

"This got so fucked up, Zuk," Max said, hands on top of his head like he'd run a marathon. "It just—"

"If you say 'it just happened,' so help me, I will scream the fucking campus down right now."

Max snapped his mouth shut. "It was one night, at a party. You weren't there . . ." he dropped his arms and settled his hands on his hips, letting his head sag between slumped shoulders.

"Then what was this now?"

"Carrie was . . . uh . . . asking me to hang out. I said no."

"Hang out? You mean *fuck*." Alec's voice sounded foreign to his ears.

Max flinched but didn't answer.

In one long stride, Alec was in Max's face, their matching heights giving them the opportunity to look in each other's eyes. "How could you do that to me? You know how much she meant to me and how I felt about her."

Max's jaw clenched, but he shook his head.

"And then you pull this macho bullshit with Kat? You don't even understand . . ." Alec took a deep breath. "I chose you over her. I chose you, my best friend since first grade, who I thought had my back, over Kat Caruso, the first girl I actually loved."

Max sucked in a breath. "What?"

"Fuck you, Max. You lost the right to know anything about me or my life. Fuck. You."

Alec wanted to punch him, do something to get this aggression out because he thought he was going to combust, but he wasn't a violent guy and that was what Max wanted. For Alec to hit him and then they'd make up and everything would be okay.

But it wasn't okay. And Alec wasn't going to hit him. Instead, he turned around and walked away. He didn't look back to see Max's face, even when he heard his name in Max's broken voice and Carrie's tearful one.

As Alec walked, his swift strides quickly turned to jogging, which turned into all out sprinting by the time he reached the edge of campus.

He kept running all the way back to his town house, wishing he wore his running shoes instead of his beat up

Converse. The cold air burned in his lungs, but the thump of his feet on the pavement, the familiar movement of his arms and legs and rhythm of his breath cleared his head.

Max had been acting odd since the summer. Alec had chalked it up to his strained relationship with his dad. He never thought it had something to do with *him*, and with Carrie.

But the betrayal was only one source of the sick feeling in his gut. He kept picturing Kat's face when he denied everything in front of Max. He had seen the flash of hope in her eyes. That no matter how mad she had been at him, she'd still wanted him to claim her as his.

By the time he walked in his front door, he knew there was one place he could go to clear his head. Twenty minutes later, he had a bag packed and was starting up his clunker of a car.

It'd been a while since Alec had been home, even though he lived less than an hour from campus. When he first enrolled at Bowler, he'd thought about commuting from home, but his mom insisted he get the "full experience" of college life.

His house was a ranch in an older community of smaller homes. The down payment was provided by his father's life-insurance policy, the rest put in an account that paid what tuition wasn't covered by his scholarship. Alec walked up the steps to his front porch, the third stair creaking no matter how many times he fixed it.

He opened the door, taking his shoulder to it when it stuck because the wood always swelled in the winter. He'd meant to plane it last summer.

His mom was in the small galley kitchen, washing dishes. She glanced over her shoulder. "Alec? Why are you home?"

He sank into a chair and put his head in his hands, the sound of her voice like a sigh of relief. She knew him well enough to walk to the refrigerator, pour him a glass of chocolate milk, and plunk it down in front of him.

But this time, he glared at it, because all he could think about was Kat telling him it was cute. He stood up and poured it down the sink.

His mom stared at him, her fingers frozen in the middle of drying them on a kitchen towel.

He collapsed back into his chair.

"The chocolate milk not to your liking? Wrong brand maybe?" She raised an eyebrow at him.

"I don't want any."

"Can you please tell me why you're pouting and sulky?"

He haltingly began his Max and Kat Saga, eventually gaining speed until he was spilling his guts and cursing Max to hell and back.

His mom's face was lined with concern. "Oh honey, I'm so sorry about Max. I can't believe he'd do something like that. Well, I can believe it, since he admitted it. But I don't want to."

"Yeah, I really didn't want to believe it either."

His mom held up a cereal bar between two fingers and waggled it. He nodded and took it from her, unwrapped it and began to eat. "I don't understand why. I'll ask him one day, when I don't feel the urgent desire to strangle the life out of him. And to think I didn't go after Kat out of guilt." He scoffed at himself.

"What are you going to do about her?"

"I don't know. I want to blame her, I want to blame Max, hell I want to blame Carrie for all of this, but I screwed up a lot of decisions with Kat. I don't know. Maybe she doesn't want me?"

The wrinkles around his mom's mouth tightened. "Not every girl is like Carrie—"

"I'm not comparing her to Carrie, Mom."

She bit her lip. "Okay, but—"

"Can we talk about something else?" He cut her off again.

She sighed loudly and leaned a hip on the counter, crossing her arms over her chest. "Sure, if you stop interrupting me."

He looked down at their scarred butcher-block countertop and traced a long gash he made one time while trying to chop an onion. "I'm sorry," he muttered, feeling like a five-year-old for getting scolded.

His mom lashed out the kitchen towel she was holding and snapped him on the side of the head. "Ow!" he protested.

She grinned and went back to washing the dishes. He took the towel from her and began drying the dishes she placed in the rack.

His phone buzzed at his hip and he pulled it out, holding out hope it was Kat. But nope, it was Max. Alec purposefully declined the call, sending Max right to voice mail. He didn't leave a message.

When they finished drying the dishes, Alec turned to head to his room.

"Alec?"

He turned around to see his mom fidgeting with the kitchen towel, wringing it through her hands. "Yeah, Mom?"

"You really care about her?"

"She's . . . yeah, I really care about her." *I think I might be in love with her.*

His mom folded the kitchen towel and carefully placed it on the counter, smoothing it flat. "Your father was . . . a little wild when he was younger." Alec remained motionless as she talked, her eyes still on the towel. She rarely opened up much about his father. "I turned him down every time he asked me out. But he was persistent. So stubborn." She huffed out a laugh and raised her eyes to look at Alec. "He wore me down. He showed me how much he cared about me and how much I could trust him. After two years, I finally agreed to go out with him. He kissed me on our first date and I was his ever since. I look back now and I wish I could get those two years back."

"Mom—"

She shook her head, cutting him off. "If he were here today, he'd tell you not to give up. I know it. So, if you really want her, go after her. Show her the kind of man you are. The kind of man I know you are. Your father's son."

He opened his mouth and then closed it. His eyes burned behind his lids and his chest felt tight, like his heart was pumping too much blood.

But he had a plan. He could work with a plan. And

he wouldn't give up. He strode to his mom and gathered her in a hug, running his hands up and down her back. "I love you, Mom."

"I love you, too."

She sniffed loudly and he chuckled. When he pulled back, she took his face in both of her hands. Looking into her eyes, hearing her talk about her husband, his father, with love rather than grief was enough for him to know he needed to move on.

"I'm not going to write to the parole board," he said abruptly.

Her smile faded and her eyes darted over his face. "What?"

He shook his head to dislodge her hands. "It's time to move on, Mom. MacEnroe is almost seventy years old now. I don't forgive him, but I don't have room in my head and in my heart to hate him anymore. I don't have the energy for this all-consuming bitterness. I just . . . need to let it go. If he gets paroled, he gets paroled. If not, he can die in prison. I can't care anymore. And I finally realized it's not traitorous to Dad's legacy to feel like that. From what I remember of Dad, and what you've told me about him, he wouldn't want me to be this angry all the time. He'd want me to move on, fill myself with love and not all this anger." He took a deep breath. "So that's it. That's my decision."

Tears streamed down her face, incongruous with the openmouthed smile. "Oh Alec." Her thumbs swiped his cheekbones. "You really are a man."

"Mom . . ."

She blew out a laugh. "My father used to say that you didn't really grow up until after your parents passed. You were always an old soul, such a serious baby. And when your father died, you were such a little man, at five years old. You used to lie in bed with me and stroke my hair while I cried . . ." She hitched sobbing breath.

"Mom—" he murmured.

"You are a man, Alec. You are a wise, loving man and if your father could see you now . . . Oh!" She gasped another breath, her shoulders shaking now with renewed sobs.

"Please, don't cry." He hugged her, tucking her head under his chin. He didn't realize he was crying until tears splashed onto the top of her dark head.

He didn't know how long they held each other. Their tears slowly dried and his mom's body relaxed beneath his hands.

She finally pulled back and held his face in her hands again. "I'm so proud of you."

"Thanks, Mom."

"Go get your girl, huh?"

He smiled. "Yeah, Mom. I'll go get her."

He drove to campus and parked as close as he could to Kat's building. When he passed the library, his swift walking turned into a jog and by the time he reached the campus suites, he was sprinting, his messenger bag slapping painfully on his hip.

He tore up the stairs and banged his fist twice on Kat's door, bracing himself with his other hand on the door frame. He sucked in deep breaths of cool air, his back heaving. When no one answered, he banged again, this time not letting up until the door swung open in haste.

"Jeez, take it easy—" Shanna stopped talking when she caught sight of Alec.

"Is Kat here?" he said between breaths.

"Um . . . do you need a water or something? Or, I dunno, an inhaler?" Shanna eyed him like he was going to drop dead.

"No. Is Kat here?"

She turned her head back into the apartment. "Tara, is Kat here?"

"No!' came the shouted response.

"Where is she?" Alec demanded.

"Where is she?" Shanna yelled into the apartment to Tara, and Alec thought this was the stupidest communication system he'd ever been a part of.

"No, she went home," Tara said, coming out of the bedroom and walking toward Alec.

"She went home?"

Tara shrugged. "She was upset about her midterms. Said she was over it and needed to get away."

Over it? Like she was dropping out? Oh hell no.

"I need her address," he demanded.

Tara raised an eyebrow. "Really?"

Alec nodded. "Yes, I need to talk to her. I mean, I need to see her. Please. I swear I'm not crazy, we—"

"I know who you are, Zuk." Tara smirked, then waved her hand and turned away from him. She was back minutes later, an address scrawled on a piece of pink-flowered paper. "Happy driving."

Chapter Twenty-Two

WHEN HER PARENTS walked in the door after work, Kat was stirring the simmering *feijoada*, her favorite Brazilian dish, made of black beans, sausage and bacon. Her mom had prepared it that morning so it could stew all day, and the smell drove Kat crazy. She could barely wait to pour it over rice and dig in.

But once the meal was served and her father perused his newspaper while her mother tapped away on her iPhone, Kat had had enough of holding her tongue.

"So, I went to see Mrs. Ross today," she said pushing around the rice on her plate.

"Mrs. Ross? Your middle-school teacher?" her mom asked.

"Yep, one and the same."

"That's nice, *minha flor*," her father said, then turned to her mother and pointed out some mind-numbing news on the day's NASDAQ closing.

"She mentioned something interesting, about how she thought I had dyslexia," Kat said quickly.

Her mom's fork clattered onto her plate and both her parents stared at her.

"She said she mentioned it to you when I was in sixth grade. I don't remember anything about that."

Her mother glanced at her husband nervously, but he seemed suddenly enraptured with his burgundy napkin. "You were always a little behind when it came to reading and writing, but we thought it was because of moving from Brazil when you were young and growing up in a bilingual household . . ." Her voice trailed off and Kat's parents exchanged a look she couldn't decipher.

"But Mrs. Ross mentioned this to you in sixth grade." Kat said. "Why didn't you do anything about it?"

Her father took a deep breath. "We were concerned about you fitting in and we . . . didn't want you singled out any more than you already were. You know, with special classes or a teacher's aide or anything like that."

Kat gripped her fork so tightly, the metal cut into her palm. "I wish you would have told me—"

"But honey," her mom said. "You were eleven years old. We didn't think you were old enough to make any sort of decisions—"

"But this decision you made for me has affected me my whole life!" Kat struggled to keep her voice down. "You were worried about me not fitting in? It didn't matter, because I've *never* felt like I fit in. Everyone around me could read their textbooks and write their papers and take their tests and then there was me—struggling to get through a paragraph about . . . I don't know . . . the Revolutionary War that should have been read a month ago."

His father glanced at her mother's pale face before turning to Kat. Regret was etched into the furrow of his brows. "But, Katía, you have so many other talents. You're a beautiful girl, charming and funny with a huge heart. We didn't think studies was one of your talents. And that's okay."

Something in his tone, while loving, bordered on placating, and it shoved a steel rod in her spine. She straightened and jutted her chin out. "I'm sorry. But I'm . . . I'm not willing to accept that. I want it to be one of my talents."

Silence. The only sound was the refrigerator kicking on to fill the depleted ice-cube trays.

"But Elijah—"

"For God's sakes, Mom!" Kat exploded, slamming her hands down onto the table so hard her knife clattered to the floor. "I saw Mrs. Carter this afternoon. Elijah is interning this summer at a software developer. He's graduating a semester early. He's spending spring break in *Vegas*." She hissed the last word. "Yeah, that label and that stigma really killed his future, didn't it?"

Her mom's eye twitched, a tell that meant she was about to fracture.

"I took a test online," Kat said quietly. "I scored moderate dyslexia in all the areas."

For the first time in the conversation, her parents looked guilty.

"Is there something we can do now?" her mother asked.

Kat shook her head, ponytail whipping in her face. "No. Absolutely not. I'm doing this on my own. I have a meeting with the learning disability center on campus, and I'm going to find a way to get the help I need. And pass statistics."

"Well, if you need me to make a call—" her father started.

Kat shoved her chair back and stood up. "I think it's a little late for you to 'make a call,' Dad. You know, I know tons of kids who always complained about their parents' high expectations of them. Well, parents having low expectations sucks, too."

She carried her plate to the sink, her parents murmuring quietly to each other in hushed, chagrined tones. Kat stopped at the kitchen table on her way back. "By the way, I'm considering declaring my major as education. I think I'd like to teach, like Mrs. Ross."

Her father nodded, looking like he was going to say something else, but she walked away before he could.

Kat headed up to her room to do a little research on changing her major to education. But before her laptop booted up, her cell rang. She answered it without checking the caller. "Yeah?"

"Kat?" Alec's voice was unsure.

"Alec?" Kat's heartbeat sped up. She didn't know how much more emotion she could take in one day. "Um, hey."

"Hey . . . uh . . . so . . . do you know where"—he paused—"Lucky Strikes is?"

That was the last thing she expected him to ask. "The bowling alley? Yeah."

"Oh!" He blew out a breath into the phone. "That's what it is. Damn, that sign is—"

She waved her hand, even though he couldn't see her. "I know. I know. The pin and bowling balls look like a weenis and balls. It's an incredibly unfortunate sign. Although, the T-shirts are arguably worse."

Silence.

"Alec? Still there?"

"Did you just say *weenis*?"

"Um . . . yeah?"

"Kat, you are twenty years old and you use the word *weenis*. That is not okay."

"What? I don't like *penis* because it sounds, I don't know, medical. Like 'let me insert the catheter into your penis,' and *cock* sounds so . . . erotic novel-ish. Like 'he stroked her feminine petals with his mushroom-tipped cock.'"

More silence.

"Alec?"

"Is it wrong that I'm kind of turned on right now?"

"Oh for God's sakes. Why are you calling me asking me about Lucky Strikes?"

"Um . . . because I'm here. In the parking lot. Sitting in my car. Because I ran out of gas."

That still didn't make sense. "Why are you in Cross Keys?"

There was a pause. "For you, Kat. I drove here for you."

Those words sent a flurry of activity in her belly that rose quickly to her head, sending her reeling.

"I'll be there in twenty minutes," she whispered.

"I'll be here," he whispered back.

BY THE TIME she reached the bowling alley, the threatening clouds that had hung around all day finally opened up and unleashed torrents of rain. When she spotted Alec's car in the far corner of the parking lot, she wondered if they could reenact that scene in *The Notebook* where Rachel McAdams jumped on Ryan Gosling and they made out in the rain. It was pretty much the most romantic movie scene of all time. But when she pulled up alongside his car, his door opened, a jacket thrown over his head, and he quickly scooted into her passenger seat.

Okay, so no-go on the rain make-out scene.

"Hey," he said, tossing a duffel bag in the backseat.

"Hey."

He licked his lips, opened his mouth and then closed it, staring out of her windshield. She'd turned her wipers off, so the rain made everything outside a watery blur like they were in a watercolor painting. It was very isolating, the two of them in the car, the outside world unreachable.

"You drove here to sit in my car and stare at the rain?" she asked.

He snorted a laugh. "Shit, I had this whole thing planned in my head on the drive here but then my car ran out of gas and then that damn sign threw me and now I'm all screwed up."

His skin was pale, his eyes red and face pinched, like he was in pain. "Are you okay? Did something happen?"

He laughed bitterly, the sound grating to her ears. "Yeah, something happened. Max happened."

"I don't—"

"Fucking asshole."

"What—"

"I would have punched him in the face if I didn't think I'd break my hand on his steel-beamed jaw."

She threw up her hands. "Alec!"

"Max slept with Carrie."

Kat thought she could hear every single raindrop that hit the car, the sound reverberating around the car and into her head. Her deep breaths. Alec's stomach gurgling. "What? When?"

"Oh, you know, when she was still my girlfriend."

Kat felt the punch in her stomach, as she was sure Alec did. "Oh, no. How did you find out?"

Alec audibly ground his teeth. "I overheard them talking and confronted him. Turns out he was the guy she slept with last summer."

"That's . . . that's horrible. I'm so sorry."

"And he had the fucking balls to give me guilt about you." Alec clenched his fists on his lap.

Hope bubbled in her belly. "So, you found out and drove here?"

He turned to face her. "I went to your apartment and Tara said you came home. Kat, please don't drop out of school. I can help you and—"

"Wait, what?"

"—we can make sure you pass this class—"

"Alec, stop!"

He snapped his mouth shut.

She took a deep breath. "I'm not sure what Tara said, but I'm not dropping out. My statistics midterm was really hard, and I just needed a break from school."

He exhaled and leaned back in his seat, rubbing his forehead. "Oh, thank God."

Is that why he . . . "Is that why you drove here? To talk me out of dropping out of school?"

He lolled his head, grinning. "Well, yeah. You're my star student, you know?"

Right. He didn't come to her to declare his undying love. He came to make sure the girl he tutored didn't drop out of school. Of course.

He raised his hand and cupped her cheek, his thumb swiping her cheekbone, reminding her how little time she had his affection and how much she missed it. "I'm so sorry, Kat. For trying to be this stupid know-it-all who thought he could fix everything. For not owning up in front of Max. Just . . . fuck . . . for all of it. I missed you."

The warmth of his touch, the look in his eyes and his voice, his beautiful deep voice saying those words rasped along the raw edges of the hole in her heart. Marked by Alec Stone.

Relief and longing pushed back all the other emotions fighting for attention. Right now, with the world outside a watercolor in the downpour, all that mattered was his possessive touch on her cheek. His apology and his confession that he missed her. She'd worry later about the doubt that still lingered in the flanks of her mind—that horrible, self-sabotaging emotion. The killer of hope. "I missed you, too."

The corner of his lips twitched, like he read her mind—because she was brain-naked in front of him—and he leaned in, brushing his lips still wet and cold from the rain right over hers. He pulled back but she hadn't had enough yet. Plus, she needed to warm up those lips. It was only polite, right? So she chased his retreat and mashed her lips to his again and he smiled against her mouth, then opened up so she could reacquaint her tongue with his. He felt the same and tasted the same—smooth, sweet Alec.

When he pulled back the second time, she let him. "Wanna come home with me?"

He laughed. "What else am I gonna do? Go bowling?"

She smiled and started her car. But as she pulled out of the parking lot, that doubt crept in again. Fear clawed up her throat and her palms dampened on the steering wheel. Alec was about to enter her house. Her own turf. How in the heck was she going to protect herself?

KAT DROVE THE dozen or so miles home while Alec fiddled with all the controls in her car. It fit her, a convertible in a cheery red color, and smelled like something called freesia according to a little plastic circle attached to her dashboard.

Britney Spears blasted from the speakers but Kat didn't sing along. In fact this was a subdued Kat, a toned-down, muted version, which bothered him. He wanted to ask about her midterm and her other classes. He wanted to ask a whole lot of things, but her posture was closed off. And he knew, if she threw up the sex kitten mask, it'd break his heart.

When she pulled into her driveway, Alec stared out of his window at her house and wondered if they'd ended up at Hogwarts.

He slowly opened his car door and stepped out, staring up at her large, three-story home. He slung his a tattered duffel bag over his shoulder as she stepped to his side.

"What's up?" she asked.

"How come you never told me you're, like, Brazilian royalty?"

She rolled her eyes. "Brazil isn't a monarchy."

"No, really. What do your parents do?"

She squeezed his hand and bumped him with her hip.

"What?"

"Bonus points for not asking me what my *dad* does," she said, her smile genuine, and it sped up his heart that he'd put it there.

"Oh, well, you know me. Burning bras in my spare time."

Kat grabbed his hand so he had to follow as she trotted up the stairs. "Come on. I guess you get to meet the King and Queen of Brazil now." She shot a wink over her shoulder.

When Kat opened up the large oak door and Alec stepped onto some sort of fancy-looking tile floor, he was instantly aware of his worn jeans, scuffed Converse and thin T-shirt. At least he'd done his hair. Kat must have noticed him inspecting himself because she told him, "Quit it, you look fine. My parents are far from intimidating."

One look at Kat's father as he strode down the hallway proved her wrong.

He was about Alec's height, skin the color of Kat's and hair a blue black, dressed impeccably in navy slacks and a white polo shirt.

Mr. Caruso smiled, his straight teeth bleached white, his dark eyes missing nothing as they roamed Alec's face. Kat introduced Alec as her "friend from school," which stung. Her dad held out his hand, which Alec promptly shook in a firm handshake. "Rafael Caruso."

He then turned his head to his wife, whose heels clicked down the hall toward them. "Helena! Come meet Mr. Alec Stone."

A pretty woman, with hair the same as Kat's, wearing a tight gray dress walked up behind her husband, smiling warmly at Alec. He instantly liked her as she hugged him. She looked like a grown-up Kat, all blue eyes and delicate features.

They invited him into the kitchen, a massive room with high ceilings and gleaming appliances and black granite. Alec sweated, worried he didn't belong here.

Mr. Caruso motioned him to sit at the counter on a stool and asked about his major and what he wanted to do. There was tension in the air between Kat and her parents. Alec could feel it, but didn't know the source.

The only time Kat came to life was when her father asked Alec what his parents did.

Kat stiffened beside him like a little pit bull and turned icy eyes on her father. "Dad, quit it with the grilling, okay?"

Mr. Caruso paused mid-sip of his water, blinking at her, clearly surprised at his daughter's outburst.

Alec didn't want to brush Kat off, because she was trying to protect him. He placed a hand on her thigh and said sincerely, "Hey, it's okay. I don't mind."

She searched his eyes for a minute, then nodded.

He turned to Mr. Caruso. "My mom is a manager at a day care and my dad passed away when I was five. He was a police officer."

Kat's dad placed his glass gently on the counter. "I'm sorry to hear that."

After her parents excused themselves to do whatever important things they needed to do on a Friday night, Kat turned to him. "Are you hungry?"

His stomach rumbled at the thought of food. When did he eat last? Hell, did he eat at all today? It'd been the longest day of his life, it felt like.

She stuck her head in the refrigerator and rummaged around, speaking over her shoulder. "What do you want? I can heat up some leftover *feijoada*. Or I can make you a turkey and Havarti sandwich. I think we have some of that good stone-ground mustard . . ."

"Kat." He laughed. Havarti? What *was* that?

She ignored him. "Ooooh, it looks like there is some left-over—" she paused, taking a sniff of something in a container. Then she made a face and gagged. "Okay, that's a no-go on the left-over lasagna. Because it's not lasagna. It's beef stew and that white stuff is not cheese. It's mold. Okay, so—"

"Kat!"

"What?" She whipped around, hands on her hips.

He took a breath. "I don't care. I can eat a bowl of cereal."

"You are not eating a bowl of cereal for dinner. Mom would kill me. Do you like *feijoada*?"

She said the word so fast, with a slight accent. It turned him on and confused him at the same time. "Fay what?"

Kat paused, a blank look on her face before she laughed. "I'm sorry, I wasn't thinking. Oh, it's a Brazilian dish. Black beans, sausage, bacon—"

He held up a hand. "You had me at sausage. And bacon just added to my excitement."

She smiled with a faint blush and he wondered if it meant something to her that he wanted to try a dish from her family's country.

Kat plopped a large, foil-covered dish on the counter and began scooping contents onto a plate before popping it into the microwave. "Then that's what you're getting."

Feijoada—however it was said—was delicious. It tasted like it'd been cooking all day and Alec ate two helpings. Kat avoided him while he ate, wiping down already clean counters and rewashing the same dish three times, running water and drowning out his attempts at conversation with her. He didn't realize what changed between the parking lot of the bowling alley and driving to her house.

Did she not want him here? What kind of relationship did she have with her parents? The knowledge that he didn't know—that he didn't know all there was to know about Kat Caruso—bothered the hell out of him.

He was in so deep with this girl.

By the time he was finished eating and the kitchen was back to sparkling, it was nearing midnight. Kat led him upstairs, directly into a room that was so brightly painted, it was blinding.

Kat pointed to a walk-in closet. "You can throw your stuff in there."

Alec stopped in the doorway and glanced around. "Where am I going to sleep?"

"Um . . . the bed," she said slowly.

"What bed?"

She pointed to the pink monstrosity in the center of her room. "That bed."

He'd rather sleep on the floor. "Where are you going to sleep?"

She put her hands on her hips. "Where in the heck do you think I'm going to sleep? In that bed!"

He clutched his duffel to his chest like it was a parachute and he was thirty thousand feet in the air and stared at the bed like it was the open door of the airplane. "We're going to sleep in the same bed with your parents in the house? No way. Your dad probably has some sort of weird Brazilian way to torture and kill people."

"Alec, my parents do not care if you sleep in my bed with me. Trust me."

He narrowed his eyes, wondering if he could trust her.

She threw up her hands. "I'm twenty years old! They don't care!"

He dropped his parachute-duffel and mimicked her action. "Well, sorry! My mom wouldn't even let us be in the room with the door closed, let alone sleep together. She'd probably be serving us milk and peanut butter and jelly with the crusts cut off."

Kat chuckled. "Well, welcome to the house of heathens." She pointed to a door off to her right. "There's the bathroom."

With a furtive glance into the hallway for any roaming Brazilian bodyguards or something, he ducked into her room. They readied for bed in silence and after the emotion of the day, Kat looked half asleep by the time he crawled in beside her.

He rested his hand on her hip as she cuddled back into him. "I like to be the little spoon," she murmured.

"Kat, we have some things to talk about . . ."

"Tomorrow." She yawned. "Sleepy."

He took a deep breath, hoping she'd be back to the Kat he knew. Then he nuzzled his nose into her hair and breathed in her familiar citrus scent. "Okay. Tomorrow."

Chapter Twenty-Three

KAT WOKE UP to a weight against her back, hot breath coating the hair at her neck. Alec's fingers were still laced with hers, and she ran her fingers over his blunt, bitten-off nails.

He stirred behind her. "You awake?"

She rolled over to face him. "Nope."

Alec's hair was sticking up on one side, smashed down on the other. Without his glasses and face still slack with sleep, he looked like a teenager.

"I have morning breath," she informed him.

His grin was adorable. "I do, too. We cancel each other out, like if we both had onions for dinner."

"I don't think it works like that."

He ignored her and pressed his lips to hers for a chaste kiss. She fingered the corner of his mouth, loving the feel of the ridges on those full lips as he pulled away. He darted out his tongue like a lizard and licked her fingers.

She laughed and lowered her fingers to his collarbone, watching the skin shift under her touch. "So what happened with your car? I thought you never ran out of gas with that high-tech pencil-and-notepad system."

He chuckled. "I drove to my mom's before I came here and I guess I was distracted. Forgot to write everything down." He grabbed her hand and brought it up to his mouth, kissing her ring finger, and she wondered if he picked that finger on purpose. He drove here to talk her out of dropping out of school, right? He'd said it himself. Despite what he said to her in the car and the way he held her last night, she struggled to believe it was all real. And that it'd last. But then he laced his fingers with hers and rested them on his chest. Her heart warmed at the sight. Maybe this could be . . .

"I know most people would just cough up the money to get it fixed and wouldn't want to keep track of all the numbers like I do."

Something about his words or his tone scraped under her skin like a splinter. "You mean most people aren't smart enough to do it, right? Like me." Her voice threatened to crack. "That's what you're thinking."

Alec's eyes blinked, awareness replacing the sleep haze. "Wh–what are you talking about?" he stammered. "No, that's not what I meant."

It was like she'd flown too close to the sun. And as the heat melted the wax of her wings, she plummeted to the cool depths of the earth. Of course she couldn't keep track of those numbers. He knew it and she knew it. The reminder chilled her to the bone. She wanted to go back to last night when he kissed her with rain-coated lips. But her guard had been down then, drained from the day and so eager to see him. But now she'd had a full night's sleep and was well-rested enough to fend him off.

She yanked her hand, but he held it fast. "Shit, hold on. I didn't mean it like that."

His hand rose, and she braced. Because if he ran his thumb over her cheekbone, she was a goner. As much as she wanted to stay in bed, snuggling with him, hands linked, she needed to get out. She needed time to get her bearings. And her barriers.

Kat tugged her hand again and this time he let go. But it hurt, like she'd left a strip of skin behind in his.

She rolled off the bed gracelessly. "I need to pee."

"Kat—"

"Be right back!" she called over her shoulder, tripping over clothes on the way to the bathroom.

Once she closed the door, she leaned on the sink and took deep breaths. And then flashed back to another time she holed herself up in a bathroom with Alec right outside the door. Except this time, she knew what he looked like under those black boxer briefs. And she knew what it felt like to be the focus of those intelligent green eyes. What would it feel like to fall even deeper for him and see those eyes turn cold or exasperated or irritated? And worse—sick of her? Max had done it, every other guy had done it. Why not Alec?

She bit her lip as her eyes welled with tears, so she

turned on the shower to cover the sobs. Then she stripped out of her clothes and reached to pull back the shower curtain when a knock rattled the door.

"Kat! Come on, let me in. We need to talk."

She debated. Get in the shower? Lock the door? Or throw on a towel and face him?

"I'm coming in," he announced, making her choice for her. She turned off the shower and then whipped a lush pink towel off the rack and covered herself.

He could already see inside her brain, she didn't need to be naked in front of him, too.

The doorknob turned and Alec strode in, slamming it shut behind him. He hadn't put on pants or a shirt. *Jeez.*

"What's going on?" He squinted at her, having left his glasses back in the bedroom.

"I need to shower." She announced.

His eyebrows rose. "You need to shower. Right now."

No, what she needed to do was cry. And then eat a lot of ice cream and watch some sappy romance movie while she leaked tears onto her pillow. "Yep, right now."

"That was a stupid thing for me to say—"

"It's fine. Everything's fine." She hated how that answer was so remote.

Alec's eyes flashed and his jaw clenched. He shook his head. "Don't do that. Don't say you're fine when you aren't."

Kat swallowed, and stared at her pink-painted toenails. There was a chip on the big toe of her right foot. She needed to fix that.

"Kat . . ."

She didn't want to talk about it. She wanted to be alone to think in peace because she couldn't with his body and skin and hair and eyes taking up all the space in the bathroom.

So she changed the subject. "I have a lot on my mind."

Alec's anger faded rapidly, interest taking its place. "Oh?"

She took a deep breath. "I went to visit my sixth-grade teacher yesterday. Turns out she mentioned she thought I had a learning disability to my parents. Specifically dyslexia. They didn't do anything about it because they didn't want me 'labeled.' " She raised her eyes to his. "So, I could have been getting help this whole time. I didn't have to struggle so much."

Was that sympathy in his eyes? "Shit. I'm sorry."

She shrugged and looked away. "Yeah, me too. But, I made an appointment with the learning disability center on campus. I explained my situation and they're eager to see me."

Alec smiled and took a step closer. "That's great. I'm so proud of you. I'll help you out. I actually researched dyslexia and wrote a whole outline of techniques you can use. Did you know dyslexia can often be diagnosed along with attention-deficit disorder? We might want to look into that . . ."

He rambled on, his eyes barely even focused on hers, lost in some nerd-world where he had a pet project, some cute girl he could rescue from the depths of the class rank and push to the top. He didn't even realize she was in the room, drowning in the blood from the reopened wound in her heart.

What was happening? Was this all she was to him, a problem to be solved? Alec had a huge future ahead of him. He'd surely graduate from Bowler summa cum laude. Then he'd go on to attend an elite law school where he'd meet some lovely female brainiac with shampoo-commercial hair who understood nerd puns and dreamed of bestowing her children with names like Aurora and Ender. Kat would just be some story he could tell his socialite wife and his judge friends when he was forty and drinking hundred-year-old Scotch in a ritzy country club. *I dated this dyslexic girl in college and helped her pass her classes. She's a teacher somewhere in Jersey now . . .*

All her fears had been realized. Once he found out what she was really like, he hadn't pushed her away like all the other guys, but it was still all he saw—the defective Kat. Did he see the witty Kat anymore? The fun Kat? The Kat he slept with?

Nope, all he saw was how to fix her. She vowed to herself—no more guys who couldn't see past her gray matter to who she really was.

He finally stopped his monologue. "What do you think?" he said, taking a step toward her. He was too close and those eyes too knowing. This was too much and too real and she didn't want it. Kat clutched the towel at her chest, knowing this was going to hurt her as much as it hurt him, but she was on the defensive now. And she blocked him the only way she knew how.

She curled her lips into her most sultry smile and cocked a hip. "So, like I said, I need to shower, so you might want to leave . . ." She dipped the towel a little so the tops of her breasts peeked out, then waggled her eyebrows. "Unless you want to watch."

And that was it.

Her block thrown. Her walls up. And Alec knew it.

His face crumbled, his eyes closing slowly, painfully, and his whole body slumped, like someone had liquefied his bones.

If she could hear over the thunderous shattering of her own heart, she was sure she'd hear Alec's break, too.

Through it all, she kept that fake smile in place. Because although she stood in front of him in only a towel, that smile was the only thing preventing the nakedness of her heart. But behind that smile, and behind that towel, she was bleeding from the inside.

Alec shook his head, running shaking hands through his hair. "You're shutting down." His jaw clenched, the green in his eyes flashing like cold peridot. "I can see it. Don't pull this bullshit on me."

This had to end soon because she didn't know how long she could keep this up. But she couldn't give up now. It was almost over. She let the towel slip a little. "So, you want to watch then."

Disappointment. That's what showed like a harsh headlight in his green gaze. "Jesus Christ, Kat."

His words bounced off her smile. "Okay, then, your choice." She forced herself to keep her voice light and breathy, like Marilyn Monroe. But to hide the tears gathering in her eyes, she turned around before dropping the towel. Seconds later, the bathroom door slammed and she didn't have to turn around to know she was alone.

She turned on the shower and stepped inside to let the pelting water muffle her sobs.

ALEC SAT ON the edge of her bed, dressed in jeans and a T-shirt, listening as Kat turned off the shower and rattled around in the bathroom.

How could she take his words so wrong? How could she think he'd call her dumb? He hadn't meant it that way. She had to know that. But then in the bathroom . . . fuck, what was that? She'd turned on the sex kitten he knew she relied on when she felt cornered.

He wished she'd just show her claws instead. Then they could scratch and hiss at each other until they were weak and then make up.

But instead she shut him out.

The door opened and Kat stepped out in just a towel. Fresh-faced, she was the most beautiful thing he'd ever seen. But she wasn't his. She'd made it clear he didn't have permission to get inside her head.

Her face twitched with nervousness when she saw him before she straightened her shoulders and twisted her lips into that sultry smile.

She walked over to her dresser and rummaged around, pulling out a pair of jeans and Bowler University sweatshirt. With her back to Alec, she tugged her pants on under her towel, then dropped the cover to pull on a bra and sweatshirt.

He tried not to watch but everything she did captivated him. Even when he was furious at her.

She ran a comb through her hair and turned around. "You need me to run you to a gas station to get gas for your car? I have things to do, as I'm sure you do."

Why was she pushing him away? "What kinds of things do you have to do?"

She straightened her spine and ticked off her tasks on her fingers. "I need to confirm my appointment with the learning disability center. I need to meet with my advisor. I need to talk with my statistics professor and figure out how I'm going to pass the class so I can stay in school and graduate."

Her voice rose a little at the end, like her stress level had reached its limit.

He stood and took a step toward her. He needed to fix this. "I can help you with that. In fact, helping you pass statistics is my job, so—"

Kat shook her head, wet strands of hair flinging droplets around them. "Look, you did your job, okay? You made sure I was staying in school. You helped me figure out why I was doing poorly. I'll take it from here. You don't have to deal with me anymore."

He did his job? His *job*? His whole body flushed cold as realization dawned. Here he'd been some lovesick puppy over her—he'd admitted to Max he'd fallen in love with her—and she saw him as her tutor and some guy to have fun with at a party.

He'd just been a stepping-stone in her life. A guy who helped her plump up her self-esteem. But he'd served his purpose, he guessed. This was Act Three, and he was no longer needed.

Exit stage left.

He wondered who would get to hold her hand and bow with her in the finale.

What had he been thinking? Kat wasn't his type. Cheating high-school sweethearts were.

Fuck this.

Suddenly the room was too small, the pink walls too bright. The anger boiled up his throat and out his mouth. "You know what? I'm done trying to figure out how your mind works. I don't even think you know. So fuck it." He grabbed his duffel bag and rooted around blindly for his things, shoving them inside. "Let's go. You're right. I got a lot of shit to do and we're wasting daylight fucking around here."

When he glanced up, Kat's head was turned and she stared out her bedroom window, eyes wide and teeth gritted. He had no idea what she was thinking. And he was done trying to guess.

She didn't want to let him in so he didn't want in.

This had been a huge, giant mistake. Him driving here in some sort of grand gesture. God, how embarrassing.

When she finally turned to him, that fake smile was in place. He wanted to scream.

They rode in silence to the gas station and then back to his car. As he filled his tank from the container, Kat stood leaning against her car, toeing the ground.

When he was finished, he started up his car, listening for the familiar old engine rattle.

He turned to face her. She watched him with a searing gaze, and he tried to read her thoughts on his face before he stopped himself. It wasn't his business to try to get inside her head anymore. She'd made this call. She'd asked for this.

When he drove away, he didn't look in the rearview mirror; he refused to witness how fast Kat got in her car to get away from him.

Chapter Twenty-Four

KAT WOKE UP the next morning with the feeling of eyes on her. She rolled onto her side and turned her eyes to the doorway. Marcelo leaned against the doorjamb, arms folded over his chest, one ankle crossed over the other.

He was every inch his father's son, from his black hair and broad shoulders to his golden skin. But like Kat, he had their mother's eyes, big, blue and wide-set. Marc was dressed casually in a pair of track pants and an old college T-shirt.

Kat rubbed her eyes. "What are you doing?" She rarely had the intellectual capacity to spar with Marc. This was a pre-coffee ambush. It wasn't fair.

Plus she had puffy eyes and an upset stomach from her ice-cream-eating, sad-movie marathon last night.

"Hey, munchkin." He uncrossed his arms and walked into the room to sit next to her in bed. He scooted backward until he could lean against her pillows. She propped her head up on her hand.

"You didn't answer my question," she said.

He flicked her on the forehead, a gesture originally designed to antagonize her when they were kids but had morphed over time to a sign of affection. "Mom and Dad called me."

She groaned and flopped her hand over her face dramatically. Her parents had called up their best weapon. She could never say no to her big brother.

"They really do have a lot of regrets, you know," he said. "And if I would have known, well, things would have been different."

"I know," she muttered from under her arm.

"Look at me."

She moved her arm and opened her eyes to look into her brother's face. Those eyes so like her own studied her closely. "Who was the greaser and why isn't he here anymore?"

"Greaser?"

Marc waved his hand above his head. "Dad said he had some old-school hairstyle or something. Said he looked like a Shark out of *West Side Story*."

Kat sighed. "I like his hair."

Marc wiggled his eyebrows. "Yeah? What else you like?"

Kat smacked his thigh. "Gross, I'm not having this conversation with my brother in my bed. When I'm not wearing pants."

Marc recoiled. "Ew!"

"I have underwear on."

He rolled his eyes. "Come on, what's the deal with the guy?"

Kat rolled onto her side to face her brother. "His name is Alec," she said quietly. "And he's . . ." It wasn't possible to describe Alec in simple terms. He'd hurt her. Treating her like a project and then throwing that last lovely parting shot. But she'd done the same thing, hadn't she? Intentionally done and said things she knew would hurt him? But then she remembered how it'd felt to be in his arms, to be the one to make him laugh.

Then tense lines on Marc's face softened. "Oh, munchkin."

She found her voice "What?"

Marc's lips turned in a wry smile. "Your silence said it all. So, if he's *the guy*, why isn't he here?"

"He's not *the guy*," Kat mumbled, picking a stray hair off her pillowcase. It was dark. And it wasn't Marc's. Her heart squeezed painfully.

"Kat—"

She sighed and rolled onto her back to stare at the ceiling. "He made me feel like when he looked at me, all he saw was what I'm not."

Marc slid down to lie beside her, his head propped on a fist. "I don't know what you mean."

"It's not like it's the first time a guy has done it. And before I never really cared. But when Alec looked at me and talked *at* me like I was just some project, I couldn't take it." Her voice cracked. "Not with him."

She rolled her head to the side and Marc's eyes were

filled with sympathy. He reached over and smoothed her hair off of her forehead. "I'm not taking his side at all, but just hear me out. When you look at yourself, really look, is that all you see? What you're not?"

Kat opened her mouth and then shut it again. What did she see? Her life had been so consumed with her failure at school, it seemed like forever since she'd thought of anything else. Had her self-esteem really sunk that low? God, she was too tired and uncaffeinated to figure this out.

Marc sighed and flicked her on the forehead. She scowled and rubbed the spot while he chuckled. "Munchkin, I mean this in the nicest way, but you can be dense."

"Thanks a lot, Marc, seeing as I'm trying to deal—"

"Shut up." He clapped his hand over her mouth. She tried to bite his fingers but his grip was firm on her jaw. "I'm talking about your heart, you dumbass. I'm going to take my hand away. Now listen and don't start spewing stupid shit."

She growled but nodded.

He took his hand from her face and kept talking. "Remember that park Mom and Dad used to take us to? The one over by the elementary school?"

"Pleasant Valley?"

"Yeah. That's the one. There was always that little boy there, with the coke-bottle glasses. He was tiny for his age."

Kat smiled, remembering her little buddy. "Sam. He could make the best sand castles in the sandbox."

Marc huffed a laugh. "Yeah, see, that's what you remember. He was quiet and had weird clothes and all the other kids picked on him. One time, this bigger kid shoved him down the slide and I'll never forget it until the day I die, the sight of you, all four feet tall, stomping over to this kid who was a foot taller than you. You shook your finger in his face and called him a bully and told him to apologize to Sam. And he did. You looked like a little teacher."

Kat shook her head. "I don't remember that."

"Of course you don't. Because that wasn't abnormal for you. Kat, your heart is huge. I don't know this Alec guy, but Dad said he seemed really into you. Did you ever think there's more to you than what a guy sees and what your IQ is?"

Kat's mind raced back to the time she cried when he told her about his dad. "Oh," she said, her eyes drifting over Marc's shoulder. Both times she'd talked to Alec about his dad, when she'd shown him her "heart," he'd told her how amazing she was. She shook her head. "But still, as soon as he found out about the possible dyslexia, it's all he saw. If you heard him talk, you'd understand. He wanted to *fix* me."

"I believe you feel that way. I really do. But I don't believe that's all he sees. I'm sure he cares about you and he's a guy. Guys like to fix."

She fidgeted because she hated that word. "I don't want to feel like I need fixed. And I can't *be* fixed. I most likely have a learning disability. It's not something that goes away." Alec had to understand that. No matter what he did, there was no fixing her.

Marc shook his head. "You don't *need* fixed. But this guy is, what, twenty-one years old? Cut him some slack."

"You're taking his side," Kat grumbled.

"I'm not taking his side, just offering an explanation for the actions of a member of my kind." He flicked her forehead again. "And the best way to get back at him for making you feel this way is to kick life's ass."

Kat laughed. "What does that mean?"

"Get back to campus and sort your shit out. Take some time to remember all the reasons you're a kick-ass girl."

That had been her plan and Marc's words ignited the fire in her belly. "You give the best pep talks ever."

"Eh, only to my little sister. And I heard you might declare yourself as an education major? That's perfect for you. I don't know why none of us ever suggested it."

"Thanks, Marc."

"If you need another ass-kicking pep talk, you'll call me?" Marc said.

Kat nodded. "You bet."

"And I'll get to meet Greaser Boy?"

"Alec!" she yelled with a laugh. "Alec Stone. And I don't know. I think we both need this time to step back and decide what we want."

He grinned. "All right. And Alec Stone, huh? Solid name."

The best, she thought with a grin as she hugged her big brother.

KAT DRAGGED HER heavy suitcase downstairs later that day, then headed to the kitchen to say good-bye to her parents. Her dad was sitting at the kitchen table, drinking coffee and reading the newspaper.

"I'm heading back to school," she said. "Where's Mom?"

"She's running some errands," her father said.

"Okay, well, let her know I left. And, thank you for calling Marc."

Her father put down the paper and clasped his hands together on top of the table. "Your mother and I are sorry."

"I know that."

"We were very shortsighted."

"I know that, too." Kat cocked her head. "Marc told you off, didn't he?"

Her father's jaw tensed, but he didn't answer. It was okay. She knew the truth.

"Well, I'll call and let you know how the appointment goes and all of that . . ." Kat said, heading out of the kitchen.

"*Minha flor*?" Her father said softly.

"Yeah?" she glanced over her shoulder.

"Tell your young man we said hello."

Her young man. She gave her dad a noncommittal nod and lugged her suitcase out the front door.

Chapter Twenty-Five

ALEC STARED AT his computer screen, blank document open, cursor blinking. He should be working on a paper for his mock trial class about the case he and Danica presented, but all he could think about was the girl he left back in Cross Keys.

How had he twisted all their moments in his head, imagining she was the love of his life? Because if their conversation before he left her home wasn't a kiss-off, he didn't know what was.

But he couldn't stop thinking about her voice and her laugh. What it felt like to hold her in his arms and breathe in the familiar citrus scent that was all Kat.

Fuck, this hurt worse than the breakup with Carrie. Everything with Kat had been bigger, more real, from their conversations about his dad to her confessions about herself.

He *saw* her. She'd told him herself. When did that change? Or was it ever true?

It was the Monday of spring break and it was killing him that he didn't even know if she was back in town yet. He hoped she drove safely. Wore her seat belt. Didn't text and drive. Kept her hands at ten and two and didn't take her eyes off of the road.

He thunked his head onto his desk. He was going crazy.

The front door opened and closed downstairs. He waited for the footsteps, by now able to determine from the sound whether the arrival was Max or Cam.

As the heavy footfalls ascended, his heart sank. Max.

The footsteps stopped outside his room. Just when he thought Max would move on to his own room, there was a light, hesitant knock at the door. Alec closed his eyes, reminding himself to keep his temper in check and cleared his throat. "Come in."

There was a rustling, then a slow turning of the doorknob, until the door swung open slowly. Alec swung in his chair to face his best friend—*former best friend?*—in the doorway.

They locked eyes and Alec held it, refusing to be the one who looked away first. Max lost the battle of staring chicken, slowly lowering his gaze to the floor. His shoulders rose and fell with a deep breath before he took a couple of steps farther into the room.

Max bit his lip and glanced around the room. He smiled sadly and picked up one of Alec's photos he had stuck on a corkboard. It was a picture of them from middle school, with their arms around each other's shoulders. Alec was smiling but drenched in sweat from completing his first 5K. Max was shirtless, a big A painted on his chest. Alec remembered Max was so proud to cheer him on, and Alec didn't have the heart to tell him that he should probably read *The Scarlet Letter* before he walked around with a big red A on his chest.

Max pointed to the picture and smiled. "Remember that?"

Immediately, Alec bristled. Because sure he remembered it, but Max couldn't bring up all the good times and instantly be forgiven.

"I'm not interested in taking a trip down memory lane with you," he said.

Max's smile immediately dropped off, and his shoulders slumped. He walked to Alec's bed with heavy steps and sank down on the edge. He widened his feet and stared at the stained hardwood floor. "I'm sorry."

"Yeah? Well you should be."

Max bit his lip so hard, Alec was sure he'd tear a hole in it. "Quit biting your lip like that."

Max jerked his head up. "What?"

"You're biting your lip . . . just quit it, okay? It's annoying."

His eyes darkened. "Well, I'm sorry to annoy you," he said bitterly.

"Don't play a victim, all I said—"

"Of course, because the martyr card is all used up by Alec Stone—"

"What the fuck? Where did that come from—"

"Because it's always about you!" Max roared, effectively quelling their shouting match.

Alec sat stunned in his chair, finally seeing his best friend in a light he never had before, and it wasn't flattering. "What are you talking about?"

Max's fingers curled into the mattress, his lips in a sneer, his voice dipping into a low tone that sent a chill down Alec's spine. "Why can't you be like Alec? Why don't you get his grades? Why can't you find a nice girl like Alec instead of those bimbos you usually date?"

There was only one person who would say all those things. Jack Payton.

"I don't . . . are you jealous of me?" The idea was ludicrous. Max, despite recent behavior, had always been well liked, the most popular in school. Alec was always happy to blend into the background behind him.

Max snorted and looked away. "You know, I actually think it would be easier if I was jealous of you. Because then I could hate you." He sighed and faced Alec again. "Every time something good happened for you, I was happy to be along for the ride. Glad that you included me in your life. But my dad . . . well, he would have been happy with only my two brothers as kids. Or, if I have to exist, at least more like you."

"I don't understand, Max, you—"

He waved his hand. "Stop, okay? We all know you're a better guy than I am." He grimaced, the lines in his face etched with self-loathing. "I fucked your girlfriend, Zuk. Pretty sure that makes me a complete asshole."

Alec winced at the curse. "You don't have to drive the point home."

Max shook his head. "But that's the point. That's what I did. That's who I am. You have every right to hate me—"

"I don't hate you." Alec cut him off. Because no matter what, Alec couldn't throw away fifteen years of friendship. "Am I pissed at you? Fuck yeah. Do I forgive you? Fuck no." He leaned forward and braced his elbows on his knees, running his hands through his hair. "If Carrie could cheat on me, then we weren't going to stay together anyway. I just . . . I still can't believe you, of all people, would do something like that to me. I don't want details, but what happened?"

Max leaned forward as well, mimicking Alec's posture with his elbows on his knees. Their heads were about a foot apart, so Max spoke barely above a whisper. "It was a bad day at the shop with Dad. He was bitchin' about school and loans and 'why couldn't you get a scholarship like Alec' and complaining about fucking everything. I went to that party, started drinking. I got drunk and instead of being pissed at my dad, I was pissed at you. So when Carrie walked in, I just . . . I wanted one thing, *one thing*, that was yours for myself." Max huffed a bitter laugh. "I never told you, but she flirted with me when you weren't around. So, I knew I could get in there. So I did. And then the next day, I woke up, and I hated myself."

"Is that why you were so . . . off . . . since last summer?"

Max rubbed his palms together and nodded. "Guilt's a bitch."

Alec couldn't help it, he blew out an ironic laugh. "You think?"

Max jerked his head up, a frown creasing his forehead, then his face cleared. "Oh, right, you mentioned that back when . . . yeah. So. Kat."

Hearing her name from the lips of her ex-boyfriend and his best friend was like a dagger to the chest. But he talked through the pain.

"Back in January, I started tutoring Kat. It was a coincidence we got paired together, and she asked me not to tell you. Well . . . things just . . . damn. I fell for her. Hard."

Max leaned back on his hands. "I knew it."

"You did?"

"I saw the way you looked at her. When I asked you to watch her for me at the party, it was almost like some fucked up part of me wanted you to mess around with her. Then maybe we'd be even."

"That wouldn't make us even, Max. It'd make us fucked up *and* dysfunctional."

Max kicked the side of Alec's desk. "Yeah, I know. I saw the looks you two gave each other sometimes, and I think a sadistic part of me liked having something you wanted."

"That's . . . brutally honest."

Max shrugged. "Yeah, well, you finally deserve honesty, don't you think? You deserve to know what an asshole I am."

Alec frowned. "But that's the thing. That isn't you, Max. I know it's not."

Max leaned back on his hands and tilted his face up

to the ceiling. "Glad you think so, but I don't really know what I am."

"You'll figure it out," he said softly. Max shrugged.

Alec scratched the back of his neck. "Speaking of that party . . . she spent the night here. With me. And then when I saw your face, I denied it. I chose you over her."

"Oh shit." Max's mouth dropped open.

Alec squirmed in his chair. "Yeah well, I went to visit her during spring break and . . . yeah. It's not going to work out I guess." He held off on explaining Kat's disability. That was her story to tell.

Max cocked his head. "Not going to work out?"

Alec shrugged. "I think I was more into her than she was into me."

Max shook his head vehemently. "No."

"What?"

"No, absolutely not. Fuck, Zuk, the way she looks at you? She never looked at me like that. I'd bet my truck that girl is in love with you."

"You hate that rust bucket."

"Right, but it's still a working rust bucket and I don't have money to buy a newer rust bucket, so it's still good collateral."

"So, if I bet my rust bucket, are we just going to trade them? That seems really stupid because no one wins."

Max rolled his eyes. "Whatever. Look, Kat's great, but we weren't right for each other. But you two? You belong together and I'll kick your ass if you don't fight for her."

"What's the point in fighting for her if she doesn't want me?"

Max stared at him. "Are you seriously this dense? She does want you, asshole. She might have something else going on that's making her act like she doesn't, but she does. Mark my words."

Alec smiled. "If you were this passionate with a girl, you might actually keep a decent one around for a while."

Max laughed and shoved Alec. "Shut up." He looked down at his hands and then tilted to face Alec. "I bet you'd treat her like a queen."

"Who?"

"Kat."

"Oh, yeah. Close. A princess."

Max cocked his head in confusion.

Alec chuckled. "Never mind."

They fell silent, each studying the floor at their feet. Alec peeked at Max from under his lashes. His friend looked troubled, but less tense. "Look, Max. I need some time. If you still want us to be friends—"

"Fuck yes!" Max's eyes were wide, a naked plea.

"Then, just give me reasons to trust you again, okay? And you need to find some way to sort your shit out. You're not going to be me. You don't want to be me. You gotta be you and you need to figure it out. Yourself."

Max nodded, picking at the ever-present calluses on his hands from a lifetime of lifting weights. "Yeah. Yeah, you're right."

When Max left, Alec slumped in his chair. Their friendship used to consist of deciding which ice-cream shop to haunt on a hot summer night, or which house to study at after school Now it was all talk of finding jobs in the same town and adult conversations. Part of him wanted to go back to high school, when life was easier. But this was life now, and they had no choice but to grow up.

He turned back to his computer and typed *The*. That was as far as he got until he started thinking about Kat again.

He thought back to every interaction with her.

When she'd opened up to him in the library and flashed him that beautiful, real smile. When she'd told him at his house that he saw the real her. When the rest of the world disappeared when he held her in his arms and danced.

When she'd taken him in his bedroom and let him inside her.

Alec wasn't a genius when it came to females but he wasn't completely ignorant. And he knew Kat felt something. If he reached deep in his broken heart, he felt that she fell for him just as hard as he'd fallen for her.

So what had happened to make her throw up her walls? He'd apologized for the teasing so it couldn't have been that.

But he'd fucked up somehow. And that last insult he hurled at her sure hadn't helped either. He cringed, thinking about it.

His mother's voice rattled in his head. *If you really want her, go after her. Show her the kind of man you are.*

He had to do something to show Kat he cared about her.

He picked up his cell phone and opened a blank text

message. Then he tapped his fingers on his desk. "Make it count, Alec. Make it count," he muttered to himself.

Then he began to type.

I want to ride covered Segways with you and make fun of your hair whispies.

Then he typed in Kat's name and hit SEND.

He imagined her face when her phone read the message out loud to her. And he wished he could be there to see her mouth open in that loud, unabashed laugh she had. The laugh he loved.

Chapter Twenty-Six

I WANT TO eat candy and watch football with you while we make jokes about tight ends.

The voice reading the text on her phone sounded nothing like Alec's, but Kat could picture his eyes sparkling, his full lips sounding out the words.

It was Friday of spring break and this was the fifth text message she'd received. They'd started Monday. Yesterday's was, *Despite what you think, I bet you look hot in yellow.*

She had no yellow shirts, but she dug a yellow bra out of the bottom of her drawer and wore it. Just for Alec.

She loved the texts. They warmed her heart and made her laugh. But she still hadn't heard the words she wanted to hear from him. *I'm sorry. You don't need fixed. I see you.*

Until then, she had to stay focused on forgiving herself. On seeing herself.

On loving herself.

"Ready to go?" Tara asked as she pulled a T-shirt down over her head.

In a moment of lunacy, Kat had agreed to try running. After she told Tara everything—about her possible dyslexia and fight with Alec, she'd been near collapse with stress. Tara had shoved a pair of leggings and T-shirt at her and told her to grab her earbuds and mp3 player.

"Running has a way of clearing out the clouds so nothing's hiding in shadow," she'd said.

Kat mumbled something about sunscreen but she'd changed and now she stood uncertainly in the middle of their room, shifting from foot to foot on rarely used sneakers. The last time she'd worked out regularly was in ninth grade. She had a gym membership and quit after she contracted ringworm from the locker room.

And Tara had finished her marathon the previous weekend with a great time. Kat figured the least she could do is get off her sorry butt and run with her friend.

Tara glanced over at her as she tied her shoes. "We'll go easy okay? A slow jog."

They started out on a path that looped around campus. Tara said she didn't like to talk while running, so Kat shut her mouth and turned on her playlist she'd made special, really quickly just for the run.

Britney's breathy voice rolled into her ears and Kat eased into the rhythm of the run. Beside her, Tara shot her a thumbs-up and Kat returned it.

March was a toss-up in Maryland. Some years, the month dumped a last blizzard on them. Other years, tulips began to poke through the ground in response to warm temperatures.

This was a tulip year.

As her feet pounded the pavement, Kat's mind did clear. Maybe it was the music in her ears or maybe it was because the physical act focused her, disallowing distractions. Because all of the tasks she hoped to accomplish next week didn't seem so daunting anymore. Her appointment with the learning center on campus was first thing Monday. And she'd made an appointment with her advisor on Wednesday to talk about declaring her major.

The thought of being on the "other side," standing in front of a group of students, as the teacher and not the "teachee" was terrifying and exhilarating at the same time.

And then there was Alec . . .

She shook her head and blew out a harsh breath, following Tara around a bend in the path. Tara smiled over her shoulder and Kat smiled back. This running thing wasn't so bad. If she ignored the stitch in her side.

When they got back to their apartment, Kat braced herself with her hands on her knees as Tara opened the door. "So, how was it?"

Kat followed her roommate in and shut the door behind her. "You were right. Running has a way of bringing out the sun, doesn't it?"

Tara grinned. "Told you."

After their showers, Tara waved Kat over to her bed. "Sit down. I want to show you something."

Kat flopped on the bed, comfortable in pajama pants

and an oversized T-shirt Alec had left at her house. God, she was pathetic.

"Why do you run?" Kat asked.

Tara pulled her laptop on her lap and opened it up, a chime sounding from the speakers as it woke up. She twisted her lips. "Well, I like feeling physically fit. And it was something I could do that didn't cost any money. I mean, just a pair of sneakers and I could take off. You know I live with a bajillion people. When I'm running, I can hear myself think. I've worked out so many of my problems while running."

Kat picked at the frayed hem of the T-shirt. "That makes sense."

"Thanks for that, by the way," Tara gestured to her ceiling above her bed. Kat had cut out "26.2" in poster-board and sequined the crap out of it with a glue gun. It was tacky and gaudy, but Tara laughed so hard when she saw it.

Kat shrugged. "It was fun."

Tara pulled up Skype and a dial tone rang out in the room. "So, I'm calling Amy. She wants to show you something."

Kat leaned forward and looked at the screen. "Oh really?"

The call connected and Amy's vibrant, six-year-old smile filled the screen. She waved, her movement blurry and too fast for the program. "Hi Kat!"

Kat waved back. "Hey sweetie!"

Amy's hair was pulled back into a bun held in place by a pink ribbon. Her lips looked redder, like she wore lipstick, and then she stepped back from the screen so Kat could see her whole body. She twirled and her pink skirt swirled around her hips and thighs. Kat had worn that same skirt long ago.

"Hot stuff! Looking good," Kat beamed.

"Go ahead, Amy." Tara turned to Kat and whispered, "She wanted to thank you herself, for the lessons."

"But I didn't—"

Tara elbowed her and she shut up.

Amy stopped her twirling. "This is what I learned so far." She pulled over a chair and held onto the back of it, like it was a barre. The she brought her heels together, little brows furrowed as she bent her head and watched her feet. Then she looked up, beaming. "First position!"

"Excellent!" Kat squealed. "Now make sure you keep your knees straight."

Amy immediately complied. "Better?"

Kat gave her a thumbs-up.

Then Amy spread her legs, toes pointed out. "Second position!"

"Oh, that's wonderful form, Ames."

The little girl smiled as she completed third, fourth and fifth position. Then she ended with a plié, her arm movement fluid and very well done for a six-year-old. When she finished, she blushed while Kat and Tara whooped and clapped.

"If I was there, I'd be throwing flowers onto your stage, Ballerina Amy," Kat said.

Amy took another hesitant plié and then sat down in front of the computer. "Thank you, Kat."

It was amazing how watching Amy show her the things she learned was all the thank you Kat needed.

The knowledge that something she'd done, no matter how small, had a made a positive impact on this little girl's life filled her heart. And she knew she wanted that feeling again and again.

"You're welcome, sweetie," Kat said, her voice thick.

After they said their good-byes and Tara shut down her computer she looked at Kat. "Are you finally starting to see yourself the way we all see you?"

Kat nodded. "I think I am."

Chapter Twenty-Seven

THE NEXT DAY, Kat stood outside of Danica's door, wringing her hands.

Even though she'd initially been angry that Danica and Alec had talked about her behind her back, she now had the perspective that the whole situation had opened her eyes. She owed Danica a thank-you. And maybe part of her wanted to fish to see if Danica knew anything about Alec. The day's text had said, *I want to lay in bed with you and eat non-soggy PB & J sandwiches.*

She knocked and after some muffled muttering, Danica flung the door open. She was surprisingly casual, in a pair of black sweatpants and pink camisole. No wig. Surprise flashed over her face, then she smiled. "I knew you'd come around. Just thought it would take you longer than a couple of days."

Kat's eyes drifted over Danica's shoulder.

"Don't worry, Stone isn't here."

"I wasn't—"

"Yeah, you were." Danica left the door open and turned to walk back into her apartment. "Come in."

Kat took a deep breath and followed Danica, shutting the door behind her. In the kitchen, Danica was scooping cookies onto a cookie sheet. Every five or so, she plopped a hunk of dough in her mouth. Kat wondered if her cookies were as good as Max's.

Danica dropped her cookie scoop in the batter bowl and slid the cookie sheet in the oven. She set the time and turned to Kat, drumming hot pink nails on the counter. "So, I want to apologize. Alec told me about the e-mail, and I'm really sorry. I don't even remember how it happened, but Alec and I were talking about tutoring you, and then he mentioned some things, and since my dad has dyslexia, I mentioned it to him."

Kat sat down at the stool at the counter and swiped her finger along some batter at the top of the bowl, then stuck her finger in her mouth. "Don't worry about it. I'm not angry with you. In fact, I wanted to say thank you."

"Oh?"

"Well, long story short, I have an appointment with the learning disability center on campus Monday to get tested."

The nails continued their drumming and Kat shifted. Maybe Alec had already visited Danica, to tell her all about the situation.

"Did Alec already tell you all of this?"

Danica shook her head. "Honestly, no. He said he

went to visit you and that you had a disagreement. No other details were given despite my threats."

"Really?"

"I solemnly swear. You going to tell me what happened?"

"Do you promise not to talk to him about this? Because I don't . . . I'm not trying to test him but I'd really like him to figure out why he hurt me on his own."

Danica swiped some batter, rolled it into a ball and popped it into her mouth. "I promise. And I like your style."

So Kat explained her meeting with her teacher and how Alec reacted. Danica didn't hide her wince.

"Oh man, that explains why he's been so mopey."

"He's mopey?"

"Well, he's not a whole lot of fun to be around."

"What do you think?"

Danica cocked her head. "About What Stone did?"

Kat ran her hands over the smooth counter. "Do you think that's all he sees when he looks at me? A project?"

Danica sucked in a breath and then blew it out. "First of all, this is a conversation you should have with him, you get that? This clearly isn't resolved between you two. And Kat, if he only saw you as a project, why would he be this hurt? Alec isn't a macho guy who's upset because his pride is wounded. He's upset because he cares about you. He wouldn't be hurt otherwise." She cocked her head. "You get that, right? You have the power to hurt him because he cares about you so much."

Kat hadn't thought of it that way. No one had ever cared enough to give her any sort of power to hurt them. But Alec had, hadn't he? God, they'd given each other the power. And hurt each other in the process.

When Kat didn't say anything, Danica kept talking. "I think he said what he did from a good place. He meant well, but he didn't think about how it would make you feel. And I'm not going to excuse him because 'he's a guy.' That's bullshit. He needs to see where you're coming from, too."

Kat missed Alec with an ache that intensified every day. So hearing Danica's affirmation this torture was right helped a little.

"You going to give him a second chance?"

"He texts me every day. Really nice, sweet things. And I think he's trying to show me why he cares about me. But he hasn't said I'm sorry. That's all I want to hear, really."

Danica rolled her eyes. "Men."

"Anyway, um, I have a meeting with my advisor. To declare my major. Early education."

Danica jerked her head up from checking on her cookies in the oven. "No way! My roommate's an education major." She turned and yelled down her short hallway. "Lea! C'mere!" Turning to Kat, she said. "You'll like Lea. She's a sweetheart."

Seconds later, a door opened in the hallway and a very petite, dark-haired girl slowly made her way toward them. Her hair was long, thick and straight, and a fringe of bangs touched her eyelashes. She had high cheekbones, round cheeks and a small, bow mouth. As she grew closer,

Kat noted she was limping. The girl turned large, round dark brown eyes onto Danica, but didn't speak.

Danica gestured toward Kat. "Kat this is Lea Travers. Lea, this is Kat Caruso, Alec's . . . something. She's declaring her elementary-education major. Maybe you can help her out with which profs to get and which to avoid."

Kat turned in her stool to face the pixie-faced girl and clapped her hands with a squeal. "Oh yay! Really?"

Lea smiled. "Sure, I'd be happy to help."

Kat grinned. "I already have a BFF, but you can be my MBF, or major best friend. This is awesome."

Lea's eyebrows rose into her forehead and she visibly shuddered. "Yeah, sure, but . . . could you go easy on the acronyms? OMG. BFF. TMI. They make me break out in hives."

Silence.

The three of them remained motionless while Lea's face reddened, and she clapped her hand over her mouth.

Danica's snort of laughter was a catalyst for Kat to double over in laughter, slamming her palm down on the counter while Danica stomped her foot on the tiled floor. Through her tears, Kat saw Lea start to giggle, her face still red. When Kat was able to compose herself, she reached for her phone.

"What are you doing?" Danica asked.

"I'm texting Tara to let her know she's been replaced as my Best Friend Forever. Spelled out." She turned to Lea. "Okay, Miss Anti-acronym. I need your number. We're going to be tight. I can feel it."

Lea's face was still red, but she also seemed pleased,

stepping closer to Kat and reciting her number. She braced herself on the counter, shifting her hips to take the weight off of one of her legs. Kat finished entering her number and set her phone on the counter. She hopped down off of her stool. "Go ahead and take my seat. I'm tired of sitting."

Lea hesitated, then hopped up onto the stool.

"So, what happened to your leg? Did you trip on that stupid crack in the sidewalk outside of the library?" She turned to Danica. "That happened to me. I e-mailed the maintenance people about it. I was in a crowd of rugby players when it happened and it was like a dandelion falling in a forest of redwoods. No one could see me and I was having flashbacks to that time I saw the running of the bulls in Pamplona, convinced I was gonna get trampled—"

"Kat," Danica said patiently.

"What? You do know about the running of the bulls, right? Because—"

"Kat!" Danica shouted and Kat snapped her jaw shut. She turned to Lea, who had her mouth open like she was trying to speak, eyes glittering with amusement.

"I didn't fall," she said, her soft voice musical. "I was in a car accident when I was younger and my leg got crushed."

That wasn't what Kat expected and now she felt a little nuts for going off about that dang crack in the sidewalk. Even if it was a total safety hazard that she needed to call someone about. Again.

"Oh, no," she said. "I'm so sorry."

Lea smiled and rubbed her leg below the knee. "Thanks."

Kat took a step closer. "Um . . . can I see it?"

Lea blinked in surprise. "Really?"

"Oh shoot, is that rude? I just never met anyone—"

Lea waved her hand. "No, it's fine. No one ever asks me, that's all. When I tell people, they usually just look uncomfortable and try to change the subject as fast as they can." She lifted up the leg of her jeans, showing a series of red and white scars which traipsed up from her ankle and disappeared beneath the denim.

"Oh wow." Kat stepped closer.

Lea shrugged. "Hey, the scars mean I survived."

"Does it hurt?"

Lea dropped her jeans back in place and shrugged. "Sometimes. It gets stiff a lot. Depends on how much walking I have to do."

"Do you have a cane or anything?"

"Not that I use on a regular basis. Sometimes on bad days or rough mornings."

Kat nodded. "Okay, I'm going to change the subject now, but it's not because I'm uncomfortable, it's because I want to ask you some questions about our major before I forget."

Lea cocked her head. "Acronym usage aside, I like you, Kat Caruso."

"I know, I'm totally likeable, right?" Kat laughed. "I like you, too, Lea Travers. So, what grade do you want to teach?"

"I'd like to teach high-school English. Eventually, I'd

like to get my master's in library science, to be a librarian."

"That's so cool. I have no idea what I want to teach. I was thinking kindergarten, but I'm not sure how good my patience is. And then I was thinking fifth grade, but that's when my school did sex education and I'm not sure I'm down with handing out Maxi Pads and deodorant and talking to boys about their boners."

Lea's raised her eyebrows and the corners of her mouth quirked up.

"I just know I want to teach, you know? For once in my life, I finally feel like I know what I'm supposed to be doing, and it's awesome."

The oven beeped, signaling the first batch of cookies was cooked. Danica grabbed her oven mitts. "Great, let's celebrate this newfound introspection with some cookies, huh?"

"Best way to celebrate." Kat grinned. "Where's the milk?"

Kat spend the rest of the afternoon with Danica and her roommate. Lea talked to her about the best advisors and professors in the education major and which campus clubs she could join to connect with other students.

By the time Kat left, she felt better about declaring her major and was prepared to face Monday's appointment.

Chapter Twenty-Eight

ALEC SAT OUTSIDE the learning center on campus, bouncing his leg. The sun shone in a bright, clear spring glare and a light breeze blew through the budding leaves of the campus trees. He'd tried to sit far enough away that Kat wouldn't see him when she left her appointment. He'd had to bribe Danica with a pair of purple fur-lined boots she'd been eyeing to get her to divulge Kat's appointment time.

The only reason he knew Danica and Lea had been talking to Kat was because he had seen a text message on Lea's phone from her. He was sure she'd been nervous for her appointment, but he could picture her, walking in with her head high. He was so fucking proud of her.

The doors of the center opened and Kat stepped out, sliding her mirrored sunglasses over her eyes. His chest ached. He hadn't seen her since he had left her in the bowling-alley parking lot, when tears stacked up in those blue eyes.

She looked good now. Her hair was down, blowing in the wind. She wore tight jeans and knee-high brown boots. She'd traded in her heavy red pea coat she loved so much for a light khaki jacket over a blue sweater.

He had to grip the bench to prevent himself from running up to her. He couldn't tell from her expression the outcome of the meeting.

The door opened behind her and Lea came out. Kat flashed a huge smile and hugged her, that beautiful, familiar laugh lilting over the campus to his ears.

The ache in his chest eased at sight of that grin and the sound of that laugh. They began to walk, heads bent in some sort of conversation. He knew he should get up and walk away now, before Kat spotted him, but he couldn't bring himself to stand up. Another couple of seconds. He had to make sure Kat was all right.

As Kat drew closer to his hideout, she jerked her head up, as if she could feel his eyes on her, and looked right at him.

He held his breath, unsure of her reaction. Last night, lying in bed, he was so sure of her feelings for him, so confident they could make this work. But in the light of day, all the doubts crept in. What if he *had* misread every moment they'd spent together?

She probably only looked at him for five seconds, but it felt like an eternity to him, until she turned her head to say something to Lea, then walked away from her, in Alec's direction.

He stood up and shoved his hands into his leather jacket. Kat stopped a few feet away from him and cocked her head to the side, pushing her sunglasses into her hair on her head.

They stood in silence, until Kat said, "Danica?"

He shrugged. "She'd sell out anyone for a pair of purple boots."

Kat laughed and looked away, her eyes following Lea as she walked away.

"So. Hi." His grand moment to talk to her and that was all he could come up with to say.

She turned back to him. At least she hadn't turned on the sex kitten. "Thanks for the text messages," she said.

That's all she said. She gave him nothing else. "Sure." He jerked his head toward the building behind them. "What did they say?"

"The psychologist said I have dyslexia," she said simply, her face calm.

"Yeah?" he asked. "So, you okay with that?"

"It took me some time to work out in my head. To get over that this is what's best for me. But yeah, I'm okay with it. I feel . . . understood. For once. I have some hoops to go through yet, but I can get extra help now. I told them about statistics and we had a conference call with Dr. Alzahabi. I did, in fact, fail the mid-term, but he said considering the circumstances, he'll allow me to make up the grade by giving an oral presentation. My choice of research topic, as long as it relates to statistics, obviously. Total bummer because I really wanted to do a science project on which nail polish dries the fastest."

Alec laughed softly. "I also heard about you wanting to declare an education major."

Kat narrowed her eyes. "I'm going to take a marker to those stupid purple boots."

"Actually, it was Lea who let it slip."

"Hm, well I can't be mad at my MBF."

"MB what?"

She waved her hand. "Never mind."

"Well, I do want you to know, I think that's great. You'll make an awesome teacher."

Her eyes softened. "Thanks." She fidgeted with her bag. "So, I need to get going—" she began.

Now that he had her in front of him, he didn't want her to walk away. "I'm proud of you," he blurted out.

Her body jerked and she blinked, her eyes glassy one minute, then clear again the next. "Thank you," she said quietly. "You know, I'm starting to be proud of me, too."

Keep her here. "And you know, I can help you with that project, if you want. I have some ideas from when I took the class . . ."

He let his voice die when Kat's entire posture went rigid. He'd fucked up again. Dammit.

And that was it. She dropped her sunglasses back over her eyes. "See you soon," she said before walking away.

He held on to that *soon* like a life preserver.

He watched her until she was out of sight and then stood there for another couple of minutes, biting his lip and thinking of all the things he should have said.

"Hey," a voice came from behind him and he whipped around to see Danica, dressed in some sort of steampunk getup, tight pants and a leather corset over a white blouse.

He raised his eyebrows at her clothes and she grinned, fingering some massive headpiece, birds and flowers welded onto a metal gear.

"Where do you find this stuff?"

She sat down on the bench and leaned back. "Oh, young man, the Internet is a great and many-splendored thing."

He sat down beside her. "Yeah, it has cool stuff like news, you know, not just places to find . . . whatever the hell that is you're wearing."

She ignored him. "Did you see her?"

He looked down at his hands. "Yeah."

"Why isn't she here, then, laughing at your awful jokes and messing up your hair with her wandering fingers?"

He glared at her. "You're just on a roll today, aren't you?"

"Answers, Stone."

"I don't know. I fucked up again, I guess. It's like every time I offer to help, she shuts me down. If she doesn't want my help, why doesn't she just say so?"

Danica's blue eyes searched his before she exhaled in exhaustion and slung an arm around his shoulder. "Oh, Stone. My misguided, left-brained friend."

He bunched his shoulders so she'd drop her arm. "Let go of me."

She held on tighter. "I tried to let you figure this out on your own. I really did. And in fact, I promised Kat I'd leave you to your own devices but this is getting ridiculous. I'm tired of seeing the two of you act like someone killed your puppies."

"What's that supposed to mean?"

She kept talking. It's like he wasn't even there. "What happened when Kat told you about her teacher and parents?"

"Um." He frowned. "I talked to her about it."

Danica shook her head. "Specifically, what did *you* say?"

"I . . . I tried to come up with a plan, to fix her statistics grade and get her off academic probation and—"

Danica held up her hand. "How do you think that made Kat feel?"

He paused. "Um, I thought at the time she'd be grateful for the help but now I'm thinking that's the wrong answer."

Danica leaned in and patted his cheek. "You'd be correct."

His mind whirled as he remembered that scene in her bedroom. He'd wanted to forget it, but every night it replayed in his head like a bad movie. She'd shut down right when he'd gone into tutor mode and offered suggestions on how to fix it. How to . . .

Oh shit.

"Fix her," he blurted.

Danica, who still had his face in her hand, squeezed her fingers. "What?"

He met her eyes. "Oh God, I'd made her think I wanted to fix her. Right? Like . . . like . . . she was just some sort of student to me. Not the girl I . . ."

He closed his eyes as Danica's hands dropped from his face. She tugged his head into the crook of her shoulder. That stupid blouse had laces that tickled his nose.

"I know you like to fix things," she said quietly. It's who you are. It's why you want to be a lawyer and why you're smart and so good at what you do." She exhaled roughly. "But you can't fix her. She's a person, not a math problem. You can't solve her for X."

He didn't care who walked by and saw him cradled in Danica's arms. She'd probably snarl at anyone who dared to look at them askance anyway.

Finally he straightened. "How do I show her I don't see her as a project? That I don't think she needs fixing?"

Danica smoothed his hair back. "Oh no, you're on your own there. I'm not good at the romance thing, either. Monica says my idea of romance is 'Take off your shirt.'"

Alec huffed. "Well clearly, I suck at it, too."

Danica shook her head. "You care about her. You see her—all her parts—and that's all she needs. No grand gestures, no flowers or anything. Just find a way to show her how amazing she is."

He leaned in and smacked a kiss on her cheek loudly. "Love you, Dan."

She smiled and squeezed his hand. "Love you, too."

Chapter Twenty-Nine

"AND THAT IS my conclusion on the distribution of animals in a box of animal crackers. I am ninety-five-percent certain of my findings that the tiger has the highest percentage of probability at ten percent and the lion has the lowest, at two percent."

Kat bit the head off a monkey animal cracker and grinned at Dr. Alzahabi. He sat in a desk in front of her in an empty classroom, hand wrapped around his jaw, elbow on the table, looking at Kat like she was from another planet.

"Want an animal cracker?" she asked.

He dropped his hand onto the desk and leaned back, clearing his throat. "No thanks, Ms. Caruso, but I appreciate the offer. I looked over the paper you submitted to me already and despite your odd choice of topic, this was well researched and presented."

Kat finished chewing her monkey head and swallowed. "Thank you."

"Because of that, I'm going to excuse your midterm test grade and use this grade instead, which will give you a B plus for your midterm grade."

Kat gawked, her mouth open, bits of animal cracker probably on her lips. A B plus? In statistics? She didn't know whether to cry, laugh or dance a jig.

"I—I don't know what to say," she stuttered. "Thank you so much for this opportunity to bring up my grade."

Her professor rose slowly from his chair and stepped toward her, his stern expression warming. "I commend you for taking the initiative to get a diagnosis, and for your desire to pursue an education degree."

She was still gawking, so she closed her mouth. "Thank you," she mumbled.

Dr. Alzahabi's face returned to his impassive status quo and he gave her a curt nod. "Right, well, we'll do this again for your final and that will be sufficient to pass this class, I think. Thank you, Ms. Caruso, and good luck."

Kat picked up her book bag and slung it over her shoulder, still processing her professor's words. He was already at his desk, packing his papers into his briefcase.

"Thanks, Dr. Alzahabi. Thank you so much," she said again, before darting out the door.

She walked down the hall in a daze, dumbfounded she had managed to pull off that project. She had thought of the idea while watching an airing of *Armageddon* with Tara over the weekend. Ben Affleck's character got frisky with Liv Tyler's character with an animal cracker, and Kat had begun to think about which was the sexiest animal available in an animal cracker (lion, obviously). Then she thought about the odds of getting said sexy lion and then she had her statistics project.

By herself.

In pure Kat style.

She had never been more proud of herself as she had been when she completed that project.

The learning support center appointment was eye-opening. The exam the psychologist gave her covered an intelligence test and reading/writing test, which resulted in a dyslexia diagnosis. She talked to them about her attention problem, and she planned to go in for further testing to determine if she had an attention deficit disorder. They suspected, however, that it was part of her method for coping in a world she didn't always understand. She'd been given some additional coping methods, such as chewing gum during tests—a trick that supposedly could help her focus.

And as she worked on her project, she learned her wandering mind, which she had previously cursed, could be creative.

No, there was no cure. She'd always have dyslexia. But it wasn't an academic death sentence. The diagnosis was freeing, releasing her from the prison of constant misunderstanding.

She had begun to realize her struggles and newfound knowledge of learning disabilities were an asset to her future as a teacher, not a hindrance. Thanks to Lea, the last two weeks had been productive. Kat had met with a great advisor who helped her declare her elementary-education major. She was officially out of the "undecided" club and squarely in the "I finally know what to do with my life" club.

It was a good feeling.

And last night, Alec's text message had said, *I still owe you a date. And then I can tell you in person how sorry I am.*

The message swelled her heart, but she kept her guard up, because she didn't know if he knew what there was to be sorry about.

When she burst out of the doors of the math and science building, a set of nervous, familiar brown eyes waited for her.

"Max?" She walked up to him where he was seated on a stone bench under a blooming maple.

"Hey," he said.

She sat down beside him. "Everything okay?"

"Yeah, sure. Everything's fine. I ran into Danica at the TUB and she said you'd be here. I . . . uh . . . wanted to talk to you."

She nodded hesitantly. "Okay."

He tapped his fingers on his knees and pursed his lips. Kat waited for him to speak, staring as he worked his jaw. "Max—"

"I'm sorry," he said quickly, finally looking up at her. "I know I was a dick to you, and I'm sorry."

This was unexpected. He didn't want to get back together, did he? Because that would be awkward. "Max, it's in the past now—"

He shook his head roughly. "No, please don't brush it off. Can you accept my apology? I was an asshole. You know it and I know it."

"Okay, fine. I accept your apology, and I appreciate it."

Max smiled, and it was the smile she remembered from October when he'd first asked her out. He'd been so charming then. He'd make some girl really happy once he sorted himself out and realized what he had to offer.

She returned his smile and patted his cheek, then quickly withdrew her hand. She didn't want to give him any ideas. "But we can't get back together, I—"

"Whoa whoa whoa," he held his hands up, palms out and leaned back. "No, that's not why I apologized. Alec told me about you two."

You two. Like she and Alec were a real couple. She pushed that aside and focused on something else. "You two are talking?"

Max's faced reddened and he looked away. "He told you."

They didn't have to mention the betrayal. "He told me."

"I didn't cheat on you, just so you know."

That was good to know, but she cared more about what he did to Alec than the thought he'd done something to her. "Okay."

Max's jaw twitched. "I apologized to him, too. Been saying 'sorry' a lot lately."

She dug her nails into her thighs. She wanted to yell at him, to tell him that's what happened when you were a jerk to your girlfriend and slept with your best friend's girlfriend, but Max looked like he knew all that. She didn't need to tell him.

"By the way," Max said, "You gonna call Alec anytime soon? He's mopey."

Kat laughed. "Are you and Danica teaming up? She used the same word to describe Alec. You guys at least need different adjectives next time you launch your offensive."

Max wrinkled his nose. "Danica and I are not on the same team. Oh wait, maybe we are, since we both like girls. I'm not sure." He furrowed his brow and stared off into campus, as if he was trying to figure it out.

A phone rang and Max reached into his pocket. He swiped his thumb across the screen to answer it. "Hey Cam." Pause. "What do you mean he won't come out?" Max stood up and put a hand on his hips "Well, fucking bang the door down, take off the hinges or something!" Kat placed her hand on his arm. Max looked at it, eyes squinted in concern, then he raised his head and met her eyes. "Never mind, Cam. I got a secret weapon." He shoved his phone into his pocket and grabbed her hand. "Let's go.

She had to run to keep up with him as he dragged her across campus. "What? Where are we going?"

"To my place," he said irritably, like he couldn't be bothered to explain why he was kidnapping her.

She tried to dig her heels in to stop but Max was too strong. "Why?"

When they reached his truck, he opened her door and pushed her inside. "Because Zuk needs you."

"Me?" she squeaked, but he'd already shut the door and was rounding the front of the truck. Why would he need her?

When Max started the truck, she tried to plead her case, that she was sure there was nothing she could do, but Max cut her off, explaining Cam said Alec got a phone call from his mom. He had answered it in the living room and while talking, his face had paled. He'd run up to his bedroom and locked the door, refusing to answer except to say "I'm fine, just go away."

Cam wasn't pacified by that.

Kat gripped the seat with white knuckles as Max sped through the town like a demon, violating about a dozen traffic laws in between his road-rage curses.

Kat pushed aside the insecurity over her ability to fix the situation. She wrung her hands because now there was a new, bigger worry. She hoped there wasn't anything wrong with his mother. Alec didn't need to lose another parent.

Max took the turn onto his street with a screech and on what Kat could have sworn was two wheels. He parked and didn't wait for her, flinging his door open and sprinting for the house. By the time she had followed him into the house and up the stairs, he was banging on Alec's door, a fretting Cam beside him. "Let me in, Zuk! What the fuck?"

Some sort of slow, depressing emo music, which Alec didn't normally listen to, could be heard through the door. She didn't know if he had searched Pandora for a "sad song" station or what.

Elbowing Max out of the way, she placed her palm on

the door. Unsure what to say, she went with the easiest thing. Her favorite word. "Alec."

The music stopped, followed by silence.

She licked her lips and tried again. "Alec."

There was a rustling and a creaking, which she knew was his bed. There was movement at the corner of her eye and the doorknob rattled as he unlocked it from inside.

Kat eyed Max and Cam, who both stepped back, conceding defeat. She gave them a small smile and walked in, shutting the door behind her.

Alec was in a cocoon of sheets on the bed, his dark, glossy hair peeking out at the top where it rested on his pillow. She didn't hesitate to go to him because no matter what, she cared about him. And he needed her. So she'd put aside her own fears and worries and do whatever she could to comfort him. She put a knee to the bed and crawled to him, lying on top of the covers, her front to his back, wrapping an arm around his waist, the other petting his hair.

His breaths were even and deep. She would have thought he was asleep if he hadn't just stood up to let her in his room.

As she touched his head and ran her fingers over the hair at his temples, he shuddered, then turned to face her.

There were no tears, but shadows lurked in his eyes. "How'd you get here?" he asked.

"Why did you shut yourself in your room?"

"How'd you get here?" he repeated.

"Why did you shut yourself in your room?" she shot back.

"I asked first," he mumbled.

"Max saw me on campus. We were talking when Cam called him. Your turn."

Alec bit the inside of his cheek. "He's dead." His eyes darted back and forth, begging her not to make him say a name. He didn't have to. She knew.

"How did he die?"

"Heart attack. Didn't even make it to his parole hearing."

Her breath left in a rush. "Wow."

"Yeah." His eyes were hard to read, searching hers like she held the answer to a question he wasn't asking.

She squeezed his arm tighter. "I can't read your mind. Are you happy? Sad? What?"

"That's what I'm in here trying to figure out," he said, his brows furrowing and the green in his eyes darkening in confusion. "I feel oddly empty right now. I don't feel justified, I don't feel happy. I just feel . . . nothing. It's all very anticlimactic." He rolled onto his back and stared at the ceiling. "Shouldn't I be dancing on his grave or something?"

Kat scooted closer and buried her face in his neck. She had an excuse to get close to him and she wasn't above exploiting this moment to do so. She was only human. And she needed something, his fresh scent, the feel of his skin on hers, to take with her when she left. "It's okay to feel this way. It's not wrong."

He swallowed and she felt his Adam's apple bob against her cheek. "I never wrote the letter to the parole board. I realized I spent a lot of time being angry about what happened, hating MacEnroe. You said it wasn't a travesty to my dad's legacy to let the anger go and you were right." He took a deep breath and exhaled roughly.

"We should mark on the calendar that I was right, because it doesn't happen often." Kat fingered the collar of his T-shirt and wondered if she could also steal one on her way out. The other shirt she took from him needed to be washed sometime.

He chuckled. "I feel like an idiot for holing myself up in here. I didn't want to have to deal with Max or Cam ..."

She wanted to ask why he let her in. What was it about her? But she didn't talk as he sorted his thoughts out loud. "Feels sort of good to be empty, actually. Like my heart is drained of all the bad so I can fill it with the good." He bit his lip.

She brushed her lips against his neck, just once. "Your heart was always full of good."

He turned to her and smiled, once again focusing that intelligent, all-knowing gaze on her and she knew it was her turn to make her exit. She couldn't do this again, get sucked into Alec's orbit. She'd come too far in the last couple of weeks for a man tell her she "needed fixed."

Even if he held her heart. "You going to venture out of your room now?"

He nodded, eyes still locked with hers, holding her there like some sort of force field.

But this wasn't a sci-fi movie, so she dropped her gaze. "Well, that makes me happy. She scooted back and up on her knees. "So, I guess I'm going to go now—"

He jolted up, one hand braced behind him, one out as if to touch her. "Wait, are you leaving?"

She nodded and stood beside the bed. "Yeah, I have some things to do and so . . . yeah."

"Wait, Kat—"

"I'm glad you're okay with everything." She fumbled with her bag on the floor. "And say hi to your mom for me!"

And then she ran out, like a coward. Jogged down the stairs, almost tripping on the bottom step as a thump and a curse sounded from Alec's room, followed by her name. Max walked in from the kitchen, a sandwich halfway to his mouth as she opened the front door.

"Don't let her leave, Max!" Alec hollered from upstairs, followed by another thump, and Max's eyes narrowed on her.

"Bye!" She yelled and hauled her butt out the door as fast as she could, then took off down the street. Thank God she'd worn flats today and had been running, because she needed speed.

She made it all the way to the Pizza Box before feet pounding the pavement caught up to her and a voice called her name.

She stared up at the sign of the restaurant, buzzing faintly in the afternoon sun, and remembered weeks ago when she stood right here and wished with all her might she'd hear her name spoken by that voice.

She'd gotten her wish. But it was too late now.

She slowed to a stop because her shoes were starting to give her blisters and her bag was heavy.

When she turned around, Alec stood five feet away, barely breathing hard, and she wanted to smack him just for that.

"Why'd you leave?" he asked.

"I have things to do."

His jaw clenched. "If this conversation goes the same way it did at your house, I'm going to scream, Kat."

Did he think that was fun for her? She wanted to scream, too.

He stepped closer and she took a step back. He did it again and she took another step back. He sighed and pleaded with her with those eyes, the ones she never could resist. And there she was again, sucked right back into Alec Stone's gravitational pull.

Stupid science.

He took a step forward, slowly, and this time she held her ground. A small smile tugged at his lips. "Why'd you come to see me?"

It was on the tip of her tongue to make a joke, like, *I wanted to see you in your boxer briefs*, or *I left my underwear behind your desk*, or *Was that a gun in your bed or were you just happy to see me?*

But she was tired, oh so tired of the barriers and the games. And she had come so far in loving herself for who she was. She wouldn't let anyone knock her down to where she had been.

"Max said you were upset and he thought I could help, so I came."

Alec cocked his head. "Just like that. Because you thought I needed you and you could help, you came."

She nodded.

He took another step closer and now he was so close that if she extended her index fingers, she'd brush his.

"Kat."

She raised her eyes from staring at their barely touching hands to see his gaze on her, soft and so full of . . . no, it couldn't be . . .

He grasped her hand and brought it to rest on his chest, over his heart. "Don't you feel it? All that negative crap I'd been holding inside is gone because of you. And the good I'm filling it with? That's you."

The people walking around them didn't exist, and it was just her and Alec now, in a little private force field, connected by her hand on his chest. She inched closer, so their chests brushed, her hand between them.

His other hand rose and cupped her face. She blinked slowly as his thumb swiped her cheekbone. He done it before outside of the Pizza Box and walked away. But he wasn't walking away now. "Kat, I was working on a plan to talk to you but then I got that phone call and everything kind of got shot to shit." He took a deep breath, his eyes locked in hers. "But you have to know. I'm sorry. You have to know when I look at you, I see a girl who laughs at her own jokes, who's so funny and adorable, she makes me smile after I talk about losing my dad. A girl who drops everything to comfort a guy, even though he made her feel like a project that needed to be fixed. And I see a girl who's so brave because she goes to college knowing it's going to hard, but she wants to make something of her life." He leaned down and dropped his voice. "And I see a girl who most definitely does *not* have the best ass on campus."

Her laugh bubbled out of her throat. She never thought she'd hear words like that from Alec or from any guy, really. And for some reason her mind processed the whole situation as hilarious. What started as a giggle turned into full-blown hysterical laughter as she threw back her head. Alec laughed with her until they were both bent at the waist, wheezing through the last of their chuckles.

Kat straightened first and wiped her eyes. Her chest itched as the hole in her heart he'd made weeks ago healed, and she wanted to scratch at the scar. "That was amazing. Did you practice that?"

He ran his tongue over his teeth and smirked. "I did, actually. Did I do okay? I winged the last part."

She stepped back into that force field, realizing finally that it was two ways. She had her own force field, pulling him to her. "You did great." She touched her lips to his, just briefly only a brush but the feel of his ridged lips was home.

He cupped her check again. "I'll spend the rest of my life proving you should love yourself as much as everyone else loves you."

God, he was too much. She felt the blush creep up her cheeks. "I know I still have some work to do on myself. Statistically, I love myself about seventy-five percent as much I should." She took a deep breath and went for it. "But I want to conquer that last twenty-five percent with you." She laid her hand on his chest.

Alec's smile split his face and he grabbed her head with both hands. "You talking in percentages about how much you want to be with me is a total turn-on."

Kat laughed and gripped his wrists. "How turned on?"

"Oh, I'm at about eighty percent and quickly gaining."

"I've been at a frustrating ninety percent for two weeks. I walked in a drugstore and got hot and bothered in the hair-products aisle."

Alec threw back his head and laughed. "Holy shit, Kat. My life was boring as hell before you."

He reached for her face and she closed her eyes as he swiped her cheekbone with his thumb, the touch full of tenderness and possibly something that started with a big L. She'd think about that later.

"I know I said some stupid shit to you at your house when I was mad and I'm sorry for that," he said. "But the thing is, what I like about you is that I don't know how your mind works. I don't know what you're going to do and say next. You make my life interesting."

They were like the justice scales tattooed on Alec's back, balancing each other out. Alec kept her grounded and she kept him on his toes.

"Well, you balance me, so I guess we do something for each other," she said.

Alec smiled. "You know, when I first met you, I thought you were this girl who rode the edge of a wave. One push, and you'd fall in." He met her eyes. "All I wanted to do was keep you up on that wave. Brace you so you'd stay stable."

She closed her eyes briefly and leaned into his touch.

"I'm not on that wave anymore. I'm right here, on solid ground with you." She leaned in and brushed her lips over his. "And that's right where I want to be."

He sighed into the kiss, then pulled away a fraction to whisper, "Ditto, *meu coração*."

Her breath caught in her throat. His pronunciation was a little off, his *r* not as fluid, but just the fact that he had obviously looked it up and probably practiced threatened to melt her into a pile of goo at his feet.

She placed his hand on her chest. "You're my heart, too."

They stumbled back to his town house, the walk a blur of giggles and stolen touches and kisses that probably weren't appropriate for public consumption.

And then they were at his front door and up his stairs and collapsed into his bed.

They stripped each other, taking their time, relearning each other's bodies.

When the touches became more urgent, she stretched her arm and rummaged in his nightstand.

Teeth clamped on her hipbone and she yelped, then looked down to see Alec releasing her skin from between his teeth, smirking. She narrowed her eyes at him and held the condom above her head. "I'd watch where you put those, because I'm the one who's in charge of our prophylactic situation."

He grabbed her ankle and easily hauled her down the bed under him. Then he ripped the condom from her hand and held it between his index and middle finger, raising an eyebrow. "You were saying?"

She huffed. "You really suck at seduction. Because I'm not sure annoying the crap out of the girl who is naked in bed is a good idea."

He hummed in response, dropping the condom on the comforter and then dipping his head. His lips began nibbling behind her ear and then ran down her neck. When he made it down to a nipple and she arched with a moan, a chuckle breezed over her skin. He raised his hand to her head and ran it through her hair. "You're so beautiful. Your skin, your hair. Those lips that have driven me crazy since you sucked on that damn smoothie straw in the library."

Her body shook in silent laughter. "It was so easy to tease you."

"I knew you were doing it on purpose."

He kissed her again, thoroughly, his hands roaming, touching every inch of her skin until her whole body tingled. Then finally, finally, he rolled on the condom and entered her slowly, while she clung to him, her arms around his shoulders, one leg around his thigh and the other around his hip.

She concentrated on his eyes, those beautiful orbs hidden as his eyelids fell to half-mast. Everything about him felt right, from the way he filled her, to his gentled nibbles on her lips, to his soft words telling her how beautiful she was. How amazing. How perfect. How she was his.

She'd never viewed sex as much more than something fun. But with Alec, it was about reconnecting, about showing each other how much they cared in every way possible.

It was beautiful.

As his thumb rolled between them, her climax built slowly, starting at her toes and creeping up her legs until it shot up her spine. She cried out and he kept his eyes on her face, only releasing himself when the aftershocks of her orgasm were over.

She stayed wrapped around him, rubbing his back with her fingers, appreciating the hardness under the soft skin.

Chapter Thirty

IT WAS LIKE music. The baseline thud of his sneaker-clad feet on the street. The steady beat of his exerted heart. The swish of his pumping arms against his shirt. The background orchestra of college-town bustle.

It'd been so long since the weather had been nice enough to stretch his legs for a run. Too long.

He didn't know how many miles he'd run. His lungs burned and his muscles ached, but he picked up the pace.

Because his finish line was Kat's apartment. For the first time in his life, he wasn't racing to outrun that threatening dark cloud. He was racing to get to the sun.

The last month had been amazing. The more time Alec spent with Kat, the more ways she amazed him. She told him everything that went through her head now, since she told him she didn't feel self-conscious or that he would judge her. He woke up every morning smiling, wondering what Kat would say or do that day.

When she told him she beheaded a primate at the end of her statistics animal-cookies project, he thought he was going to die laughing.

He hadn't realized life could be this fun. He hadn't realized he could find a girl like Kat, who understood him.

He hadn't realized a girl like her would love him.

But she did, somehow, and he thanked the Fucking King Fuck of all Fucks she did.

Not that it was a surprise, but thankfully, his mom was a full member of the Kat Caruso Fan Club. They'd driven home to have dinner with her a couple of nights ago. His mom had been in a tizzy, e-mailing him dozens of recipes, asking him what Kat liked to eat, what she didn't, if she had food allergies . . .

Alec finally wrote her back, told her to throw some barbecue chicken on the grill and be done with it.

She didn't listen, and when they showed up, she was half in a panic attack, pulling him aside and wringing her hands because her chicken cordon bleu wasn't "pretty." He'd hugged her and told her it didn't matter.

Kat hadn't noticed a thing, ate everything on her plate, then asked to see family photo albums.

When his mom showed Kat a picture of his father holding him as a baby, Kat had stroked the photo, a thoughtful look on her face. Then she turned to him, her smile shaky, and said, "You look like your father. Wish I could have met him."

His mother had to excuse herself. When he went to check on her, she was in her bedroom, sitting on her bed, twisting his father's wedding ring, which she wore on a chain around her neck.

He sat down beside her and she'd said, "She's one of the good ones."

He hadn't disagreed.

Alec didn't slow until he spotted Kat's apartment. His body urged him to keep running, but he knew he needed to cool down a little and stretch. He'd told her he'd take her for ice cream, a reward for getting an A on a history paper. When he had his breath back and muscles relaxed, he knocked on Kat's door. She let him in with one hand on top of her head, a bobby pin in her mouth.

He walked past her and grabbed a bottle of water from her mini-fridge. She walked up behind him and touched her nose to his back.

He jerked away. "Did you just smell me?"

She didn't even look embarrassed. "Yeah, I did. How do you not smell?"

"Uh . . ."

"You run miles in seventy-degree weather and you don't smell." She cocked a hip and his eyes strayed to how amazing she looked in her thin cotton dress. "You're like a ferret. Did you know that ferrets at some pet stores have their scent glands removed?" She turned and walked into her bedroom, rambling on about ferrets and he followed her, shaking his head and laughing.

He picked up her laptop off of her desk. "Hey, before we go, can I check my e-mail?"

Kat rummaged in her closet. "Sure."

Alec sat on her bed and booted up her laptop while

she busied herself spreading purses around her.

"Alec?"

He hummed in response, half paying attention while typing a quick e-mail to Danica about a project.

"Where's my ID?" She pawed through her purse, the contents strewn on the floor around her.

His fingers froze momentarily as a twinge of regret nibbled at him. "Your driver's license?"

"No, my fake ID. I'm changing purses, from my winter purse to spring purse, and I can't find my fake ID." She huffed, a dark purse in one hand and a lighter-colored one in another. He had no idea there were different purses for different seasons. If he would have known there was going to be a Great Purse Exchange, he might have tried to hide his theft a little better.

He kept his fingers on the keyboard, afraid to look at her. "Oh, I shredded it at the computer lab."

It'd been a momentary lapse in judgment. He'd seen the ID and it had reminded him of the night he'd fallen in love with her—he knew that now for sure—and how helpless he'd felt. And now that she wanted to be a teacher, getting an underage drinking violation was a serious cramp on getting a job. So he'd taken it. And shredded it. And now he realized that might have been a bad idea to do behind her back. *Shit.*

She slowly pivoted to face him. "Okay, let's rewind." She made jibberish sounds, like a tape was being replayed backward. "Repeat that again?"

He exhaled and shut her laptop, leaning over to place it on her desk beside her bed. He deserved the wrath, he guessed. Leaning back against the headboard, he folded his hands behind his head and met her eyes, enunciating each word. "I. Shredded. It."

She dropped her purse on the pile on the floor and took a step toward him, hands straightened at her sides. "You shredded my ID? Why the heck would you do that? It cost me two hundred dollars!"

"You're not using a fake ID, Kat. You turn twenty-one in a month anyway. If you get an underage drinking arrest, you could get in a lot of trouble, especially now that you want to be a teacher. There's no way I'm cool with that."

He was only digging his hole deeper. Her face was so red, he thought steam would shoot from her ears. "You're not cool with it. You're not cool with it? You're not cool with it!" She sputtered.

He chuckled. "No matter what punctuation you put at the end, that's what I said."

"I can't believe you!" she screamed at him and turned to grab his bookbag. "Let's see what precious belonging of yours I can shred!"

He moved, hooking her around the waist and hauling her back to his chest on the bed. She went into full freakout mode, like his cat did one time they tried to give it a flea dip, jabbing him in the ribs with her elbows and jamming her heels into his shins.

"Holy shit, Kat! Chill! You're going to poke my eye out or something."

"Good, then maybe I can shred it!"

"Calm down!" He slapped her arms at her sides and hooked his legs around hers to hold them in place.

She renewed her efforts, going into some sort of crocodile death roll to dislodge his grip. "No other guys I ever dated cared. They liked that I could go to the bars with them!"

Alec grunted as she slammed her head into his chest and growled, "That's because none of them loved you enough to look out for you!"

Both of them froze, sweaty limbs under clothes tangled with Kat's flannel sheets. The only sounds in the bedroom were their gasping breaths.

Alec's thunked his chin onto the top of her head and rubbed it on her hair.

She spoke first. "Did you just—"

"Yeah, I did."

"Did you mean—"

"Yeah, I meant it."

She dug her nails into the skin on his arm. "You love me enough to shred my fake ID?"

"Yeah, I love you enough to shred your fake ID."

He couldn't see her, but he knew she smiled. "I love you enough not to retaliate and shred your eyeball after I poke it out."

He chuckled, her head bouncing on his chest, and then she started laughing, and then they were both rolling in the sheets, tears streaming down their faces.

Then their lips met and then they rolled around some more. Under the sheets. Clothes removed. Limbs still sweaty.

They never made it to the ice-cream shop.

Chapter Thirty-One

ALEC REACHED ACROSS the backseat and grabbed her hand. Smiling at her with retro sunglasses over his eyes, slouched against the door of the truck, Converse-clad feet spread and the sun shining off his pompadoured head, he looked like a model on break from some fifties photo shoot.

Kat wanted to climb him like a tree, but Cam was driving and Max was yelling at one of his brothers on the phone so it wasn't the most appropriate time to be thinking impure thoughts about jumping her boyfriend. She squeezed his hand back and shot him a wink.

Kat now felt justified for complaining that Max never held her hand. Because holding Alec's hand, walking across campus, in the car, in bed, was *awesome*. Hand-holding was such a big deal in high school. It was the widely adopted symbol for officially "going out." When soccer forward jock Carter Lewis held hands with goth

Laura Hillenbrand, the whole school went into a tizzy. It lasted two weeks, but that had been an infamous hand-hold. Admittedly, not as famous as when Carter Lewis had held hands with the goalie from his team, Nick Durgess.

Alec holding her hand didn't feel like a high-school statement, an official claiming. It felt natural to have the physical connection to him.

"I left one hour early, Cal, get off my fucking back," Max spat into the phone. Kat stiffened, not used to hearing Max that angry. He gripped the back of his headrest in front of her and his knuckles were raw.

Her eyes shifted to Cam's in the rearview mirror and he shook his head once. She pursed her lips and looked away, gripping Alec's hand tighter.

Max's mood had definitely darkened the last month or so. He kept up the outgoing, love-life attitude but the warmth wasn't in his eyes anymore, his smiles a shade fake. Despite their rocky past, Kat cared about him, and it pained her to see him hurting. Alec was sick to his stomach about it, but he said family issues had always been off-limits with Max.

Which was why Kat and Alec agreed their bet date—which was altered because in the end she passed her midterm and the class—would be a group affair. They'd invited Cam and Max, and Tara and Danica, who were meeting them there a little later. Shanna refused to come since Cam blew her off after the night at the party. Kat didn't blame her. Cam Ruiz was gorgeous, with his golden skin and liquid brown eyes, full lips and deep dimples. But his "love 'em and leave 'em" philosophy was harsh.

Max ended his call and threw his phone on the dashboard with a hissed curse.

"Hey, don't take it out on Maggie," Cam said, caressing the steering wheel of his beloved beast of a white Dodge Ram.

"Pretty sure Max doesn't want to hear about your anthropomorphizing your truck right now, Cam," Alec said.

Three sets of eyes stared at him.

"Never mind," he mumbled, sinking into his seat.

Kat giggled.

"So, let me just get this straight," Max said. "We're driving an hour and a half to go bowling. Because we have to go to this specific bowling alley."

Alec straightened. "Yeah, it's in Kat's hometown."

Cam squinted in the rearview. "And what's so special about this bowling alley?"

"It's the sign," Kat blurted. "Great . . . signage."

She looked at Alec and raised her eyebrows and he threw his head back on the seat and burst out laughing.

Max turned around and scowled at them. "This *is* a bowling alley, right?" His scowl turned to a smirk and the familiar humor heated his eyes. "Is *bowling alley* really code for 'strip club'?"

Cam smacked his head.

"Ow!" Max protested.

Kat turned to Alec. "I actually always wanted to go to a strip club."

The truck fell silent, the only sound a classic rock song wailing through the speakers.

Alec's mouth was open and it took him a minute to talk. "Fuck, I love you."

Kat blushed as Max turned back around to face out the windshield. "Great, now we gotta hear lovey-dovey bullshit the rest of the way."

Kat watched the scenery flash by outside her window. Finals were over and this was the last Saturday they had together before moving back home for the summer. Her stomach hurt thinking about being away from Alec, but he assured her they didn't live far and would visit as often as they could.

Max cleared his throat. "Uh, so, just checking because no one actually confirmed we aren't going to a strip club—"

"For fuck's sake, Max, we aren't going to a strip club," Alec said.

Kat giggled again.

THEY PULLED INTO the parking lot and Max peered up at the sign. "Holy shit. That is the most amazing sign I've ever seen." He turned around, a goofy grin on his face that made him look like a teenager. "Do you think they have T-shirts?"

"It's been a while since I bowled here," Kat said, "but I'm pretty sure they do."

Max pumped his fist. "Score."

They climbed out of the truck and Kat smoothed her shirt. Despite the warm weather, she'd worn jeans because bowling shoes with a skirt or capris wasn't a good look.

Alec stepped beside her and grabbed her hand, his eyes even lighter in the bright sun.

"This isn't much of a bet payoff," she said, as they walked behind Cam and Max toward the front door. "I mean, you get to choose between bad pizza and old hot dogs at the food stand."

Alec laughed. "You think I care about the food? You're the reward."

She wrinkled her nose. "You're getting so sappy in your old age." She bumped him with her hip. "Senior."

He reached between Cam and Max and swung open the door, ushering her in ahead of them. "Ladies first."

She rolled her eyes but secretly adored the chivalry.

Seconds later, she found out why.

"Surprise!" The shouts rang out in a semicircle of people crowding the lobby. It took a minute for her eyes to adjust as she stood frozen.

"Happy Birthday!" said a voice from the back she recognized as Marc's. And a whistle made her turn her head, so she spotted Danica and Lea, grinning like fools.

Her parents stepped forward and Kat couldn't hide her surprise. She hadn't spoken to them much the last couple of months. She'd been busy with classes and changing her major.

"*Minha flor*," her father said, wrapping her in his arms. "Happy birthday to my sweet, brave girl."

Her hands flapped at her sides, trying to hold back the well of tears that threatened to spill over her lashes. She gripped her father's shirt to keep them steady. "Thank you, Daddy."

When he released her, he stepped back so her mother could greet her as well. "Katía," she said, kissing her cheek.

"Hi Mom," Kat whispered, doing her best to maintain her composure.

Her father glanced over her head. "Thanks for inviting us."

She looked over her shoulder as Alec nodded. "Of course."

Alec had done this? Gathered her friends and family together to celebrate her birthday? And that was it. The dam lifted and tears dampened her cheeks. Alec saw it and grabbed her, clutching her face to his chest. "Hey, it's okay. We all wanted to do something nice for you. It's been a hell of a year."

That was an understatement and it made her laugh. She pulled back. "Thanks."

He swiped the wetness from her cheeks with his thumbs. "No problem."

She turned around and waved. "Sorry for blubbering, everyone. I'm just surprised. Thank you all for coming!"

One by one, she greeted cousins and aunts and uncles. A couple other friends from college. Marc walked up to her and flicked her forehead. "Hey, munchkin. You gonna introduce me to the guy now?"

She swatted his hand away and grabbed Alec's arm, pulling him forward as she made the introductions. They shook hands, Marc's cool gaze on Alec's.

"I like this," Marc said, gesturing to gathered friends and family. "Good job."

Marc's attempt to play hard-ass annoyed her but Alec just grinned. "Thanks."

Marc excused himself as Lea and Danica walked over. They each hugged her, laughing about how long they'd been bowling but congratulating Alec on a successful surprise birthday party.

Danica wore a long purple wig with low pigtails trailing down her shoulders. Her eyes matched her hair and she wore a tight rainbow shirt, a short black tulle skirt and rainbow knee-high socks.

"And this look is . . ." Kat raised her eyebrows.

Danica performed a mock curtsy. "I was going for a derby-girl look. Did I pull it off?"

Kat chuckled. "I think so."

Alec clapped his hands to get everyone's attention and then let them know pizzas and snacks were available at the food stand. As they walked over, Kat slapped her hand on his chest. "This isn't fair, I was supposed to buy the food."

Alec grinned. "I like knowing you owe me." When she glared at him, he shrugged. "Actually, once I told your parents I wanted to do this, they decided to foot the bill."

She raised an eyebrow. They'd had a lot of discussions about her parents. Alec tried to convince her that while misguided, their hearts had been in the right place. They'd made the wrong decision, but it didn't mean they didn't love her. "Really?"

"Kat," Alec sighed patiently. "You're their daughter."

She pursed her lips and Alec directed her to sit at a

table while he fetched their food. Kat plopped down in her seat and rested her chin in her hand.

The last couple of months with Alec had been like a dream. Not a Kat-land dream, because there had been a disappointing lack of bubbles, but as close to perfect as it could be. They got along, they argued, they made up and life went on. She'd never been with someone where she felt loved every minute of every day. But Alec never failed her, by the way his eyes searched her out in a crowd, his muscles visibly relaxing when he knew where she was, the way he deferred to her when making decisions that affected them both, the way he held her at night, their once-frantic sex now full of sweet words and soft touches.

Unless it was make-up sex. That was still awesomely aggressive. Like the time he refused to spend the night because she was procrastinating over writing a paper. So she poured her soda all over his head. Then, naturally, he had to shower. And naturally, she had to help him because she was the one who got him sticky. And naturally, that resulted in her pressed against the wall with her legs wrapped around his waist. Which naturally resulted in mutual orgasms.

"Hi, Katía." Her mom's voice took her out of her thoughts and she blushed at being caught daydreaming naughty things. Her mom took a seat across from her.

"Alec told me," Kat looked around, "about you guys helping out with the party. Thanks for that."

"Oh, of course. We were happy to help out." Her mom grabbed her hand, rubbing the back of it with her thumb.

"We're proud of you, too, you know. Both your father and I."

Kat squirmed and tried to shift away.

"No," her mom said, tugging on her hand. "I'm sorry we didn't take your teacher's words seriously to get you the help you needed. And we're so, so proud of you for doing it yourself, and for choosing such a wonderful vocation. You'll be a great teacher."

Kat bit her lip to hold back the tears. She hadn't realized how much she wanted to hear those words until her mom said them. She wouldn't know if she'd made it off academic probation until she received her final grades for the semester, but with the extra help and techniques she'd been learning, she felt much more confident in her academic future.

"Oh Mom," she murmured. "Thanks."

"Love you, Katía."

"Love you, too, Mom."

When Alec returned to the table with their food, her mom murmured she had people to talk to and left them alone. As he sat down beside her and she took a bite, Lea and Danica sat down across from them.

"I can't believe you two kept this a secret," Kat said.

Danica narrowed her eyes at Alec. "Stone threatened my life."

"Well that's not very nice," Kat said to him.

He rolled his eyes.

"Check it!" A deep voice hollered and Kat looked up to see Max strolling toward them, chest thrust out, pointing both thumbs at the front of his T-shirt.

"Christ, Max, you bought one already?" Alec said.

"Best shirt ever," he declared, swiping a fry from Danica's plate.

"Hey, get your own, jackass," she said, covering her plate.

He leaned down. "One shot at my ass and I'd turn you straight."

Danica coughed and fake dry-heaved. Max straightened up, a smirk on his face until he caught sight of Lea.

Surprise crossed his face before the smirk returned and Kat knew what was coming. Max sauntered over and pulled up a chair beside Lea, straddling it with his arms over the back. "Hey there, doll."

Kat opened her mouth to tell him to leave Lea alone, but her friend spoke up first. "You steal one of my fries, and I'll castrate you."

Max's body jerked before he threw back his head and roared with laugher. "Is that your way of saying you're kinky? I think I could handle it."

Danica snorted. "I'd like to see you try to handle Lea."

Kat opened her mouth to explain Lea had been enrolled in martial arts since she was a kid but Danica shook her head and made a zipper motion over her lips. So Kat kept quiet, thinking it would be amazing if next time Max said something obnoxious, Lea executed a painful karate chop to his throat. She looked over at Max and Lea, who were locked in some stare-down.

"I'm Max," he said, voice low, and held a hand out.

Lea ignored the proffered hand and scrunched her lips. "Hmm. I've heard about you."

Max's smirk didn't falter. "Oh yeah? All good things I'm sure."

Lea shifted to face him fully. "If you call arrogant asshole a good thing."

His mouth dropped open and he placed a hand on his chest in mock affront. "I'm hurt."

Kat spoke up before things got ugly. Or ugly-er.

"Sorry, Lea, this is Max, Alec's roommate. Max, this is Lea, my—" Kat bit her cheek.

Now Lea's narrowed eyes were aimed at her.

"Every time I have to avoid an acronym, a part of me dies inside," Kat whined.

Lea sighed. "Go ahead . . ."

"MBF!" Kat crowed. "She's my MBF!"

"MB what? You still haven't told me what that means." Alec said.

"Major Best Friend," Kat explained.

Lea rolled her eyes.

Max opened his mouth but a shout from behind them cut him off. "Hey!" Cam yelled, sitting at a computer in a bowling lane. "I'm going to enter you as Maxi Pad, sound good?"

"Asshole," Max muttered as he shoved out of his chair and stalked off toward a laughing Cam.

Lea's eyes were on Max's retreating back and Kat thought maybe there was a spark of interest.

Alec leaned in and kissed her her cheek. "I know what you're thinking. Don't try to play matchmaker."

"What? I wasn't thinking that." She said in mock offense.

"Liar," Alec said softly, leaning in to kiss her lips.

After they ate, they got their shoes and walked to their lane, picking their bowling balls along the way. Alec triumphantly showed her a god-awful electric blue bowling bowl with tacky neon yellow—glow-in-the-dark, he told her proudly—lightning bolts, and she chose a sparkly, glittery hot pink ball. After much deliberation and full-on debate with an excellent rebuttal by Alec, it was determined he won the unspoken Ugliest Bowling Ball competition.

She bowled horribly for the first five frames trying to think of how to get back at him. Losing was no fun.

She ended up bowling three strikes in a row, beating Alec as well as a grumbling Cam. Max probably would have grumbled if he'd been paying attention to the game and not staring at Lea with a softened expression as she laughed with Danica.

As Kat hopped up and down shouting about her victory, Alec laughed and grabbed her around the waist. His eyes darkened. "I so do not want to make out with you right now."

She gripped his shoulders. "No?"

"Not at all."

She leaned in and pressed a kiss to his lips. "Details."

"I definitely do not want to find the nearest flat surface and hook your legs around my waist. And squeeze your ass. And kiss that victorious smug smile right off your face . . ." He trailed off as he buried his face in her neck. She felt lips, tongue and a little bit of teeth.

She bit back a moan. "Well, that's good, because I

don't want to get naked right now. I ate like three brown-
ies last night."

Alec laughed and nipped her earlobe.

"And you're the aspiring lawyer," she said, "So you
know that I'm definitely not worth the risk of a public
indecency arrest."

He pulled back and chuckled, cupping her face to
swipe his thumb over her cheekbone. His lips quirked
into a smile. "Nah, definitely not worth it."

She ran her fingers along his jaw, then placed her hand
over his heart. "Ditto, *meu coração*."

Enjoyed Megan Erickson's *Make It Count*?
Good news! There's so much more
from Bowler University to come!

Next up, can popular, cocky Max Payton
redeem himself in

Make It Right?

Read on for a sneak peek!

Make It Right

Bowler University, Book 2

MAX PAYTON WOULD like nothing more than to forget his junior year of college . . . and yet, senior year isn't looking to be much better. After graduation he'll still be under his overbearing father's thumb, helping run the family business as he's always been expected to do.

When Max volunteers to help teach a self-defense class after a rash of assaults and thefts on campus, one of the other instructors is the pixie-faced girl he hasn't been able to stop thinking about since last year. His dad always taught him size and strength always win a fight. But while Max is lying on the mat at Lea Travers's feet after a skilled blow to his carotid artery, he begins to revise that thought.

Lea Travers avoids guys like Max—cocky jocks who assume she's a fragile doll because of her small stature and disability from a childhood car accident. She likes to be in control, and Max challenges her at every turn. But during the moments he lets his guard down, she sees a soul as broken inside as she is outside. Trusting him is a whole other problem ...

When the assaults hit close to home, both Max and Lea have to change their assumptions about strength and weakness before they can get the future they want—together.

Coming September 2014

Chapter 1

THE CAT WAS back.

Its left ear was shredded but healed, and that scar on its chin a hairless C amid the black fur.

But it was limping and Max could see a dark, wet spot on its haunch. Small red footprints marked its path leading to Max's back door.

He crouched down and held a hand out. "If you could talk, bet you'd say, 'You should see the other guy.'"

The cat sat down ten feet away and licked its black lips as if in an affirmative answer.

"I bet you got some good licks in, huh?" He said, reaching behind him for the can of tuna he'd opened when he saw the cat through the window of his college town house.

The cat didn't move, just studied him, yellow eyes glowing in the setting sun. From what Max knew of cats—which was limited since his dad threatened to be in control, and Max challenges her at every turn. But during the moments he lets his guard down, she sees a soul as broken inside as she is outside. Trusting him is a whole other problem . . .

When the assaults hit close to home, both Max and Lea have to change their assumptions about strength and weakness before they can get the future they want—together.

Coming September 2014

Chapter 1

THE CAT WAS back.

Its left ear was shredded but healed, and that scar on its chin a hairless C amid the black fur.

But it was limping and Max could see a dark, wet spot on its haunch. Small red footprints marked its path leading to Max's back door.

He crouched down and held a hand out. "If you could talk, bet you'd say, 'You should see the other guy.'"

The cat sat down ten feet away and licked its black lips as if in an affirmative answer.

"I bet you got some good licks in, huh?" He said, reaching behind him for the can of tuna he'd opened when he saw the cat through the window of his college town house.

The cat didn't move, just studied him, yellow eyes glowing in the setting sun. From what Max knew of cats—which was limited since his dad threatened to

shoot any potential feline pet when Max had been a kid—
the cat must be hurting to let the injury sit without clean-
ing it thoroughly. So he quit the small talk, scooped out
the tuna onto a small plate and shoved it toward the cat.

Then he waited. And the cat didn't move.

This wasn't their normal routine. Max always left
right after supplying the food, like he was the cat's dirty
secret and if its big cat-gang buddies found out it had a
human on the side, it'd be laughed out of the alley.

But he didn't like the way the cat was favoring his leg.
And he was tired of being a dirty secret. Next he grabbed
a plastic bowl of water and shoved that alongside the food.

Then he waited. And still the cat didn't move.

"Come on, buddy," he whispered, hearing the concern
in his voice. "I'm your friend."

The cat's yellow eyes never left Max as it dipped its
head and slowly crept forward, body tense, clearly fighting the flight instinct.

Max didn't move.

The cat reached the plate of food and crouched, then
scarfed up bits of tuna in between glances at Max. He ran
his eyes over the sleek, battered body and sighed.

When the cat ate all the tuna, he gave Max a long look
before lapping at the water.

He was close, only like two feet away, and if Max just
stretched out his arm . . .

There was the bang of the screen door behind him and
the cat took off like a shot, bounding down the alley and
disappearing through a hole in the neighbor's shrubs.

"Dammit!" Max swore, jumping up from his crouched

position and whirling to face whoever interrupted the moment. "Could you be any louder—"

Kat Caruso stared at him, eyes wide, empty gallon of chocolate milk dangling from a finger. Then those blue eyes—which would darken when he used to lower his head to nuzzle her neck—narrowed. She dropped the gallon in the recycling bin and wiped her hands. "Excuse me for helping to clean your kitchen, Max."

He winced. When they'd dated, she'd taken his bad attitude without a peep. But since she'd fallen in love with his best friend, she didn't let anyone give her crap. As it should be.

And that just depressed him further, because he never inspired someone else to be a better person. He couldn't even inspire himself. So he tightened his jaw and stayed silent. He should apologize for swearing at her, but the words stuck in his throat.

Kat cocked a hip. "What are you doing out here anyway?"

Before he could answer, movement behind Kat caught his eye. Lea Travers's big brown eyes focused on him below her thick fringe of dark bangs. "I heard yelling, what's up?" Her voice, as always, was soft and musical and did something weird to his gut.

Kat glanced at her friend and waved in Max's direction with an eye roll. "Max being Max. Come on, Lea."

Kat turned and walked back into the house, light brown hair swishing behind her.

But Lea didn't follow Kat. Her eyes landed on the

empty plate of food and bowl of water, then roamed past his shoulder. The scrutiny unsettled him. Made him cranky. Okay, crankier.

It must have shown on his face, because Lea's pixie features hardened into an indifferent mask. He waited for her to leave so he could clean up after his cat—shit, his cat—and get to class. She crossed her slender arms over her chest. "It takes time, you know?"

"What're you talking about?" he snapped.

Lea didn't flinch. She nodded toward the cat's dinner area. "Cats. Takes a long time for them to trust. And sometimes feral cats never trust humans."

Who died and made her an expert? He'd get that cat to trust him if it killed him. "Well thanks, Miss Veterinarian. Didn't know you were studying that on top of your Shakespeare and Dickens."

She dropped her hands at her sides, fingers curled into little fists. "Why do you always have to be an asshole?"

"Why are you still bugging me?" he shot back.

Those liquid brown eyes fired. "Grow up, Max." Then she turned around and walked back into the house, her limp more pronounced then he'd ever seen it.

He didn't watch the way her ass looked in her tight jeans. Or how her hair shone in the sun. The sight of her eyes—so alive and challenging, calling him on his bullshit—didn't linger in his mind.

He knew Lea despised him. All she knew of him was that he'd dated Kat and treated her like crap. And before that, he'd slept with his best friend's girlfriend and kept it from him.

Although it had worked out in the end, because now Alec was with Kat and neither had ever been happier.

But Max was still an asshole.

His phone rang in his jacket pocket and he pulled it out, eyes still scanning the road to see if the cat came back. He glanced at the caller ID and sighed. "Yo."

"Max," Calvin's voice grunted in his ear.

"Who else would it be? You called me."

His oldest brother ignored the question. "Friday afternoon, you don't have class, right?"

As a senior at Bowler University, he'd had his pick of classes, so he'd made sure to keep his Fridays open. That was his day. A day for himself. One where he didn't have to attend class in a major he hated or work in his dad's automotive shop, doing work he hated. A constant reminder he was about to be stuck doing that same work he hated for the rest of his life. Unless he crawled out from under Jack Payton's steel-toe boots. Which he didn't see happening.

"You know I don't," was all he said.

Another voice murmured over the line and Max recognized Brent's voice—the middle brother. "That's what I'm doing right now, assface," Calvin's voice was muffled as he spoke to Brent, and Max rolled his eyes.

"Max," Calvin's deep voice came back on the line, clearer.

"I didn't go anywhere. You called me. What the fuck do you want?" Max growled.

Silence.

"What crawled up your ass and died?" Cal asked.

"Cal—"

"Can you drive to Dad's Friday? That big dying tree in the backyard finally cracked under last week's ice storm. Dad wants it cleared out and if we don't do it Friday, he's going to do it over the weekend. And then he'll throw his back out and be even more miserable than usual. Brent and I don't want to deal with that shit, so we need to get this tree taken care of. You in?"

Max gritted his teeth and rubbed his eyes with his thumb and forefinger. His older brothers had to work with their dad every day at the shop. And sparing them from their father's wrath was the only reason he said what he did next. "Sure."

Cal's voice was muffled again. "Will you quit yapping in my ear? I asked him and he said he'd do it. Fuck, you're annoying . . . What? . . . Fine, Brent." More muffled sounds and again the clearer voice. "Max?"

This time, he didn't even dignify it with an answer. Cal continued, "Brent wants some of your cookies."

He couldn't help but grin. "Last time I saw both of you, looked like you needed to lay off the cookies."

"Fuck you," Cal said, laughing, and Max grinned wider.

"I'll be there. With cookies."

"Later, bro."

Max ended the call, took one last look at the alley and then gathered the cat's dishes before trudging into the kitchen. As he washed the dishes, voices filtered in from the living room, Kat's laughter, Lea's quiet murmuring, Alec conversing with their other roommate, Camilo Ruiz.

Amazing how the voices of a full house made Max feel even more alone.

A breeze ruffled the back of Max's T-shirt. He glanced over his shoulder at the open screen door and frowned. He must have forgotten to shut it. He dried his hands, pulled the door shut, and then walked into the living room.

Lea and Kat sat on the floor in front of the coffee table, books open in front of them. Alec sat behind Kat, his spread legs on either side of her as she leaned her head on his thigh.

Alec Stone, his best friend since elementary school, turned his head when Max cleared his throat. Alec's face turned wary, and Max hated the fact that he'd been such a prick lately that even his best friend was cautious around him. "Hey, man," Alec said.

Max nodded. "What's up, Zuk."

Alec smiled, clearly loving that Max used the old nickname, which Max had given him years ago because of his pompadour hairstyle—like Danny Zuko from Grease.

Alec's fingers absentmindedly shifted through Kat's hair. "Cat let you touch it yet?"

Lea's eyes were on him. He could feel them, like twin heat-seeking missiles. "No," he said.

Alec nodded encouragingly. "He will. Just give it time."

Max shrugged, playing it off like he didn't care.

"Wanna play?" Cam asked, tilting the controller to his video-game system, eyes on the TV as his army guy dodged a grenade and took aim at a sniper.

Max chuckled at their roommate. "No thanks, man. Got some studying to do." Even though he didn't give a shit about his major, he was so close to graduating, he could smell it.

He took one step forward, when a black blur flew past him and raced up the stairs. "Holy shit!" Max yelped, losing his footing and crashing painfully into the coffee table. The girls screeched. Cam threw his remote control, and Alec joined Max on the coffee table, the two of them clutching each other like it was some B-rate horror movie.

"What was that?" Alec's low voice vibrated in Cam's ear.

"A raccoon?" Cam guessed.

"A dog," Lea said.

"A real big dog," Kat added.

"I think it was a bear," Max said.

Alec's nails dug into Max's biceps. "I don't think bears move that fast."

"Okay, so, like a freak bear." Max gently pushed Alec off of him before he could develop bruises.

Cam stood up slowly, eyes on the stairs. "I wish I had my gun."

Alec rolled his eyes. "We are not in a combat zone."

"I'm going to get a broom," Max declared, heading for the kitchen.

"A broom?" Alec called after him. "What the hell is a broom going to do?"

Max grabbed the wooden-handled broom from the corner of the kitchen and walked back into the living room, brandishing it like a sword. "I don't know, I'll poke it."

Alec narrowed his eyes. "I'm sure this freak bear is going to love being poked."

"You have a better idea?" Max retorted.

Alec was mute.

Kat tapped her finger to her lips. "Should I grab the fire extinguisher? That seems like something someone would do if this was a movie."

Alec sighed and laced his fingers with Kat's. "I'm thinking we don't need the fire extinguisher."

Max drew his eyes away from the couple to see Lea quietly climbing the flight of stairs. "Hey," he said, shouldering past her, broom held out in defense. "You don't know what that thing is. Don't just march up there alone."

Lea eyed the broom, then him and raised an eyebrow. "You're going to protect me, then? With a broom?"

Max's cheeks warmed. "Well, I don't keep bear-protection weapons lying around so . . ."

Lea snorted a laugh and then waved him on. "Fine, you first, then."

Max walked slowly up the stairs, broom handle out, while the caravan followed him, Cam bringing up the rear. Alec's room was at the top of the stairs and Max poked his head in, looking around.

"All clear!" He called out.

"For the love . . ." muttered an exasperated Alec behind Lea.

"All clear!" Kat echoed, followed by a "Roger that!" from Cam.

Next was the bathroom, and Max used the broom handle to slowly push aside the shower curtain. The only creature in there was a wad of hair Kat had left behind. "All clear except for a Kat hairball!" Max called.

"Hey!" Kat protested.

"Roger that!" Cam repeated.

Lea giggled behind Max and he decided he liked that sound.

Next was Max's room and the door was definitely open wider than he had left it. He held up a closed fist and Lea bumped into him. "Don't you know the hand signal for stop?" he whispered over his shoulder.

Those eyes pierced him. "Excuse me. Your massive head is blocking my sight and I can't see anything."

"Hey," Max said, affronted, "Cam, you gotta teach Lea the military hand signals or whatever."

"Roger that!" Cam called again with a laugh. He was in the Air National Guard and knew all that fancy stuff.

Max focused back on the task at hand—ridding their campus apartment of unwanted wildlife.

He motioned for Lea to stay outside his bedroom door and peeked in, broom handle at the ready to defend his person.

And right there, in the center of his unmade bed, was a ball of black fur. Yellow eyes blinked at him and a pink mouth opened to reveal white teeth and a chipped fang.

"Well fuck me," Max said, lowering the broom handle and releasing the tension in his shoulders.

"What's going on?" Alec called and Max poked his head out into the hallway to survey his makeshift backup.

"It's him," he said, still in awe.

"Who?" Kat asked.

"Him," Max waved a hand toward his bedroom. "The cat."

Kat's eyes widened. "How the hell did he get in the house?"

Max bit his lip. "I left the back door open while I washed the dishes. I guess he crept in and hid or something, then we saw him when he ran up here." He shifted his weight. "And he's hurt. I saw him bleeding."

"You just going to leave him in there?" Kat said.

Max shrugged. "Sure. I mean, he could use a break from the cold and he seems to be loving my bed."

Alec slung an arm around Kat's shoulders. "All right, well, we'll leave you alone with your cat, then. Let us know if you need anything." They walked downstairs, Cam at their heels. "I'm glad it's not a bear," he muttered.

Max stood in the doorway of his room, staring at the cat on his bed. He seemed right at home, lounging on the worn gray comforter.

"What're you going to name him?" A musical voice said beside him, and he looked down to Lea at his side. Her head barely came up to his armpit as she gazed at the cat.

Max looked around his room, at the shelf that held his favorite hockey stick and the game puck he won when he called into a radio show and had to belch the Ocean City Devils' fight song.

Then his eyes fell back on the cat. His scarred, chipped-tooth cat. "Wayne."

Lea's head tilted, and a soft lock of hair brushed his bicep. "Wayne?"

He nodded. "Yeah, after the hockey player Wayne Gretzky. The cat's kind of . . ." he almost said *scarred* but he remembered Lea's limp, her lingering injury from a childhood car crash, and he stopped short. "He seems tough. You can take one look at him and see he's won his fair share of fights."

Lea pursed those lips, the ones he'd stared at many times, all lush and full with a cupid's bow. Her eyes searched his and he didn't know what she was looking for.

Then she hummed in the back of her throat and her hand fluttered at the thigh of her left leg. "Guess so," she said quietly. Then she turned and peered at him from over her shoulder as she left his bedroom. "I'll leave you two alone, since you have some 'getting to know you' to do."

Then, with a quick smile, she was gone.

Max turned to Wayne, whose eyes shifted from the door back to Max. "What you think of her, buddy?"

Wayne licked his lips, and Max laughed. "Yeah, me too."

About the Author

MEGAN ERICKSON grew up in a family that averages 5'3" on a good day and started writing to create characters who could reach the top kitchen shelf.

She's got a couple of tattoos, has a thing for gladiators and has been called a crazy cat lady. After working as a journalist for years, she decided she liked creating her own endings better and switched back to fiction.

She lives in Pennsylvania with her husband, two kids and two cats. And no, she still can't reach the stupid top shelf.

Visit www.AuthorTracker.com for exclusive information on your favorite HarperCollins authors.